THE
HARD
KNOCKER'S
LUCK

THE HARD KNOCKER'S LUCK

William Murray

Viking

VIKING
Viking Penguin Inc., 40 West 23rd Street,
New York, New York 10010, U.S.A.
Penguin Books Ltd, Harmondsworth,
Middlesex, England
Penguin Books Australia Ltd, Ringwood,
Victoria, Australia
Penguin Books Canada Limited, 2801 John Street,
Markham, Ontario, Canada L3R 1B4
Penguin Books (N.Z.) Ltd, 182–190 Wairau Road,
Auckland 10, New Zealand

First published in 1985 by Viking Penguin Inc.
Published simultaneously in Canada

LIBRARY OF CONGRESS CATALOGING IN PUBLICATION DATA
Murray, William, 1926–
The hard knocker's luck.
I. Title.
PS3563.U8H3   1985   813'.54   85-10628
ISBN 0-670-80621-8

Printed in the United States of America by
The Book Press, Brattleboro, Vermont
Set in Times Roman
Designed by Michèle Greiner

For Alice. Again.

"Life is hard. And then you die."

—Anonymous hard knocker, after
losing a photo in the fifth at
Del Mar one afternoon

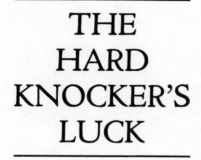

THE
HARD
KNOCKER'S
LUCK

— I —

Lifting

I was there when they arrested her. It had been a slow day in my department, and I had been restlessly pacing around my counter, literally counting the minutes until my next break, when I happened to notice her. She was a small, slender brunette with a freckle-cheeked, wistful little face set off by a snub nose and almond-shaped, dark-blue eyes. She was conservatively dressed in a green skirt, cream-colored blouse, and black pumps, and she looked, at first glance, like a thirteen-year-old dressed in her mother's clothes. I also noticed that she had a trim figure with well-shaped calves and ankles, and so it was no hardship for me to watch her wandering about the store. What else did I have to do with my time? No one was buying children's books that afternoon, and I was alone at my end of the floor. Besides, something about the woman appealed to me. I could tell that she must have been about thirty, but her gamin looks made me want to enfold her protectively in my arms. She seemed lost and helpless.

I realized, too, that she had been in the store for nearly an hour. She had been wandering aimlessly up and down the aisles, her arms full of packages and a large brown shopping bag hanging from her left shoulder. She seemed to be in search of something, but it was impossible to tell what, because she stopped first at the perfume counters, then by the shoe racks, then at notions and accessories, even the stationery and candy departments. She picked up this and that, one item after another, then put them back. She seemed fidgety and distracted, unsure of herself and slightly bewildered by her own indecisiveness. Twice she had taken an elevator to the upstairs floors, but she had come back after ten or fifteen minutes. She had apparently bought a number of items in the store, as well as elsewhere, but was still looking for something else without quite knowing what. Even though she hadn't yet come up to my end of the floor, I had just about decided to ask her if she needed any help, when I saw her pick up the purse.

It was a small, dark-brown leather handbag, one of about thirty or forty on special sale that day, and I watched her inspect it. She put some of her packages down on the counter to look at it, opened it and peered inside; then, apparently satisfied, she casually draped it over her left shoulder next to the shopping bag and picked up her packages again. She resumed her inspection of other merchandise, finally even skirted my position. I knew she wouldn't stop unless I spoke to her, so as she passed me, I muttered darkly, "Filthy children's books? Sex and violence for tiny tots?"

Startled, she looked back at me. "What?"

"Just kidding," I said. "Nobody's buying anything here. Can I sell you a nasty fairy tale?"

She looked bewildered. "I'm sorry, I'm afraid—"

"Oh, it's all right," I reassured her. "I'm just bored. And you looked like someone nice to talk to."

"Oh," she said, and smiled. "Thank you, I don't need a book. But it's very nice of you, really."

"Could I interest you in anything else? A little magic, maybe?" I took a coin out of my pocket with my good right hand and made it vanish. "I'm a little limited, I'm afraid," I continued, holding up my injured left hand, with my little finger in a splint, "but I can still do a few things."

Something about this woman made me want to entertain her, but I could see that psychologically she was simply not up to it that day. "It's very nice of you and all," she said, "but I have to go now." And she quickly turned away from me. I watched her hesitate a moment, then head for the exit to the parking lot.

I hadn't really quite grasped the implication of what was happening, when I saw Grant move after her. He was black, very young, and dressed in the dark gray slacks and blue blazer that distinguished the Amsterdam's shoplifting prevention squad. By the time I understood what was happening and followed them out into the lot behind the store, it was too late. He had come up behind her just as she reached her car.

"You have one of our bags," he said, tugging at the strap that protruded from between the pile of packages the woman had been holding in her arms. I could see the price tag still attached to it, fluttering in the air like a butterfly during this mild tug-of-war.

"What?" Her mouth was open in astonishment. "You what?"

"The bag," Grant said, keeping his hold on the strap. He seemed very serious about it, but also mildly apologetic, as if he realized now that the situation must have struck her as preposterous.

"Oh, my," the woman said, now amused as well as surprised. "I didn't know I had it." She giggled.

"Please come with me," Grant told her.

"Oh, dear. I guess I'd better speak to the manager."

He took her back inside and I caught up to them as they reached the stairway leading up to the mezzanine. "Officer," I said, "I don't think she meant to take the bag."

"I've got to take her upstairs," Grant answered, frowning. He had only been on the job a week or so, I guessed, and he was afraid of making a mistake; he was going by the book. "I saw her take the bag."

"I saw it, too. I was talking to her."

"I've got to take her upstairs," the boy insisted. "She took it."

"Look—" I began.

"It's all right," the woman said to me. "I can explain it, really. It's very nice of you, but it'll be fine."

Grant took her arm and they walked up to the mezzanine, a broad open landing that looked down over the ground floor. Amsterdam's was built in the nineteen-twenties and had a friendly, small-town feel to it, with wide staircases and slow-moving elevators still manned by uniformed operators. It was one of the oldest department-store chains in Southern California and this particular building, two blocks north of the new shopping mall in Santa Monica, was the original shop. It had been kept pretty much as it was and had a devoted, somewhat elderly local clientele. I hadn't found it depressing or demeaning to work in, but then I hadn't been there very long myself, only about a month. And I hadn't yet met Tony Cruz, either.

His command post occupied one end of the mezzanine, with a couple of desks facing each other next to the railing, from where he and his staff could peer down on the action below without getting up. The area was separated from the administrative offices by a waist-high glass partition. Mounted prominently on the wall over one of the desks was a printed motto, THOU SHALT NOT STEAL. It was the only decoration and the first thing I noticed when I walked up there, a couple of minutes after Grant and his charge had reached the premises. I was still about twenty or thirty feet away when I saw Cruz look up. "Yes, Grant?"

"I'd like to speak to the manager," the woman said, before Grant could say anything.

Cruz stared at her coldly. He was a stocky young Chicano

with a thick black mustache and dark, angry eyes. "My name is Cruz," he said. "I'm the supervisor."

"Well, I'd like to explain what happened," the woman said.

Cruz ignored her and looked at his agent. "Yes, Grant?"

"She had this bag," Grant said. "I seen her going around with it, then she went out to her car. She was about to get in when I stopped her."

"I forgot I had it," she said. "I had a lot of other stuff and—"

"You don't have to explain anything," Cruz said. "You just have to answer questions."

"Well, I guess that will be all right, of course," she answered, and sat down.

Cruz picked up his phone and punched a button. "Elena, come out here, will you?" he said, then hung up. Grant sat down at the other desk and began laboriously filling out some sort of form or report. Cruz, slouching morosely in his seat, suddenly became aware of me. "What do you want?" he asked.

"I'm waiting for Diehl, in Personnel," I lied.

"You got an appointment?"

"Not exactly, but he's expecting me."

"Haven't I seen you?"

"Yeah. My name's Anderson, Children's Books."

"You're new."

"Temporary. By the way, this lady—"

The woman turned around in her chair and smiled at me. "Really, please don't bother," she said. "This will all be straightened out."

Cruz scowled at both of us and hammered his palms lightly on the arms of his chair, but said nothing more. I sat down against the wall on the other side of the glass and pretended to go on waiting for Diehl. I made a clear show of indifference to the proceedings around Cruz's desk, but

I managed to stay within hearing range.

Elena appeared. She was a dark, pretty girl, probably also of Mexican descent, and still in her late teens. She sat down nervously next to Cruz with a steno pad on her lap and stared blankly at the woman, who now leaned forward in her chair. "Look, this is really very simple," she began. "I've—"

Cruz cut her off. "Just answer the questions," he said. "That's all I want to hear from you."

All right, he was just following accepted procedures, I told myself. But why did he have to be so truculent? What was the matter with the guy? He was short and dark, and he came from some *barrio* where they'd taught him to hate all Anglos. I was hoping she would stop trying to charm him.

"Name?"

"Allyson Meade."

"Spell it."

"M-e-a-d-e."

"And the first name again."

"A-l-l-y-s-o-n."

She gave him her home address, her work address, her telephone numbers, her occupation, her birth date, her mother's maiden name, her Social Security number. "Don't you want to know what happened, Mr. Cruz?" she finally asked.

"You have some identification?"

She rummaged about in her purse and produced her driver's license, which evidently had a photograph of her that failed to convince Cruz. "Where'd you get this?" he asked, holding the little card out in front of him as if it were contaminated.

"Where'd I get it?" she echoed. "It's my driver's license. My hair was long then."

"That's not your picture."

"Want to bet?"

Cruz silently dropped the card on the desk, then picked up her bag and methodically began going through its contents. He counted her cash and had Elena make a list of everything he found, as well as all of her packages. When he came across the store's credit card, he took a pair of large scissors out of one of his drawers and ostentatiously cut it up, then dropped the pieces into a wastebasket.

The violation of her privacy, to say nothing of this bit of psychodrama, angered Allyson Meade. "What the hell are you doing?" she asked.

"You're under arrest, that's what I'm doing."

"I'm what?"

"We've called the police. You're going to jail."

"And you're a nutty Mexican fruitcake."

"You'd better make some arrangement to have your car towed out of our parking lot."

"I'd like to make a call, please," she said, her face white with suppressed rage.

"Not from here."

"Then how am I supposed to move my car?"

"That's your problem."

"I have to call my husband."

"You can do it from the police station." He reached again into his top drawer, pulled out a form and shoved it at her. "Sign this."

"I'm not signing anything," she said.

Cruz turned to Elena. "Put down that she's being un-cooperative."

She made one more try. "Look, Mr. Cruz, you may have noticed from my charge card that I have an account at this store," she said, keeping her voice as even and as calm as she could manage it at this point. "Why don't you check my account? I think you'll find it in good order."

"That has nothing to do with it," Cruz snapped. "Besides, I don't even know who you are."

She laughed at him; it was all so ridiculous. "I have a perfectly plausible explanation that so far you've refused to hear," she said, "and now you're holding me here against my will. I demand that you let me call my husband."

"You demand nothing," Cruz answered. "You're on private property. You sit until the cops get here."

"And when will that be?"

"When they're good and ready," he said. "You think you're the biggest case they've got?"

"All right." She stood up. "Where's the ladies' room?"

"You're not going anywhere."

"No? Would you like me to do it right here?"

"Grant, you show her where it is," he said. "Then bring her back here and make sure she doesn't go anywhere." He stood up and walked out in front of them, slamming the door of the partition behind him. I watched him storm off down the landing, while Grant sheepishly reopened the door for her and ushered her out toward the rest rooms at the far end. She was so angry by this time that she didn't notice me still sitting there, and I thought it wiser not to say anything. After they had gone, though, I popped my head up over the partition. "Hey, Elena," I said.

The girl looked up, her eyes bright and jittery, like those of a bird. "Is he always like that?" I asked.

The girl shrugged and looked away. "I don't know," she said. "I haven't been here very long."

"Me neither. I guess no one has, except maybe Cruz. He probably fires everybody else."

"I don't know," she said miserably.

"No, of course not," I told this live wire, and went off in search of the terrible Cruz.

I didn't find him right away, but it worked out that he caught up to me about an hour later, when he happened to walk past my position downstairs. "Mr. Cruz," I said, coming out from behind my pyramids of Oz books and Dr.

Seuss, "I'd like to tell you something."

He turned and stared blankly at me, as if he had never seen me before. "Who are you?"

"Anderson," I said. "We met upstairs earlier."

"What do you want?"

"That woman you stopped for shoplifting—" I began.

"Yeah? What about her?"

"I don't think she was trying to steal the bag," I told him. "She was distracted and I got into a conversation with her on the way out—"

"She took it, all right."

"Yes, but—"

"But nothing. I know her kind. We get lots of these phonies in here. She ain't even who she says she is."

"You're sure of that?"

He regarded me with the contempt of the old pro for the bumbling amateur. "You ever worked in a store before?"

"Sure."

"A department store?"

"Well, no."

"Then you don't know shit," he said. "You like working here?"

"It's grand," I answered. "I've looked forward to it all my life."

"I don't like your attitude."

"I'm a magician with a broken hand," I said, "which is like a bird with one wing. My luck has not been extraordinary lately at the track either. I need this job until after the first of the year and, with the holiday rush, the presumption is that you need me. Isn't that enough? Or would you like a wholehearted testimonial on the glories of salesmanship? Or should I just say I love you?"

Cruz had frozen into his Aztec mask by the end of this outburst, and now he looked right through me to the wall. "Pick up your check on Friday," he said, "but don't come back tomorrow. You're fired."

"And a joyous wassail margarita to you, too," I told him, but he was already walking away from me and he never looked back.

It was nearly six-thirty before two officers of the Santa Monica Police Department finally showed up. One was blond, the other dark; both were very serious young men, neatly attired in dark-blue uniforms that gleamed as they walked into the store. "Thank God you're here!" Allyson Meade exclaimed, to their evident amazement.

When they found out that Allyson had an explanation that Cruz had so far declined to listen to or allow her to tell anyone else, one of the young men tugged the supervisor out into the hall, and she overheard him say, "If she's right, she could sue your ass."

Cruz peered around the corner of the wall at her. "We know she's guilty and she knows it," he said. "We're going to press a criminal complaint."

The officers gave up on him, and one of them produced a form for Allyson to sign. He informed her, in the flat monotone of a recitation learned by heart, that it was simply what is known as a standard Notice to Appear, which meant that she agreed to present herself in court in two weeks' time. He didn't tell her exactly what she had been charged with, and in her confusion she neglected to ask. Her first reaction was relief that she was not being hauled off to jail, as Cruz had predicted. She whirled on him now and unloosed a barrage of abuse.

One of the policemen took her arm. "Knock it off," he said, "or we'll take you in."

She looked into his eyes and saw that they were young and clear, as innocent as those of a fawn. "Do you realize it's after seven and nobody knows where I am?" she asked him. He stared at her uncomprehendingly.

"He'll take you to the clinker," Cruz said.

That ludicrous word, out of an old B-movie, made her laugh. She turned to leave at last, but the supervisor's voice followed her out: "And don't ever set foot in this store again!"

I saw her heading for the public phones diagonally across from Cruz's station, and I came up behind her in time to hear her say, presumably to her husband at the other end of the line, "I've been arrested for shoplifting. . . . No, I mean it. It really did happen." He must have asked her where, as if that mattered more than whether the incident had actually occurred. She told him exactly what had happened, including a colorful description of the supervisor's hostility. "I'll be home in twenty minutes," she concluded. "Take the steaks out of the icebox."

She turned around then and saw me. "I've been eavesdropping," I said, handing her a business card with my name, address, and phone number on it. "If you need to call me," I explained. "I won't be here after tonight. You may need a witness."

"Thank you, that's very nice of you," she said, dropping the card into her bag without looking at it and again reaching for her packages.

"Can I help with those?"

"No, it's all right, I can manage." She started out of the store, then looked back and smiled at me. "I hope you haven't been waiting just for me."

"Oh, no," I assured her, "I get off at nine. We're on holiday hours now till Christmas."

"Thanks again." And she walked quickly away from me.

I went back to my book counters and looked at my watch. About an hour to go now. Two towheaded California kids of about eight were wandering casually through the aisles and I beckoned them over. "Hey, guys, want to read some good books?" They stared at me, and I smiled at them.

"Here," I continued, picking up a stack of recently reissued paperback editions of the Oz series, "these are terrific." I popped them into a shopping bag and then added a handful of other good tales from the brothers Grimm and the Greek and Roman myths, all old favorites of mine. "Wonderful stuff," I assured them, "better than TV." I rang up the transaction and dropped the sales slip into the bag. "Be sure you tell your folks these are paid for," I told them. "Just tell them you met a nice crazy man who likes kids, okay?"

I patted their heads lightly as I passed them, clutching their heavy sack of books, and headed out. What the hell, I thought, the store owed me a lot more than I was giving away, at least three days' pay, and I wasn't about to come back to this dreary scene just to collect a depleted paycheck on Friday. I looked up as I reached the exit and saw Cruz looking at me from his observation post. I waved cheerfully at him and gave him a quick finger, then walked out into the cool, clear air of a perfect California December night. I was broke, of course, and unemployed again, but I was free.

2

Hard Knocks

My friend Jay Fox, the prince of handicappers, was sitting in one of his favorite grandstand boxes over the Hollywood Park finish line when I caught up to him the next afternoon, about an hour before post time for the first race. It was early and he was still alone, busily burrowing for corroborating facts among the charts of past races in one of the big, black notebooks he took to the track with him every single racing day. He had told me earlier that he had a couple of good things going that afternoon, so I guessed he was now merely making a last survey of the figures, sniffing out, if possible, the additional right or wrong number that could alter his action, however slightly, one way or the other. Basically, Jay did not believe in chance, and so he left absolutely nothing to it. "The rewards do not go to the casuals," he had once informed me. "They shower like emeralds only on the worthy."

I eased myself into the box and sat down beside him, as I had so often before in our time together at the track. "How goes the chase, Fox?" I asked. "Still like your selections?"

He looked up and smiled. "Very much," he said, snapping the notebook shut and leaning back to gaze benevolently upon me, like an elder prophet welcoming a straying disciple back to the fold. "I thought you were staying away till Santa

Anita," he said softly. "I thought you didn't like Hollywood Park."

"I don't."

"I thought you needed freshening."

"I do."

"So then?"

"So then I was a liar," I said. "Anyway, I got fired yesterday."

"For what?"

"For sticking my nose into somebody else's business," I explained, "and for making merry with a supervisor."

"Oh, Shifty," Jay clucked sympathetically, and eyed my damaged flipper. "How's the hand?"

"The bandage comes off next week, they say," I told him. "Then I have to start therapy. I might be able to get back to work in six to eight weeks."

"That's tough," Jay said. "I had no idea."

"Me neither. Do you have my loot?"

He dug into his left pants pocket and peeled off three one-hundred-dollar bills from what looked to me like a very sizeable roll. "Here," he said, handing them to me. "You won't need more than that. I want you to stick close to me today. I'm hot and I have two very good numbers on these beasts. But I won't let you in on them till just before post times, after I see them on the track." He saw me waver, but raised a cautionary, imperious hand at me. "I know it's not your style, Shifty," he said, "but, believe me, I want to bail you out. You obviously need help."

I did. In fact, I had clearly hit some kind of low point in my life. I had begun to lose early in the Oak Tree meet at Santa Anita in October, but it hadn't bothered me very much at first. I had been performing regularly at a series of conventions in the L.A. area, and three nights a week I had been appearing in the close-up room at the Magic Castle, where I had been perfecting some new illusions with coins and cards and working up a comedy patter to frame them. I was going to audition for the new Comedy Club in Encino, and I was also up for a running part, as the magician friend of a crippled female private eye, on a projected TV series coming up in the spring. I was easily carrying my losses at the track and not at all worried about them. Betting on Thoroughbreds to run according to form is a risky enterprise and subject occasionally to long losing streaks. You have to ride the arid stretches out, mainly by cutting your action down and not pressing. Eventually, the winners begin to pop up again, usually when least expected, but always on days when the Dummy God, the deity of all the little old ladies and hard knockers who bet odds-on favorites, is not in session. Or, as I had once put it to Jay during one of *his* bad times, "This game is not subject to rational analysis, Fox, but only to a certain childlike faith." It hadn't helped him, because he had his own dogmatic belief to defend. He trusted in numbers, I in the mystery at the heart of all our strivings.

And then, on that Black Monday in October, I had broken my hand. I'm still not certain how it happened, except that I know myself to be an established household *klutz*. Here I am, Shifty Lou Anderson, the Rubinstein of the broad tossers, as my friend and colleague Vince Michaels once labeled me, an artist who can cause small objects to vanish into the air and make packs of cards dance exquisite *pas de cinquante-deux* on tabletops, "dazzling miracles of manual dexterity," and I can't hammer nails into boards, mop the bathroom floor, or fry an egg without maiming myself. What I'm best at is hitting my head on things, even though I'm not that tall, just under six feet, and have perfect eyesight. Put me into any small space I'm unfamiliar with, however, and I will crack my skull against something unyielding—a sill, a closed door, a shower nozzle, a sink edge, even the wall. I carry the bumps and scabs of dozens of such encounters through most of the weeks of the year. But I can live with those, because they do not affect my work. My hands, my fingers, the only real capital I have, I protect, usually by not risking them. I employ a small, wiry Mexican woman named Rosaria to clean my one-room studio apartment in West Hollywood, and most of the time I eat out.

All I remember is that I set out to clean my screens one morning, an area Rosaria never touched. I wouldn't have either, except that, after two years of neglect, an encrustation of dead insects and dust had begun to shut off daylight. In a rush of misplaced confidence, I had set about taking them down one by one and washing them. That part of the operation I had managed brilliantly, but in putting them back up I had miscalculated. The largest of the kitchen ones had slipped and landed with a sickening crack on the little finger of my left hand, right on the big knuckle. I had soaked it immediately in ice, but by late afternoon it had swollen to twice its normal size, and I had had to go to the hospital, where the finger had been X-rayed and then immobilized in a splint. The prognosis was only fair—six weeks and then another six to eight of therapy to regain the full use of the limb. The little finger is a largely useless addition to the human physique, quite unnecessary to most functions, but not, alas, to the more delicate moves of a concert pianist or a prestidigitator.

I had obviously fallen into the hands of a dark demon. As if to mock my sudden immobilization, he now destroyed my ability to analyze the cabalistic notations in my *Daily Racing Form,* and he clouded my other senses as well. Not only did I continue to lose every day, but I went right on betting with the gay abandon of a blind tap dancer on a window ledge. I woke up one morning with no money in the bank and an unenviable streak of thirty-four consecutive losing bets. I quit, vowing to sit out the rest of Oak Tree and all of the fall meet at Hollywood Park, until the traditional reopening of Santa Anita the day after Christmas. Which is how I happened to find myself peddling children's classics in Amsterdam's, a temporary interruption of my real life from which Allyson Meade and Tony Cruz had rescued me. The three hundred dollars I had borrowed from Jay to get back in action would somehow have to last and be compelled to grow until I was whole again, making magic and picking winners on my own.

"I will tell you one thing," Jay said consolingly. "My horses don't run until the seventh and ninth. Till then I'd bet light, if I were you."

"I'm not going to bet at all," I told him. "I didn't even buy a *Form.*"

"I noticed that," Jay said. "You're getting smart, at last. Just be patient and the Fox will make all things well."

I could pardon him his ego in full bloom. When a man is on a hot streak and the money is flowing in like a riptide through a channel lock, he's entitled to revel in his success, at gambling on horses as well as in any other respectable profession. I had been with Jay when the tables had been reversed, and I had witnessed his times of despair. So I could hardly begrudge him now his moment in the sun, and my heart was as empty of envy as a suckling babe's. We were friends, we had been on the seesaw together and we had both been humbled by the Dummy God.

About twenty minutes before the first race, when Jay's entourage of daily suppliants began to stop by the box to raid his brain and he began scattering his pearls of wisdom before these helpless porkers, I moved out and took a stroll through the grandstand. I'm not especially fond of Holly-wood Park, a garishly decorated emporium in one of the drearier parts of the great smog-enshrouded L.A. basin, but I like all racetracks, really. They are like great ships embarking on a new voyage every day and in which we strive for the only forms of immortality I believe in—the achievement of ecstasy, the blinding flash of revelation, the dream made true—each day containing all the seeds of hope and risk needed to make life a renewable adventure. On all such journeys, I take pleasure, too, in communing with my fellow Argonauts.

This time I hadn't taken ten steps when I ran into Freddie Chambers, whom I hadn't seen in nearly a year. Freddie was a hard knocker, by which I mean that he'd rather bet his money on a horse race than do anything else, except possibly breathe. In the past this had kept him in a permanent state of financial disarray and had eventually broken up his marriage, but he had always remained resolutely cheerful in the face of adversity. Somehow, no matter how bad things got, Freddie never lost heart. And though he was broke much of the time, he always managed eventually to get back in action, the sign of the true horseplayer. I assumed he had some sort of a connection somewhere that yielded him a small income. Somebody had once told me, in fact, what it was, but I had forgotten. Anyway, I was glad to see him. He was a thin little man in his sixties, with the craggy, bearded face of a mischievous gnome, and nothing ever dismayed him. Laughter lived inside him, like a hidden spring under a mossy rock.

"Shifty," he said, grinning and giving me a quick hug, "where you been?"

"Around. Where have you been, Freddie?"

"Abroad. I got back three weeks ago."

"Abroad? Where?"

"Italy, mostly."

"Italy? Doing what?" I couldn't have been more surprised if he'd told me he'd been on a space shot.

"Business," he announced, "strictly business. And you know what?"

"What?"

"They got horses there, too. Only it's so crooked it makes this game seem easy."

"Now, Freddie, I have to hear about this. What were you doing—"

But he cut me off as the bugler appeared to blow the call to the post for the first race. "Listen, I'll tell you about it one of these days," he said, "but right now I gotta get a bet down. Come with me."

"Where are you going?"

"The Turf Club. I'm a member."

This was another shock; I could no more imagine Freddie in the Turf Club, that playground of the rich, than I could see myself there. Freddie, the terminal loser, in the Turf Club? Had he won a lottery somewhere? "I haven't got a tie," was all I could think of saying. "Besides, I'm sitting with Jay."

"Come on in for a race or two," he answered, taking my arm and tugging me toward the escalators. "I haven't seen you in a year. I'll get you a tie."

He left me at the entrance to the club, vanished, and reappeared five minutes later with a pass and a tie. We went upstairs together; then Freddie, who by this time was sweating slightly and had the itchy jitters of the confirmed addict, swooped away from me toward the betting windows. "I got to get down," he called back. "I'm wheeling the first to Crimson Prince in the second. I'll meet you at the bar after the race."

That sounded more like the Freddie Chambers I knew. He was betting every horse in the first race to an obvious favorite in the second, for a daily double that seemed likely to pay off at low odds, unless, by some miracle, one of the two longshots in the first happened to come in. It was the sort of wager that invoked the intercession of the Dummy God and would have made Jay Fox's eyes harden in disapproval. Freddie, I knew, had few illusions; he understood what the percentages were. "Betting every race," he had once said to me, "is like putting your bankroll into a shredding machine. Federal Reserve notes go in and torn pari-mutuel tickets come out." But Freddie always plunged ahead anyway. Basically, he was the kind of bettor who believed that if you added up enough minuses, you could somehow come up with a plus.

Three years ago, I remembered, he had tried to retire from the track. Then Hollywood Park had instituted a form of wagering called the Pick Six, in which the bettor tries to select the winners of the second through the seventh races. This is about as difficult as bobbing blindfolded for apples in a tub of beer, but the payoffs can be astronomical. The prospect of such a big score had brought Freddie out of retirement and, though he had never yet hit a Pick Six, he had continued to try, while also making his usual wagers on horses race by race to win, place, show, and in various exotic combinations. In defense of his addiction, he had always blamed the track management, even though no one compelled Freddie to bet the way he did. Like most losers, he could not admit his own responsibility.

I sat down in the bar to wait for him. It was a beautiful scene, with comfortable chairs and plenty of servile attendants. Glamor, chic, style, entrenched wealth, and privilege, none of which I had ever associated with Freddie before. On one of the TV monitors over my head, I watched an animal named Poison Gal win the first race, at odds of nine to two, which meant that Freddie stood to win very little money if Crimson Prince ran to form and to lose quite a bit if he didn't. Freddie seemed undaunted by his dim prospects when he came back, his ten-by-fifty Japanese binoculars bouncing heavily off his chest like a medicine ball, and he ordered himself a club sandwich and coffee. I asked him how he had happened to pick Crimson Prince.

"Hubie told me," he answered, naming one of the more unsuccessful touts on the premises. "He said Tony was talking to Harry, who says he got it from the stable that Crimson Prince would run real good."

"Freddie, he's the even-money morning-line favorite," I said. "You didn't need a tout to tell you about him."

Freddie shrugged and grinned. "So what if he's a lock? Better a winner at low odds than a longshot who runs last."

Dubious logic, but I kept quiet; I knew it was hopeless to argue with him. Crimson Prince proceeded to run his eyeballs out, but something called Our Sonny, at ten to one, beat him handily. Freddie told me, when he came back this time, that he was out ninety dollars on his ten-dollar wheel. He had also blown another two hundred and fifty-six dollars on his Pick Six ticket, but he remained undismayed. He got up and went to buy a ten-dollar Exacta box (a wager in which two horses must finish one-two in the exact order selected) on the favorites in the third, a race he told me he didn't like, and I looked around the room to kill time.

The Hollywood Wives were all there, I noticed, lined up at the bar, gigglers all. They were ladies in their middle years whose husbands were show-biz tycoons and who came to the track once a week or so to bet tiny bits and pieces of their play money on horses with cute names or jockeys whose looks were darling. They also worked variations on versions of Oriental betting systems they'd been told about by their gurus. You could always tell when they had backed a winner, because they shrieked like banshees. They did a lot of screaming after the third, because they brought in a five-to-one shot named Sweet Norman, which happened not to be one of the horses Freddie had used in his Exacta. "We live," Freddie said, "in a merciless world."

I looked again at Freddie. He was wearing Gucci loafers, dark-gray tailored flannel slacks, and a checked cashmere sports jacket that fitted him like a uniform. In the states, it would have cost him a thousand dollars to dress like that.

"Freddie, tell me about Italy," I said.

"Some other time, Shifty," he said. "Can't you see I'm picking horses?"

"No, I can't see that."

He ignored me and went back to scanning his *Form*. The fourth race, he decided, looked like a cinch for a maiden filly named Irish Lass, and Freddie decided to pass it. The last time he had risked money on a favorite in a maiden filly race, he told me, was sometime back in the late Truman era. He couldn't even remember exactly when, but he did remember losing the bet. He ordered more coffee for both of us, and I tried again to draw him out.

"Did you win a lottery or something?"

"Naw. You didn't know I was Italian, did you?"

"With a name like Chambers? How could I?"

"My real name is Camerini," he explained, "which in Italian means little rooms. My father Americanized his name after he got here, back in the twenties. I'm Italian on both sides. From Naples, originally."

I decided immediately that he must have inherited some money, but I didn't have a chance to ask him any more about it, because Marty Joyce came by. He was on his way to the windows to buy some tickets for a seated group of ancients too arthritic to heave themselves out of their chairs to wager. Marty, who is small and agile, sometimes picks up useful tips that way, since some of the elders he services also happen to own horses. He leaned over us confidentially.

"They're playing the O'Hara filly in the fifth," he confided, with a wink. Marty, who works as atmosphere in bad TV shows and the occasional soft-core porn movie, was convinced that the world was at the mercy of a huge conspiracy that could only be defeated by inside information.

Freddie buried himself in his *Form* again. It told him that Wood Nymph, the O'Hara filly, would be favored, so he decided quite sensibly not to play her, but then, just before the race went off, he bought two ten-dollar Exacta tickets from her to two longshots. Freddie couldn't explain why he did impulsive things like this, but I knew why. He had to have the action.

Wood Nymph ran second, and Freddie was now out three hundred and eighty-six dollars, which in the old days would have demolished him for weeks and caused his disappearance. This time it didn't seem to bother him very much. "Still four races to go," he announced cheerfully. "I've never been much good in the early ones, anyway."

I decided to help him out. "Listen," I said, "Jay has a couple of good numbers on horses in the seventh and ninth. I'll get him to tell me what they are right now. Wait here."

I knew I could get Jay to spill the beans, because he was also fond of Freddie and he knew he could count on our discretion. I was right, but when I came back to the Turf Club with my information, I found Freddie no longer alone. He had been joined by Boom Boom Hogan, a party girl with magnificent legs; Harris, an El Monte insurance salesman; Wally, a pensioned fireman; and Bertie, a retired savings-and-loan executive who dressed in black suits and lived alone with his mother in a Pasadena mansion. I nodded affirmatively to Freddie, who smiled back, and I joined his entourage.

There wasn't a winner among them. To make conversation, I gathered, Freddie asked Boom Boom why she had failed to put in an appearance the previous week. "I was in Vegas with a high roller," she explained, "but then he had to go home to his wife."

Everyone nodded sympathetically. The men Boom Boom dated all had wives, women who looked as if they had just been hit in the mouth with a mashie. For a long time Boom Boom had been kept in relative splendor by a plumbing executive, but recently the man had gone home to his wife and children. Boom Boom had compensated by having her hair pinked.

Silence reigned again while the comrades studied the charts. It was broken a few minutes before post time by the appearance of Action Jackson, a tapped-out stockbroker who holds the all-time Turf Club bar record for drinks spilled while reaching for the hors d'oeuvres. He faced the group and informed us that he had had a winner in every race. Furthermore, he couldn't understand how Freddie and the rest of us could have failed to pick each race as accurately as he. "It's an easy card, the easiest," he announced. "They're giving it away out here."

"That sonofabitch hasn't had a loser since April," Bertie said, after he'd gone. "He bets on every horse in every race. He's sick."

After the friends had separated to go and bet the sixth, I persuaded Freddie to pass the race and gave him Jay's selection in the seventh. The horse went off the favorite, at three to two, but we each risked a hundred dollars on him and he won easily. I was now a hundred and fifty ahead, and Freddie had shaved his losses by forty percent, which, he figured, put him in a good position to get out on the last two races.

"I'm only going to bet the ninth," I warned him. "Jay doesn't like the feature."

"What do I care about Jay?" Freddie answered. "He's not God, is he?"

"He's hot, Freddie. I'd go with him, if I were you."

It was hopeless; Freddie ignored my advice. In the eighth and feature race, he again came up with the favorite, at three to two, but on his way back from the window he bumped into Pinhead, a very tall accountant whose method of play consisted of listening to tips from supposedly reliable sources. "Flying Cricket is money in the bank," he announced, as Freddie brushed past him. "Got that from a

friend of a friend of the owner, a guy who really knows."
He informed Freddie that he was putting two hundred dollars
of his own money on the animal, at five to two.

Freddie followed him back to the windows and exchanged
his one-hundred-dollar ticket on the favorite for one on
Pinhead's choice. The favorite won easily and Flying Cricket
managed to stagger in fourth. "Why do you suppose I keep
doing things like that?" he asked, not expecting me to answer, and I didn't.

"Freddie, I'm going back to Jay's box," I said. "His horse
here is Ariated."

Freddie looked shocked. "Ariated? She'll stop."

"Jay figures she's the only speed in the race," I explained,
"and she'll get an easy lead. He figures she'll hold on against
this weak field of plodders."

"Well, okay," Freddie said, looking very dubious. He
liked Rightful Annie, a late-running mare that looked to
him like the class of a weak field going a flat mile over the
turf course. "You say Jay's hot, huh?" I nodded. "All right,
I'll bet Ariated straight and box her in Exactas with Annie."

I left him and only found out later what happened. On
his way to the windows, Freddie encountered Boom Boom
Hogan, who looked distressed and needed a winner badly.
Freddie told her about Ariated. "I'm going to box her with
Eager Beaver," Boom Boom said, indicating a thirty-to-one
shot no one else liked.

"Eager Beaver has no chance," Freddie informed Boom
Boom, whose ignorance on the subject of horses was just
about total.

"The bartender told me she'd run good," Boom Boom
insisted.

"That's why the guy is a bartender," Freddie said. "If he
knew anything, why would he be tending bar?"

This reasoning failed to shake Boom Boom, who went
off to make her bets. Freddie went outside over the finish

line just as the horses filed into the starting gate. He was feeling very confident, because this time at least he had stuck to his selections. He felt sorry for Boom Boom, that was all.

Ariated opened up a huge lead, just as Jay had predicted, and held it turning into the stretch. Rightful Annie was not in a running mood, but the win ticket on Ariated, at eight to one, would bail Freddie out. A few hundred yards from the wire, however, Eager Beaver suddenly closed with a rush to win going away, with Ariated finishing second. "Oh, my God, I'm rich!" Freddie heard Boom Boom scream, just before she threw her arms around his neck. "Thanks for telling me about Ariated!"

I was feeling all right about my day, because, without telling Jay (who would have disapproved), I had backed Ariated up in the place hole and so won another eighty dollars on the race, making a total of two hundred and thirty for the day. It would help to keep me alive. Jay was disgusted by Ariated's failure to hang on for the win, but he took his loss philosophically. He had also had a small winning afternoon, and he had been around too long to complain about that.

On the way out to the parking lot, I filled him in on my visit with Freddie Chambers. "Yeah, it is strange," Jay agreed. "I'd heard he was in the money, but the way he bets it won't last long."

"Did you know he was Italian?"

"No. But Mafia he isn't."

I spotted Freddie again, waiting for his car at the valet parking station. When I had first met him, he'd been driving a '66 Olds that sounded as if it had squirrels scurrying about under the hood. As I waved goodbye to him this time, an attendant stepped out of a sparkling new cream-colored Chrysler Le Baron convertible and ushered him into it. Freddie tipped him, slapped a bright-blue beret on his head and swooped out of the lot. "I'll be damned," Jay said.

I agreed with Jay; Freddie's good fortune was doomed. I thought idly about him all the way home, but then soon after put him out of my mind again. He was a sure loser at the track, that was all, and I had my own problems to think about. There was only one message that evening on my answering machine. It was from Allyson Meade, asking me to call her and leaving me both her home and office numbers.

3

Confidences

"It was so nice of you to come," Allyson Meade said, getting up to greet me as I entered the reception room. "I hope this isn't too much trouble."

"Not at all," I told her. "I didn't like the double anyway."

"The what?"

"The daily double," I explained. "Post time at Hollywood Park is two o'clock. I do have a horse I like in the fourth, but we have plenty of time."

"Please sit down," she said. "It shouldn't be long."

I joined her on the settee facing the receptionist's little glass window, which was closed firmly against us. We were alone in the silent, immaculate room, which was handsomely furnished in dark American period pieces, probably all imitations, but expensive ones. The atmosphere screamed entrenched money, undoubtedly suitable to the type of law firm Allyson Meade had apparently chosen to represent her. Harvey, Harvey and Walsh, I knew, was an old and prestigious outfit in Pasadena, with only big-name clients, some of them in politics and none of them in show business.

"We should be out in half an hour," Allyson Meade said. "It's only eleven."

"I know. Don't worry about it."

"So you go to the races," she said. "Do you go often?"

"As often as I can manage it."

"But isn't that expensive?"

"Not if you win."

"Do you always win?"

"By no means."

"Then how..." she began, but left the unspoken, embarrassing question dangling in the air between us.

"As I told you on the phone," I said, "I'm out of work. I'm not playing the horses for fun right now."

"I'm so sorry."

"Don't be," I reassured her. "I can't think of a place I'd rather be at the moment."

"But what if you lose?"

"I don't go to lose," I explained. "I need the money."

"It's all my fault," she said. "I didn't know you'd been fired. I think that's terrible."

"Mrs. Meade—"

"Please call me Allyson."

"It was not one of my big ambitions to make good at Amsterdam's. So please don't worry about it."

"I do feel responsible—"

"Don't. I guess you're in more trouble here than I am."

"Isn't it crazy? I never imagined they'd actually press charges. Anyway, Jamie Horton, my lawyer, thought it would be a good idea if you came. You were so nice to give me your card."

"No trouble, really. I'm not a great fan of the Señor Cruz."

"He was unbelievable," she said. "I tried to explain to him—"

"I know you did."

"Oh, dear." She looked ready to cry, and I hoped she wouldn't, but I had underestimated her. She looked very sweet and feminine, very vulnerable, but she had a strong jaw line and I could see it set against her impulse to let go.

She turned her head briefly away from me to get full control of herself, then swung back to face me with a cheerful little smile.

"Please forgive me," she said. "I'm upset and all, but what I really am is angry."

"Cruz was rotten—"

"It's not just that," she interrupted me. "It was so dumb of me. I still can't believe what I did." She laughed abruptly and caught herself. "I don't know why I did it. I was so confused. Maybe I wanted to be arrested."

"Why would you want that?"

She looked away from me again and shook her head. "I don't know," she said. "I've been feeling kind of funny . . ."

Before she could proceed any further along this interesting line, the reception window slid open, and the face of a motherly-looking, gray-haired woman appeared in the opening. "You can go in now, Mrs. Meade," she said. "You know the way?"

"Oh, yes, thank you," Allyson answered, bouncing quickly to her feet like a small child being summoned to a meeting with authority and anxious to get it over with. I followed her through the door.

"This must be a very expensive deal," I observed, despite myself, as we headed down a long, thickly carpeted corridor lined with presumably genuine Currier & Ives prints and framed antique maps of the Americas. I didn't know a great deal about art, but I've always had a good feel for costs.

"It is," Allyson assured me. "My husband sent me to them."

I began to get the idea that perhaps the period pieces in the reception room were not imitations at all, but the real thing. "I guess you can afford this," I said.

"I'm not sure we can," she answered, "but Julian insisted."

The lawyer Allyson's husband had found for her turned out to be a tall, attractive brunette in her early thirties named Jamie Horton. She was a junior member of the firm, not yet a partner, and she had had some experience in criminal law. This was reassuring, but apparently she had handled mostly civil cases; she had never had to go to trial or argue before a jury. This would have made me nervous, but Allyson obviously felt calmer in her presence; here at last was someone who was trying actively to help her. She was still pretty tense, however, and sat on the edge of her chair, ready to spring out of it like a deer.

The lawyer paid very little attention to me at first, but concentrated on her client. "You called the store, Mrs. Meade?"

"I went there, but nobody would talk to me," Allyson said. "Later, I did get this man Grant, the one who stopped me, on the phone, but he said he couldn't talk to me either. So I called Mr. Anderson..."

"I see." The lawyer looked appraisingly at her, momentarily puzzled. I could understand her reaction. Allyson Meade was wearing an elegant pants suit, dark gray, with a ruffled collar and cuffs. She looked very young, almost virginal, and she obviously took good physical care of herself. Also, she was clearly a woman with a strong reserve of pride, who knew who she was and what she was about. What, exactly, had happened to her? People of her class and background just didn't get themselves arrested for shoplifting, or did they?

Jamie Horton looked at me. "Mrs. Meade tells me you were in the store and witnessed the whole incident."

I nodded. "I think I contributed to it."

"Really? In what way?"

"Well, she was wandering around with all this stuff in her arms," I said, "and I tried to pick her up. I think she forgot about this bag." I smiled, determined to loosen this serious young attorney up a bit. "I must have had a devastating effect on her."

Jamie Horton was not charmed. "Undoubtedly," she said, in a dry, cold voice. She turned back to Allyson. "Mrs. Meade," she told her, "we've been all through this before, but I'd like you now to go back over it, step by step, exactly as it happened. Partly for Mr. Anderson's benefit and partly for my own again. I want to be sure we have it exactly right."

Allyson sighed and went right into her account. It sounded plausible enough; essentially her story was a catalog of small decisions and events that had each contributed to a mistake. At noon, on her lunch hour that day, she had gone to another department store, one close to her office in West Hollywood, to buy a dress and a pair of shoes. She had decided she didn't like the shoes, so on her way back to her office she had stopped in a shoe store on Wilshire and bought another pair. She had then left work a little early and dropped into Amsterdam's, which was nearer her home in Westwood. She had intended to pick up a piece of flatware she had ordered from the silver department, buy some ribbon and sewing materials, then possibly find an inexpensive bag to match the second pair of shoes she had bought earlier.

To accomplish all this she had had to go to several different parts of the store on different floors, while lugging around what she'd bought as well as her own purse. She hadn't been sure about the fifteen-dollar bag she'd selected. "I thought the strap might be too long and the color not quite right," she explained. But she took it along with her on her wanderings until she could make up her mind. In the middle of all this, I had tried to get her into conversation and unwittingly contributed to her confusion. She had been in the store for about an hour, and by the time she headed for the parking lot, the item in question had become one of six or seven bulky objects she was clutching in her arms, while simultaneously groping for her car keys. "I'd really forgotten all about it, until this man Grant tugged it out from between all these other packages," she concluded.

Jamie Horton looked at me. "And you were there and saw what happened?"

"Yes," I said. "A lot of it."

"Would you be willing to make a sworn statement on Mrs. Meade's behalf?"

"Of course."

"Or testify in court?"

"Sure."

I heard Allyson gasp, but Jamie Horton tried quickly to reassure her. "I want to be prepared for the worst," she said, "even though none of this may be necessary."

"I just can't believe this," Allyson said. "I've been in that store ten or twelve times this year."

"What happened when you went back the other day?"

"Cruz wouldn't see me, and then they shunted me about from one department to another," Allyson answered. "Nobody would talk to me. So then I left and called the guard."

"Grant?"

"Yes."

"You've never been arrested for anything before?"

"No, never. I've never even had a traffic ticket."

"What happened when you called in about your account?"

"I told them I'd lost my card, as you suggested. No problem, they said." Allyson laughed. "I'm all paid up, a client in good standing." The smile suddenly froze on her face. "What's going on, Miss Horton? I guess I'm a little scared."

"Well, security people hear a lot of stories, just like judges," the lawyer explained. "They have a tendency to accept at face value whatever an arresting officer says, simply because he has no reason to lie, whereas with a defendant, it's often a case of, 'Oh, we've heard *that* story before.' They've heard every story, believe me, including yours, which fits into the category of the 'I-forgot' defense. That's the one most favored by well-to-do people caught with the goods.''

"Oh, dear," Allyson said, looking stricken.

"Shoplifting is the fastest-growing crime in the country," the lawyer continued. "Stores are protecting themselves now by prosecuting as much as they can. They're getting a message across, if you see what I mean."

Allyson leaned forward in her chair, her small, delicate-looking hands clutching her purse. "What's going to happen to me?"

"Don't panic," Jamie Horton said. "There are a lot of things I can do. The first is to make a few calls of my own. You're not exactly a hardened criminal." She reached for a scratch pad and jotted down some notes. "What does your husband do?"

"Julian?" Allyson asked, evidently startled by the question. "Oh, he has an art gallery on La Cienega, the Masters. He used to have one in Venice called the Cerberus, which was very avant-garde and all like that, but now he sells a lot of old stuff."

"Old stuff?"

"Paintings, old bits and pieces of things, even furniture. He's begun doing very well."

I gathered from her tone that there had been a period, and not too long ago, when Julian hadn't been doing very well. I found myself beginning to wonder about Allyson Meade's marriage. I was finding her even more attractive than when I'd first spotted her in Amsterdam's.

"I want to know something," she said, still poised for flight and staring at the lawyer.

"Certainly, Mrs. Meade. What is it?"

"Do you believe me?"

"Yes, I do," Jamie Horton assured her. "The point is to make them believe you."

"Do you think you can?"

"I'm going to try very hard," the lawyer said. "You did have the purse, after all. The only thing in question is intent."

"Did I mean to steal it, is that what you're saying?"

"Exactly," Jamie Horton said, reaching again for her pad and pencil.

We stood up to go. "You know what I'd like to do?" Allyson Meade said.

The lawyer looked up. "What's that, Mrs. Meade?"

"I'd like to go back to that store and kick the shit out of that man Cruz," she said, her cheeks red with anger.

I laughed. "I'll help you," I said.

Jamie Horton was not laughing. "I don't think that would be very productive," she observed.

It was about noon when we walked out of there into Lake, a long, tree-lined avenue of stores, restaurants, and small office buildings. "Would you like a cup of coffee?" I asked, as we headed for the parking lot.

"Well..." She hesitated. "You won't be late for your bet?"

"Plenty of time," I assured her. "I need some caffeine."

"Well, that's very nice," she said, "but I'm paying."

We found a place on the corner of the next cross street and settled into a booth. Allyson ordered herself a tuna salad sandwich to go with her coffee and asked me if I also wanted to eat. I told her it was early for me and that I'd grab something at the track. "It helps to kill time between races," I explained, "especially if you're not betting."

"I've got to get back to work," she said. "This is my lunch break."

"What do you do?"

"I'm a nurse," she declared.

I was amazed. "Really? What hospital?"

"I work for three doctors in West Hollywood. I'm sort of their head honcho and all like that." I must have looked puzzled. "I take care of the patients some of the time, but I also keep the books and answer the phone, whatever has to be done. There are three other women in the office, and I kind of ride herd on them."

"West Hollywood? I thought all the rich doctors had offices in Beverly Hills."

"Who said they were rich? Not all doctors are rich. These are three wonderful men. I've been with them for twelve years now." The sandwich arrived, and she took one small, delicate bite out of it, the little fingers of both hands raised exactly as she had obviously been taught at home or at school. It was an old-fashioned gesture, curiously disarming. Everything about her, in fact, seemed soft and gentle and refined, but I had also noticed in her, when she had exploded in anger against Cruz, a certain amount of steel. Somewhere behind that lace-curtain exterior, I suspected, and not too far behind, lurked a tough, self-reliant individual with a strong mind of her own. It made her even more attractive to me.

"What do they do?" I asked.

"Who?"

"These doctors of yours."

"They all have specialties and all like that," she said. "One's a gastroenterologist, one's a cardiologist, and the third one's a nephrologist, kidneys. But basically they just practice good medicine. We have all kinds of patients, a lot of old people on Medicare, too."

"That can't be a bundle of laughs."

"Oh, there are days when I just hate it and want to quit and all," she said, "but I think I'd go crazy if I didn't work.

And sometimes, especially when we win one and save somebody's life, it can be wonderful. I mean, most of the time we have these little old complaining women who don't have anything to do with themselves but come to the doctor, and there's nothing really wrong with them, except they're old and lonely and have to talk to somebody, and they drive you crazy in the office. And then along comes some real interesting case and you get all involved and then you help to make that person well again and its wonderful. It makes you feel you've done something important, something that matters. But there are very bad days, too."

"Like what?"

"You lose people," she said. "You get a patient and you have him for years and he becomes your friend and then you lose him. That's hard. Harder on the doctors than on me."

"I thought doctors were all fairly cold-blooded about that sort of thing," I commented.

"Wrong," she said. "You're as wrong as you can be. Maybe some doctors. Surgeons, I know, can be very hard, or seem to be, even if they're not. It's like a protective shield, because if they let what happens affect them too much, they wouldn't be able to practice at all. I mean, they lose people all the time. But with my doctors, when we lose one of our patients, it's a tragedy. I've seen all three of these men cry. That's one reason I stay with them. If they were in it just for the money I wouldn't still be working for them."

"Then you don't have to work."

She looked a little uncomfortable, as if I had suddenly presented her with a dilemma she had been turning over in her own mind. "Well, not now," she said. "I mean, Julian's doing real well, but it was hard for a long time. When he had the gallery in Venice and he was trying to promote all these modern artists, we didn't have two dimes. He's doing very well now." She took a sip of her coffee and stared past me out the window.

"Why do I have the feeling you were happier when he wasn't doing so well?" I asked.

She blushed slightly and smiled, a bit wanly. "I'm a terrible actress, I guess."

"Look, I don't want to pry into your private life," I said, "but I do get the idea I could ask you out."

"That's very nice of you, but I am married."

"Lots of people are married."

"I know," she said. "I know lots of people fool around—"

"I don't want to fool around," I told her, with absolute sincerity. "I'd just like to see you again. I wouldn't ask you, if I thought you were totally unavailable. I'm picking up some distress signals on my radar screen."

"Julian and I had a very old-fashioned ceremony in a church and all," she said, "with all the old words. You know, 'richer or poorer,' and all like that. I happen to believe in them, that's all."

"I hope you're not angry."

"Oh, no," she said, smiling and reaching out to touch my hand. "I'm flattered, really. It's so nice of you. But I just can't. And anyway, I'll see you again."

"You mean, if we go to court."

"I may even see you at the races. That's where you are, isn't it?"

"Right now, yes. And much of the time, when I'm not working. You go to the track?"

"I've been a few times, on Wednesdays, with my doctors," she explained. "The office is closed Wednesday afternoons, and two of my doctors go to the races. Last year they had a horse of their own and they love to bet. So I went with them. I had such a good time. It's like you forget about everything else, especially all the bad things, at the track. That's why they go. That's why a lot of doctors gamble as they do."

"Yeah, I once worked a convention in Las Vegas, and the casino was full of medical types," I said. "I've never seen such high rollers, for a bunch of amateurs."

"They just need to blot out everything else," Allyson said. "There's a very high suicide rate among doctors, you know."

"Yeah, I can see that."

She took a couple of more nibbles of her sandwich, the little pinkies still upraised. I really loved to watch her eat. "Listen," I said, "what about this Wednesday? Will you be there?"

"Maybe. The doctors might go, and I'll go with them." She paused, as if to consider the possible complications implicit in such a seemingly trivial commitment. I thought her hesitation had to do with me, in terms of her loyalty to her marriage vows, but I had overestimated my own role in her life. "Julian might be there, too," she said.

"Your husband? How come?"

She looked vaguely away from me again. "He's been buying racehorses," she said. "He's . . . he's really getting into it now." The revelation seemed to make her increasingly uncomfortable.

"What horses do you own?" I asked.

"Me?" She looked startled by the question. "It's Julian. It has nothing to do with me."

"It doesn't? There's community property in California."

"He doesn't talk much to me about it," she said, in a tone that was clearly intended to close the door on this part of our conversation. "It's an investment, that's all." Another pause now. "That's what he tells me, and I don't ask him too much about it."

"Well, if you're both out there," I observed, "you can introduce me to him."

"No chance of that," she said, with a strained little laugh.

"Julian's in the Turf Club. I'm up in the grandstand, with my doctors. They have a box."

"Whereabouts?"

"Section Nine, above the main aisle."

"I know it well," I said. "Then I'll look for you."

"That will be nice," she answered, signaling now for the check. "Then you can do most of the talking. You can tell me about your magic and the races and all."

"I apologize for pumping you," I said. "And I hope I haven't been boorish about wanting to see you again."

"Boorish? Oh, no." She laughed, this time with genuine pleasure. "It's very nice to feel wanted. It's very flattering. Really."

4

Dancing Feet

I had a good weekend. Jay's hot streak came to an end on Saturday, when his three main selections ran second, but by that time I had recovered my own touch. *The Racing Form* no longer seemed an incomprehensible jumble of contradictory statistics, but a sensible key to the day's action. I smoked out a couple of longshots and hooked them up properly in Exactas to show a thousand-dollar profit for the two days, so I was able to repay Jay's loan and I still had about six hundred dollars to do battle with on Wednesday. Furthermore, I was feeling better about my life in general. My agent had called to inform me that the TV series I was up for had been put off until at least February, by which time I was sure I'd be back working at my magic again, and my doctor had told me that my finger was doing just fine; I'd be able to begin therapy in about ten days.

Best of all, I had had a call from Allyson Meade. She had telephoned to thank me again for my help and to tell me she would definitely be at the track on Wednesday and hoped to see me there. My cup wasn't exactly running over, but it was fuller than it had been in quite a while.

I didn't much like the card that Wednesday. The fields were short, no more than seven horses in all but two of the races, and I had checked out my estimate of the day with

Jay, who agreed with me. "It looks like the classical Dummy God day," he said. "A lot of obvious bad favorites who'll go off at low odds and probably win. I may just sit all day long, unless I can find something in the ninth, which I haven't finished doing yet. So I'll see you at the office, okay?"

The office is what Jay calls the track. "Fine," I said. "I kind of like Bombardier in the seventh. He should be three or four to one."

"Yeah," Jay agreed, but without enthusiasm. "He could win, if somebody hooks the favorite early and runs with him. Otherwise, I'd say it's another watch-it race."

It was tough to argue with the Fox. Once he'd settled on an opinion in a race, he became a mountain; it was almost impossible to budge him off it. It was one of his major strengths at the track. Playing the horses for a living takes plenty of discipline and an iron ass, and nobody knows that better than Jay Fox, who runs his business, day in and day out, in somebody's box somewhere over the finish line. "Once I've done my work and I feel I understand what a race is all about," he once said, "I have no reason to listen to anyone else or to change what I've decided to do." Moses himself, with the Ten Commandments clutched in his hands and just down from Mount Sinai, couldn't have spoken with more authority than that.

I spotted Allyson Meade before she saw me. She was sitting in a box a little beyond the finish line, two or three rows back from the aisle. She was still dressed in her nurse's uniform, white pants and a light-blue blouse, and she looked adorable. She was gazing down at the horses in the walking ring, which here was directly below the box area, and her long, graceful arms rested lightly on the railing in front of her. She didn't notice me, and I sneaked up beside her.

"Who do ya like?" I asked, in a hoarse imitation of a

diseased horseplayer I know, whose only question this is. "Ya got anything hot, baby?"

She laughed. "Hi," she said. "Would you like to join me?"

"Sure." I sat down beside her. "You alone?"

"No, my doctors are here. We arrived just after the second race," she said. "They've gone off to bet."

"You didn't bet?"

"No. I don't see anything I like."

"Very sensible of you. This is a bad race. Any one of these cheap fillies in here could win it." I pulled out my *Form* and showed her the field, as I had analyzed it. Over my notations I had scribbled "Pass." "There's no value in the race," I told her. "The three horse will probably win it, but she's even money."

"I wouldn't know about all that," Allyson said. "I just don't have a good feeling about this race."

A couple of minutes before post time, two disheveled-looking, middle-aged men, wearing huge binoculars around their necks and clutching programs and *Racing Forms,* showed up and sat down behind us. One was of medium height, curly-haired, with a long nose and the soulful eyes of a kindly pawnbroker; the other was tall, carried himself very straight, and had a round, pleasant-looking face with dark eyes and high, arched eyebrows. Allyson quickly introduced me to them, but I didn't catch their names clearly and they paid very little attention to me. Their eyes were now glued to their glasses, as the horses reached the starting gate. "It is now post time," the track announcer intoned over the public-address system.

"The four is a lock," the kindly pawnbroker said. "This pig of a favorite will die in the stretch, and the four will pick them all up."

"If the six breaks and doesn't get fanned on the turn,

she'll be right there," dark eyes countered.

The race went off and the favorite won easily, leading all the way around the course and paying $3.80 to win. Strictly a Dummy God horse. Allyson's doctors looked momentarily crushed, but quickly rebounded and reached for their *Racing Forms*.

"It was the four who got fanned on the turn," the kindly pawnbroker said.

"The six didn't break," dark eyes countered.

"Well, let's move on."

"This race is wide open."

"Mr. Anderson is the nice man I met the day I was arrested," Allyson said.

"Oh, that's right. It's nice of you to help out," the kindly pawnbroker observed, his eyes scanning the *Form*.

"Hell of a thing," dark eyes said. "She ought to sue." His finger suddenly jabbed at the page in front of him. "Look, Ed, look at the finish on this six horse here in his last race."

"That was two months ago," Ed countered. "Where's he been all this time?"

"Resting."

"Or laid up. You see any works?"

"Two."

"In two months? And what's the recency?"

"He worked on the twenty-second."

"That was three weeks ago, and it was real slow," Ed said. "What you have here, Charlie, is a cripple they're trying to unload on some poor bastard who doesn't know any better. Forget him."

"I don't know," Charlie insisted. "This trainer pulls these off every now and then."

"He's a chemist, strictly a needle man."

"He wins a lot of races, Ed."

"And he breaks down a lot of horses, too."

"I don't care too much if they break down after the race," Charlie said. "The idea is to win races, isn't it?"

"He could break down during the race, too."

"With cheap claimers, Ed, that's the chance you take."

"Not with my money, fella."

"You do what you want, I'm putting something on him at that price."

"What is he?"

"Twelve to one."

"Give me the money," Ed said. "He has no chance."

"I'm not giving you my money," Charlie said. "I'm going to talk you into betting him with me."

"No way. Forget it."

"You just don't like money."

"I like it well enough not to throw it away on some broken-down plater who's going to be eased in the stretch."

"I'll bet you ten dollars he's on the board."

"You're on."

Before either Allyson or I could intervene in this discussion, a third man joined us. He was short and on the plump side, in his late forties, with an affable-looking, troubled face and a tangled mop of dusty-looking, brown hair that kept falling over his eyes. "What are you going to do here?" he asked, his gaze shifting agitatedly back and forth from Ed to Charlie.

"I like the six horse," Charlie said.

"No chance," Ed contradicted him. "The one is a lock. I'm going to wheel him on top in Exactas and back to two longshots, the four and the three."

"The six horse is the winner," Charlie said. "I'm just going to bet him straight. Hell, he's twelve to one and he'll go off at no less than ten."

"The six won't finish the race," Ed said.

"Ed doesn't like money," Charlie observed. "The one has a lot of dog in him. He'll die in the last sixteenth."

"Oh, my God!" the new arrival exclaimed, his hands now groping wildly in his pockets. "I think I had the double. I hope I didn't throw away the winning ticket." He produced a great wad of crumpled pari-mutuel tickets and began shuffling through them. As he did so, some fluttered to the ground; others he threw away. He took his *Racing Form* out of his back pocket and more tickets fell out, also his program, which was already torn, stained, and battered, as if it had been mangled in a garbage compacter. "Jesus," the man said, "where the hell is it?" He retrieved the fallen tickets and his program, hitting his head on the railing of the box as he went down. He ignored the blow, which had been hard enough to make the metal rail quiver like a harp string, and bobbed up to resume his frantic search for his missing winner. He was sweating profusely now, and his hands were trembling. More tickets cascaded to the ground. "Christ, it must be in my box." He thrust his program back into his pocket and rushed away, nearly knocking down two well-dressed, elderly women on their way back to their seats.

"Who's that?" I asked. "I've seen him before."

"Dr. Thompson," Allyson answered. "He's a friend of ours."

"He's a doctor?"

"One of our most eminent," Charlie said.

"He's a very fine surgeon," Allyson explained.

"A surgeon? I wouldn't let him cut my cuticles."

Allyson giggled. "He's just terrible at the track."

"Terrible? He's a wreck."

"Luckily, he only operates in the early mornings," Ed pointed out. "Horses run in the afternoons."

"I'd want to know if he bets with a bookie," I said. "I wouldn't want to be on the table if he had a horse being loaded into a starting gate somewhere."

Ed and Charlie both laughed. "It's a good thing his wife takes care of the money," Ed said.

"Last year she got him to go to Europe," Charlie explained. "They spent a month in France and Spain, and it cost them twenty-five thousand dollars. When they came back, Will told us he figured he'd saved money by going over there."

I turned to Allyson. "That's one rich doctor," I observed.

"Surgeons make a lot of money," Allyson answered, "more than anyone else in the medical profession."

"That is the truth," Ed said.

"Amen," Charlie added.

"Okay now," Ed said, "we got eight minutes. Can I change your mind?"

"Nope," Charlie answered. "Let's go."

They got up and headed up the stairs toward the betting windows.

After they'd gone, I looked at Allyson. "If you hadn't told me those two guys were doctors," I said, "I'd have sworn I was sitting with some real hard knockers."

"I told you," she answered. "They love the races."

"Yes, but you didn't tell me they were a couple of madmen."

"Only at the track," she said. "You know we lost a patient last night? Charlie's had about two hours' sleep. This is where he comes to blot it temporarily out of his mind."

"Tell me their names again."

"Charlie's last name is Tanana," she said. "He's part Polynesian, on his father's side. Ed Hamner is the one who hired me. They're both wonderful men."

"Where's the rest of your triumvirate?"

"Oh, Dr. Goldberg never comes to the track. He doesn't enjoy it."

"I notice you don't call him by his first name."

"Or Ed and Charlie either, when I'm working," she explained. "At the office, it's all business. Outside of it, we're good friends."

"Do you care about watching this race?"

"Not really. Why?"

"I thought I'd buy you a drink or something."

"I'd love a diet soda."

"You don't look like you have a weight problem."

"I don't now," she said. "And I'm going to keep it that way. But I was a fat girl until I was in my late teens."

"Hard to believe."

"You'd better believe it."

We went to the main bar in the clubhouse, and I ordered a Tab for Allyson and a light beer for myself, then we stood and watched the action around us, which became increasingly agitated as post time neared. It made me happy to watch it all, and I found myself grinning.

"You really love this, don't you?" Allyson asked.

"Yes, I do."

"Do you love it as much as your magic?"

"That's a tough question," I answered. "I don't think I would love it nearly as much, if I didn't have the magic. Magic is the real world for me. It's what I do best, it's what I've built my life on. The horses, that's something else."

"Escape?"

"No, not really. I'll explain it to you sometime."

We watched the third race on the nearest television monitor. Once again it was won by the favorite, at odds of eight to five. Ed Hamner's selection finished a distant third, but, as he had predicted, the six horse broke down on the turn for home and had to be carted off the track. "Well, at least Ed won his bet with Charlie," I commented. "Maybe he broke even on the race."

"I hate that," Allyson said, her eyes focused on the screen where the crippled animal stood quietly, awaiting the arrival of the horse van. The jockey had dismounted and was standing by his head, bridle in hand, patting his neck and trying to keep him calm. "That's the side of racing I hate," she continued, turning her head away from the sight. "Will they destroy him?"

"I don't think so," I said. "It doesn't look like he broke anything. Maybe it's his suspensories or he bowed a tendon. These animals can hurt themselves so many ways. Anyway, he'll get better care from the vet now than from that butcher who trains him."

"How does he keep his license?"

"A lot of doctors break people down and they keep their licenses," I said. "Racing is not a game, Allyson. There's a lot of money at stake, and there are a lot of pretty unscrupulous people scrambling around after it, just as in real life. Because this is real life, too—just as real as what you do for a living."

"It's not life and death."

"Oh, yes it is," I corrected her. "Very often it is."

We spent another half-hour at the bar, chatting about this and that, and also watched the fourth on the monitor. This one was won by a five-to-two shot, making it four races in a row won either by favorites or the second choice. Jay had been right: the Dummy God was on his throne, scattering blessings from above on the little pointed heads of the ignorant and the trusting.

As we headed back toward the box, about twenty minutes before the fifth race, I spotted Freddie Chambers. He was on his way back from somewhere else to the Turf Club. I waved at him and he came right over, a jaunty little figure dressed in white slacks, a navy-blue blazer with gold buttons, and a red beret. He was smiling broadly. Before I could say anything, he brushed past me and hugged Allyson. "How're you doing, sweetheart?" he asked. "I haven't seen you in a hell of a long time."

"Oh, Freddie," Allyson said, hugging him back and kissing him on the cheek, "it's so good to see you! Are you okay?"

"I'm great." He cocked a finger in my direction. "What are you doing with old Shifty here? I thought you knew only a higher class of people."

"We met a few days ago."

"I picked her up in a department store," I said. "I helped her with her packages."

Freddie ignored the information. "Julian's here," he said to Allyson.

"I thought he would be."

Freddie seemed troubled, as if about to impart some other possibly unpleasant piece of information, but apparently changed his mind. He gave Allyson another hug. "Listen," he said, "I gotta get a bet down here."

"You go ahead, Freddie," she told him. "It was nice to see you."

Freddie lingered, however, and bounced on the balls of his feet, as if about to leap into space. "It's not like the old days, is it, Al?" he said. "Are you all right?"

"Yes, I'm fine."

"You sure look good." He paused again. I had the feeling he was still wrestling with some piece of disquieting news he didn't quite know how to handle.

"It's fine, Freddie, really," Allyson said. "Don't worry about me."

He looked at her and shrugged. "Well, then..."

"How are *you* doing, Freddie? You winning?" I asked.

My question cleared the air like a flash of lightning through a storm cloud. "Winning?" Freddie shouted. "I'm killing them! I haven't lost a race all day! I'm—" He stopped abruptly, as if an unseen fist had jabbed him violently in the solar plexus. His eyes widened in terror, and he suddenly whirled and rushed away from us toward the Turf Club stairway.

I turned and saw a tall, pale blond man wearing dark sunglasses detach himself from the bar and move swiftly after him. He was in his thirties, I guessed, and dressed in a dark-gray business suit. He moved with the grace of an athlete, but by the time he reached the foot of the stairs Freddie had vanished. The stranger was prevented from following him by the uniformed attendant guarding the entrance, and he turned back. The dark glasses stared blankly at us, and I thought for a moment he might come over, but he apparently changed his mind and walked quickly off through the crowd around the betting windows.

"Who's that?" I asked.

"I have no idea," Allyson said. "Maybe Freddie owes him money. He used to owe everybody money. He even borrowed from me one time."

"Could be a bookie," I agreed, "but he sure didn't look like one."

"I hope Freddie isn't in trouble."

"Well, that's his business," I said. "Anyway, he's got the money now to bail himself out. At least until he blows it back."

"He's doing so well now," she said. "I'm glad."

"Where do you know Freddie from?" I asked.

"I've known Freddie Camerini for years," she said, "from when Julian had the gallery in Venice. He was one of the original Cerberus artists."

"Really? And he called himself Camerini then?"

"That's his name—Federico Camerini. Only he always called himself Fred. Julian told me he had changed his name, but I don't remember why now."

"I've known Freddie for a while, not as long as you," I said, "but I never even knew he was an artist. A painter?"

"Oh, yes. And a very interesting one," she answered. "But his things never sold. I don't know why, really."

"What kind of pictures were they?"

"Very small, very simple. Mostly he painted still lifes—bottles, fruit, small objects. They were very beautiful and odd, really unique, but not at all flashy or commercial. That may have been the trouble."

"Doesn't sound very avant-garde to me."

"They weren't, I guess. Anyway, nothing sold, and Julian had to drop him after a while. He kind of disappeared. Then, about three years ago, he popped up again. He called the house and asked for Julian, who was out or unavailable or something, and I gathered from what he said that he'd been having some kind of success somewhere. I asked Julian about him, but all he told me was that Freddie was in business for himself and doing fine."

"Doing what?"

"I don't know. He travels, I guess, because he called Julian once, again at home, but from Switzerland, I think. Lugano?"

"That's in the southern part, yes."

"Anyway, Julian was very upset that Freddie had called him at home, but he never told me why. But isn't it nice he's doing well? He was always so hard up."

"I know one thing," I told her.

"What's that?"

"He didn't make his money at the track."

"He's bad?"

"The worst I've ever seen, on a par in every way with this surgeon friend of yours."

When we finally got back to the box, we found it shrouded in gloom. Ed and Charlie had yet to cash a ticket, and they were nose-deep in their *Forms*, trying to pry a decent winner out of the tangle of little numbers dancing maddeningly before their eyes. I prudently kept quiet while they blew another bundle on two impossible horses in the fifth and sixth, after which I invited Allyson down to the saddling enclosure behind the grandstand. "I have a horse I like in here," I said, "but I want to look at him up close. Want to come down?"

"Sure," she said, rising from her seat.

"What horse?" Ed Hamner asked.

"Bombardier," I said. "I think there's enough speed up front to make his closing move decisive. But the horse is nervous. He has a tendency to wash out and, if he's all wet, I don't want him."

"Are you coming back here before betting?" Charlie wanted to know.

"I will," Allyson said. "I'll tell you what we see."

A few minutes later, Allyson and I were standing side by side at the railing of the saddling enclosure, watching the trainers and grooms at work around their animals. Bombardier, a big, gray six-year-old gelding, looked just fine. His coat gleamed with health, and he seemed really on the muscle, ready to run his very best race. His odds, at the moment, were four to one, and I was pretty sure I was going to bet on him.

"What about that one?" Allyson asked, waving her program at the next to last horse in the parade, as the entries were led out toward the paddock, where their jockeys and owners awaited them.

The horse she had indicated was Sneaky Pete, a fast, lightly raced four-year-old colt, who was stretching out here from sprint distances to a mile and a sixteenth for the first time in his career. He was trained by Mel Ducato, whose horses were usually live, and was being ridden by Robbie Lance, a young apprentice jockey who had begun to win some races. "He's all right, I guess," I said, "but he's a speed horse. He's drawn outside and he's not going to outbreak the favorite, who's on the rail. Also, there are a

couple of other speed merchants in here, so he'll probably
go wide on the first turn and lose a lot of ground. I just
can't see him in here today. Maybe next time."

"He has dancing feet," Allyson said, as the horses disappeared into the tunnel.

"He has what?"

"Dancing feet," she repeated. "You know, like when a
horse is bouncy and looks like he really wants to run and
all like that."

"Well, that's an interesting observation. I just think this
isn't his day, that's all."

Allyson didn't answer me, but I noticed her jaw was
firmly set. When we got back upstairs, she headed right for
the betting windows, and I knew she was going to put
something on Sneaky Pete. I went by Jay's box and found
him encamped on his chair, arms folded and an expression
of benign boredom on his face. "I haven't made a bet all
day," he informed me, "and I'm not going to."

"I like Bombardier."

"Yeah, he could do it. But I think he'll run out of ground.
The speed is sticking pretty good today."

"I'm going to bet him in the place hole."

"Yeah, yeah, that's not a bad way to go," Jay said,
nodding dubiously.

"A lady I met likes Sneaky Pete."

"He has a shot, but the post is bad and he can't get the
lead," Jay observed. "What do I want him for?"

"He has dancing feet," I said.

"He has what?"

"Dancing feet. That's what the lady said."

"I don't think they pay off at the windows on choreog-
raphy," Jay said.

I left him, just as Whodoyalike and Action Jackson came
rushing up to pick his brains, and went to wager two hundred
dollars on Bombardier to place. I reached the box just as

the horses were being loaded into the starting gate and found the doctors in a high state of excitement. They had both wheeled Sneaky Pete up and back in Exactas. The horse was nine to one, and they stood to make a tidy profit if he won or ran second to anyone but the favorite, who had been bet down to six to five.

The race was run exactly as I had anticipated it would be, but with one important exception. Sneaky Pete broke well, but Robbie Lance took a hold on him and eased him in toward the rail as the horses charged for the first turn. He was fourth at the seven-eighths pole, no more than two wide all the way around to the backstretch. The favorite and two other speed horses were waging a brisk duel for the lead up front, and Bombardier was next to last, but running easily along the rail.

As the horses turned for home, Bombardier moved out and began his run. He was being carried wide now, but it didn't matter. I could see that the speed up front was dying, and I was certain that Bombardier was going to win the race. As the field reached the head of the lane, he had drawn even and by the eighth pole, a furlong from the wire, he was in front. I cursed myself mentally for not having had the courage to bet on him to win, but I had neglected to take dancing feet into account.

Robbie Lance had kept Sneaky Pete tucked in close to the rail all the way around and never more than five lengths back. Now, at the head of the stretch, as the horses up front tired and began to drift out, he shot Sneaky Pete through a hole on the rail and asked him for his run. The animal responded. He caught Bombardier at the sixteenth pole, then, with the apprentice whipping and slashing, he drove for home and won going away by a solid two lengths.

Ed and Charlie were up on their feet, hugging Allyson and beating each other on the back with their rolled-up

Racing Forms. Their Exacta tickets were each worth over four hundred dollars and put them comfortably ahead for the day.

I looked at Allyson, who was smiling and blushing at the same time. "I'm so sorry," she said to me. "I just liked him."

"Don't be sorry, Allyson. I won my bet and I'll make about three hundred myself," I told her. "What did you bet?"

"Only two dollars," she said. "I don't like to bet much. I was poor for too long."

"Listen, we all won, it's great," I said. "Dancing feet— I have to remember that."

"I don't know anything," she said. "I just had such a strong feeling..."

Dr. Thompson came by, looking like the last survivor of the Charge of the Light Brigade. He had been told about Sneaky Pete, of course, but had not bet him on the nose and had somehow managed to couple him with every horse in the race except Bombardier, whom he had dismissed as "a plodder." The man obviously needed a special Dummy God of his own, all to himself. But then, no dunce deity in the universe could be expected to lift that heavy a burden off the ground.

The doctors now turned to consider the eighth race, but it in no way diminished the glow of our big win. Allyson was as excited as if she had brought in a fifty-thousand-dollar Pick Six ticket, and I was delighted for her. When the doctors went off to bet again and I had returned from cashing our tickets, however, I noticed that she had suddenly become very quiet and pale. She was staring down into the paddock, where the horses were walking around in a circle preparatory to being ridden out onto the track. "What's the matter?" I asked, handing her her winnings.

"Nothing."

"Do you feel all right?"

She was gazing at the people milling about on the grass inside the walking ring. "I knew he was seeing her," she said, as much to herself as to me. "The bastard."

"Who?"

"My husband."

"Where?"

She sat down in her chair, her face very tense and both hands clamped on her purse, so hard that her fingers were white from the strain. "He's the tall man, on the heavy side, with curly hair. He's near the break, to the right."

I looked down and quickly picked him out. He was good-looking, all right, about forty, with thick, dark hair and strong, square shoulders. He was wearing horn-rimmed glasses and smiling broadly. He had a very white, very even set of perfectly aligned teeth that I would have been happy, at that moment, to jam a fist into. Next to him was a slender, very beautiful young woman of no more than thirty, with long ash-blond hair and fine legs and skin the color of honey. "Who is she?" I asked.

"I don't think I want to talk about it now," Allyson said. She stood up. "Would you mind driving me home?"

"Now?"

"It's all right, if you don't want to," she said. "I can wait. I came with the doctors in their car, right from the office."

"Of course I'll drive you home," I told her. "Let's go."

On our way out of the track, after saying goodbye to Ed and Charlie, I passed Jay on his way back from the men's room. "Dancing feet," I said. "I told you."

"If he didn't get through on the rail, he was dead meat," the Fox answered. "You leaving?"

"Yeah. See you tomorrow."

He hadn't noticed Allyson, who had turned her head away from us and was hurrying toward the escalators. She was in tears by that time, I realized, and there was very little I could do to comfort her.

— 5 —

Dreams

"Would you like to come up to my place and see some tricks?" I asked, smiling.

"Well, I don't know..."

"You want to know about magic," I said, "I can show you."

"That would be very nice, but, really..."

"Look, Allyson, I would love to take you to bed," I assured her, "but I promise I won't touch you. You said you wanted to know about me. There are very few moves I can pull off one-handed, but I could show you some things I have, and we could have a nightcap, and then I'll drive you home. All right?"

She nodded. "Yes, I'm sorry. You must think I'm a tease or a prude or something," she said. "After all, I did agree to go out with you."

"I didn't mistake you for Nancy Reagan," I told her. "You must know I like you a lot, but we can just be friends, okay?"

"That's very nice."

We had eaten at Saratoga West, a pleasant neighborhood meat-and-potatoes restaurant with a friendly bar, where I was more or less a regular and which was only a few blocks from my apartment in West Hollywood. It was Friday, two days after our afternoon at the track, and I had called Allyson that morning at her office to find out how she was. She had cried silently all the way home in the car that Wednesday, but then had tried to apologize to me for her behavior.

"Apologize? For what?" I had asked. "You're upset. I can understand why."

"I'm mad," she said. "I always cry when I'm mad. I hope their damn plane gets hijacked."

"Their plane? Where are they going?"

"He's taking her to New York this weekend for eight or nine days, damn him."

"He told you that?"

"No, of course not," she said. "He's going on business, about his new gallery there. But I know she's going with him."

"Why do you put up with it?"

"I'm not going to, not for long." She had hesitated a moment. "But I owe Julian a lot," she added. "I'll explain it to you sometime."

"I think you already have."

"You don't know all of it."

She had told me a good deal about herself during dinner. Her maiden name was Connors and she was born in a little town called Hope, lost somewhere in the Oklahoma Panhandle. She was raised as an only child by a widowed mother, who was fiercely determined that Allyson would move away and have a better life than she had had. They had been very poor, but somehow money had been found to send Allyson to a series of Catholic boarding schools in Arkansas, where she had received a first-rate traditional education and, simultaneously, lost her belief in a merciful, understanding God. The nuns, with their petty cruelties and prejudices, had seen to that. Then she had worked her way through nursing school in Salt Lake City, first by cleaning other people's apartments and then as a part-time waitress in the local Hilton coffee shop. Her last year in school, at the age of twenty, she had fallen in love with a marine pilot, who had come home on leave and asked her, two weeks after they met, to marry him. After the ceremony in Salt Lake City and a two-day honeymoon at the Hilton, he went back to his base in Southern California, and she continued her studies.

Three days after graduation, she received a telegram informing her that her husband had been killed in a training accident. After the funeral, she had left Salt Lake and gone to live in Mission Viejo, just a few miles from the marine base where her husband had died, and she moved into the one-bedroom apartment he had rented for them for a year in a dreary new development on the edge of a shopping mall. Walking home late one night from her job in a hospital two blocks from the mall, she had been accosted and attacked by two drunken enlisted men, and would have been raped, perhaps murdered, if her cries hadn't been heard by a Mexican maintenance man, who had shouted at her attackers to leave her alone. He had scared them off and they were never caught.

She had not been badly hurt, but she moved a month later to Los Angeles, where she got a job in another and better hospital. But she could no longer sleep at night, and she was afraid for a long time to go anywhere alone after dark. She had been forced to quit the hospital and applied through an agency for a lower-paying job in private practice, where she would be able to work regular hours. She had been hired by Ed Hamner and had been with her three doctors ever since, but at first it hadn't been easy. "I couldn't sleep," she had told me. "I kept having all these terrible dreams. I was always being chased or attacked. I was so tired I couldn't do my job right. I'd fall asleep on my lunch hour."

The doctors had called her in, and she thought she would be fired. Instead, she had told them her story, and they had

sent her to a therapist, a marvelous woman named Ellen
Ravick, who treated her for over a year. The doctors paid
for everything her insurance didn't cover. "They were wonderful to me," she said. "I don't know what I'd have done.
Of course, I still had no money and no life. I was afraid to
go out and I didn't see anybody. I just went home and sewed
or read and watched TV. My mother died, and I went home
to bury her. I had tried to get her to move out to California
and live with me, but she wanted to stay in her town, where
she had her friends and all. I saw her at Christmas one year,
when somehow we had just enough money for her to get
out to see me for a week. I tell you, Lou, I wasn't having
much of a life."

Julian Meade had changed all that. He was a patient in
her office. He came in toward the end of her first year there
for a checkup and, as she was drawing his blood, he invited
her out to lunch. "I hadn't ever met anyone like him," she
said. "He was very charming and very considerate, and he
was a wonderful lover. I mean, Lou, I didn't know anything
at all."

"About sex? And you a nurse?"

She laughed. "Oh, I knew what it was all about, but not
how much fun it can be. The nuns saw to that. And Tommy
and I were just kids when we got married. I hadn't been to
bed with anyone else." She blushed. "Anyway, Julian was
an education in a lot of ways. He knew about art and music
and literature and he taught me a lot. I think he loved me,
too. And I loved him. Maybe I still love him, I don't know.
Certainly, things aren't the same anymore."

I paid the bill, and we strolled the few blocks to my place,
her arm comfortably in mine. She had a very light touch,
like that of a child, but it warmed me. I was not anxious
for the evening to end, but I didn't want to push matters
too hard either. She must have known how I felt, but I
assumed that she trusted me, and I was not about to violate

that trust. I wanted very much to keep on seeing her, even if it meant having to be nothing more than a friend.

"When did things begin to go wrong with you and Julian?" I asked. Not because I really cared, I have to admit, but really to keep our conversation going. I was afraid of silences, because I thought she might bolt. "I mean, was it when he started seeing this other woman?"

"No, before that. About two years ago," she said. "He began making a lot of money. It changed things."

"I've never been one to romanticize poverty."

"Oh, money isn't bad, I don't mean that. But we were happier when he had the Cerberus, the little gallery in Venice," she explained. "We used to see all these crazy young artists and go to lots of parties, and it was so much fun. Exciting, too. The Cerberus was *the* avant-garde gallery in L.A., you know. Julian backed and launched a lot of artists, including a couple of really important ones. But we couldn't make it pay. Julian had some money he'd inherited from his family back East, but in four years it was all gone. After that, it was a struggle and all. And then he gave it up. He had to, I guess."

"And he went into Old Masters and big bucks."

"Not right away," she said. "He was an assistant curator at the County Museum for three years, which is where he met all these fancy society people and all like that. And then he got some backing and opened the Masters. It's been a success from the first day. I mean, it's like Julian knew just what to buy and for whom."

"The business succeeded and the marriage died."

"Oh, I don't know," she said. "I hope it's not like that. But Julian's changed, and I guess I haven't. I mean, I'm basically a redneck, I guess."

"What about children?"

"We never wanted any, either of us."

"And do you still see any of your old friends?"

She shook her head. "Not many. Julian sees Freddie from time to time, but never socially. He's just around the gallery, I guess. I don't know why."

"Yeah, that is funny," I said. "Freddie's not exactly a class act. He's always been just another hard knocker to me."

"We don't see any of our other old friends," Allyson said, "not even the artists who became successful, and there have been several of them. It's like—like Julian turned a switch off somewhere. I guess he was hurt badly by his failure. Now—well, he's just in it for the money."

"We used to call that selling out."

Allyson didn't answer, and we walked the last half-block to my apartment house in silence. When we reached my front door, she detached herself from me. "Lou, I really feel I should go home," she said. "I'm sorry."

"Don't be sorry. I understand."

"I'm just upset about all this. If I do come in, I might stay."

"I wouldn't mind."

"I would. I'd be with you for the wrong reasons." She touched my arm again. "Please, some other time. I do want to know all about your magic. Honest."

I walked her back to her car, which was parked in the Saratoga West lot. Then, to my surprise, she kissed me goodnight on the lips and drove quickly away.

Julian called her Sunday afternoon from New York, Allyson told me later. She had been out in the garden, weeding, and she was out of breath by the time she picked up the phone. "Allyson?" he asked.

"Yes."

"You all right?"

"Yes, I was out in the garden."

"You sound so far away."

"I ran in when I heard the phone."

"You still sound funny."

"It must be the connection."

"You want me to call you back?"

"No, it's fine. How is it going?"

"Very well. Did you see your lawyer again?"

"I talked to her on the phone."

"What did she say?"

"I'll tell you when you get back. We don't want to waste the phone time. It's all right, really. She's trying to take care of it."

"That's good. How's the weather?"

"Smoggy, as usual. What's it like in New York?"

"Miserable. It's cold and rainy and they say there's a storm coming in tomorrow. Listen, Ally, it's going to be terrific here."

"Really?"

"Yeah, just great. The space is right across from the Whitney, on the second floor of a brownstone. Very elegant. I'm going to sign the lease today."

"Good, Julian, I'm glad."

"Of course, I'll have to make sure about the lights, all the furnishings, the security and all. I'll have to be coming back and forth. God, it's really complicated here. Just getting anything done in New York is a big deal."

"I'll bet."

"But I should have opened a branch here a year ago. It's all here, you know."

"I can imagine."

"I've already seen so many people, you have no idea." He paused ever so slightly. "I wish you could have come with me."

"You know I couldn't."

"I'll be back probably a week from Tuesday, but I'll call you again and let you know. You won't have to meet me. I'll take a cab."

"That's fine."

"Are you sure you're all right, Ally?"

"Yes. Goodbye, Julian."

"Goodbye."

She hung up and stood in her bedroom, staring at the phone, as if expecting it to ring again. So much had been left unsaid. She shut her eyes and sat down on the edge of the bed. She had a vision of Julian's room at the Algonquin, where they had once stayed together, but this time she herself was not in the picture. The woman Julian was with came out of the bathroom. She was naked and still damp from her shower, her blond hair piled up under a towel. She walked over to the bed and sat down beside him, and then Allyson opened her eyes, bounced up again and began to shake.

Two days after this phone call, Allyson Meade spent the night with me. It happened very simply and naturally, as if we had planned it all along. She had called to tell me about the progress, or lack of it, of her case, and I had again invited her for dinner. This time we ate in a seaside restaurant in Venice, where the food was excellent and the decor distracting. Allyson had the impression that we were sitting in an aquarium. The place was full of hanging plants and miniature potted trees through which the waiters in their red jackets seemed to swim like fat goldfish. I ordered an expensive Pouilly Fuissé to go with our grilled sea bass and Allyson took my hand. "Lou, can you afford this?"

"You bet," I reassured her. "I had a pretty good weekend—three bets and two wins. I've got about twelve hundred dollars in the kitty now, and my unemployment checks should begin to arrive this week or next. Unless old Tony

Cruz can figure out a way to stop them."

"Can he?"

"No. But they did call me in for two interviews, and I had to go into a lot of detail about why I was fired. So he must have tried, the bastard."

Allyson looked distressed. "Why is he being so vindictive?"

"Just one of nature's great noblemen," I said. "By the way, what's happening with you?"

"It looks like I'm going to have to go to court."

"You're kidding."

"I wish I were. Jamie says it's almost impossible to stop these procedures once the police have been called in," she explained. "The stores are afraid they'll lose credibility with the City Attorney's office or something, and they won't back away from it."

"When is your hearing?"

"In a couple of weeks. I'm nervous about it."

"I can imagine. I'll come with you."

"No need. It's only if we actually go to trial."

"I'll come anyway. Is Julian going to be there?"

"I don't know." She looked unhappy, and I could have kicked myself. Julian Meade was the last person in the world I wanted to talk about that night.

"I spoke to him, you know," she said. "He called me from New York, and I knew she was in the room with him."

"How did you know?"

"I just knew." She told me all about their conversation. "I could actually see the room."

"You've got a terrific imagination."

"It was so clear to me," she said. "Like my dreams, sometimes. I dream a lot, usually in spurts."

"Who's the woman?" I asked. "Do you want to talk about it?"

"Sure, why not? I've kind of made my peace with it for

now," she said. "Her name's Linda Halsey."

"Halsey? Any relation to Bernard Halsey?"

"His only daughter."

"That's big money."

"Oh, yes, she's very rich. Julian met her and her father when he was still at the museum."

"Halsey's a big art collector, isn't he?"

"He has an incredible collection," she said. "His house is like a museum. It *is* sort of a museum. I mean, he opens it to the public three afternoons a week and all like that."

"That way he can write it off his taxes," I commented. "These billionaires never miss a bet."

"Have you ever been there?"

"No."

"You ought to go someday," she said. "Do you like paintings or art in general?"

"Yes, I do, as a matter of fact. I've always meant to go. Maybe you'll take me."

"We'll see. He has the finest Donabellas in the world. In fact, he has half of them."

"Who's that?"

"Giorgio Donabella, an incredible artist. He was an Italian who lived in Holland, a contemporary of the great Flemish painters. There aren't more than twenty-two or -three of his canvases in the whole world, and Mr. Halsey has eleven of them. They're really remarkable. I think Julian got him at least two."

"So that's the connection."

"What?"

"How your husband got his gallery off the ground."

"It certainly helped," Allyson admitted. "When I think that that bitch was a guest in our house..."

After dinner we walked along the beachfront promenade back toward our car. Once again Allyson's hand rested on my arm as lightly as a child's caress. I kissed her under the shadow of a towering palm tree at the corner of the public parking lot, and her arms went up around my neck. A solitary young black man on roller skates swooped past us, a ghetto blaster on his shoulder and his teeth flashing in the darkness. "All right!" he called back to us. "Well, that's all ri-i-i-ight!"

We smiled at each other, and I drove us back to my place. She sat very close to me in the car, and we didn't speak. I parked directly outside my building, a two-story California Tudor apartment house a couple of blocks below the Strip, and led Allyson inside. We walked through the patio area, with its dilapidated aluminum furniture, and skirted the empty swimming pool, which gleamed wanly under the pale moon peeking above the rooftop. I lived toward the back, on the ground floor, and I was reluctant to turn the lights on, because I had suddenly realized how shabby my quarters might look to a woman who lived in a small Spanish villa in the hills of Westwood.

I needn't have worried. No sooner had I shut the door behind us than she was in my arms. We fell on the bed in a tangle of arms and legs and spent the next two hours making love. It was one of the most remarkable things that had ever happened to me. Allyson had skin like warm silk, and she was an expert, generous, and, above all, tender partner. When at last we had had enough, we lay for a long time in each other's arms, in silence but also in what I took to be perfect understanding.

"I suppose I should ask you if the earth moved," I said at last, when she got up to go to the bathroom.

"Why do men always want to know how wonderful they were?" she asked.

"Because we're the insecure sex."

"Such fragile egos." She disappeared from view and turned on the water in the tub.

"Say it in Panhandle," I called after her.

She stuck her head out the door. "Honey, one thang I do know," she drawled, in what I took to be a parody of her native speech, "you're fast out of the gate, you make all the turns, you shift leads cleanly, and you got a good finish. What more could a gal ask for, hunh?"

I followed her into the bathroom and sat on the toilet seat beside her while she immersed herself up to her chin in suds and hot water. The building I lived in was thirty years old, which by L.A. standards made it almost a historical landmark, and the fixtures were original. My bathtub was about six feet long with deep sides, ideal for the contemplative wash, and Allyson luxuriated in it. I loved the look of her lying there, all legs and stomach and breasts, flesh peeking provocatively through foam.

"How much do you want for this tub?" she asked. "I'll take it with me."

"It's not for sale, but you can come back anytime."

"Thanks."

"So what do you think of my digs?"

"Who's seen them? You assaulted me before I could look. But I know one thing, sweetheart."

"One thang?"

"No, thing. I worked hard to get rid of the Panhandle."

"Okay, what is it?"

"Plants. You need a little living green around you."

"I'd forget to water them."

"I'll remind you. I'll post a schedule on your icebox door. You do have an icebox?"

"I think so."

"Anything in it to drink?"

"Wine?"

"Perfect."

"Coming up."

I'm not exactly a domestic type, but I do keep wine on hand for all such emergencies. I happened to have a fairly decent Chardonnay available, properly chilled, and I went to pour us both a glass. When I came back, Allyson's eyes were closed and I thought for a moment she might have fallen asleep in there. Her small, pink breasts bobbed gently in the water and her legs looked endlessly long. I resisted the impulse to jump into the water with her and gave her the wine.

"I had a dream last night," she said, taking a sip.

"About me, of course."

"Wrong. Want to hear it?"

"You bet."

"One of my doctors, Sid Goldberg, came and rang my front doorbell," she said. "He was dressed in this long, white hospital coat down to his ankles, with a big stethoscope around his neck. He said he had an emergency case and had to go, but he wanted me to bet ten dollars for him on a horse that couldn't lose, according to him."

"I've heard that one before."

"Wait. It was so clear, Lou. The horse's name was Pacific Prince. Is there such a horse?"

"I don't know. Isn't Goldberg the one doctor in your office who doesn't bet on horses?"

"Yes, right. Isn't it strange?"

"I guess. Do you dream a lot?"

"In spurts. But never about horses before. It must be your influence."

I leaned over and kissed her again; I thought no more about her dream horse that night.

She telephoned me from her office at nine o'clock the next morning. "Have you seen today's entries?"

"Not yet. I was just getting to the *Form* now."

"Look at them and call me back." And she hung up.

Pacific Prince was entered in the fifth race at Hollywood Park, a mile gallop over the turf course for medium-priced claiming horses, and he figured to be one of the longshots in the event. He was a recent import from New York, a five-year-old gelding who had once had some class, but who had done nothing so far this year. He usually ran well early, but would then fade and drop out of contention in the later stages of the race. He was trained, however, by Rod Munson, one of the younger men coming up, who had a good-sized public stable and had won more than his share of races. I called up Jay Fox to find out if he had an opinion on the animal.

"I haven't quite finished doing the race," Jay said, "but I see no reason to bet on him."

"Could he be a bleeder?" I was alluding to the fact that some horses hemorrhage in their lungs when they run and inevitably pull themselves up. In California and some other states, such ailments are treated with Lasix, a diuretic that quite often relieves this condition and enables these horses to compete, whereas in New York the drug is banned. Lasix can make a huge difference in a Thoroughbred's performance, so it is one of the handicapping factors to be considered when an animal is first transferred to California from the East.

"I don't have any information on that," Jay answered, "but I can't guess. The numbers I've got on him are poor. Why? Did you hear something?"

"A lady I know had a dream."

There was a short but deadly silence at the other end of the line. "Shifty, please don't waste my time with shit like this," he said. "I'm running late, I haven't got all my work done, and I don't need foolish interruptions." Then he hung up on me.

I had been scheduled for a third and, I hoped, final interview at the unemployment office in West Hollywood that afternoon, so I would be unable to get to the races. I called

Allyson back and told her the little I had found out about the horse.

"Oh, yes, I know," she said. "We're all going to bet on him."

"You are?"

"Well, of course. Do you want me to bet for you?"

I hesitated. "Well, two dollars," I finally said.

"Everybody here is betting five and ten."

"Two dollars, Allyson."

She giggled. "You have no faith."

"I have faith in you, but not your horses," I said. "And I think I'm in deep like with you. Everything okay at home?"

"Yes. I'll call you tonight. Will you be in?"

"I'll wait to hear from you."

I knew what had happened even before she did phone me that night. I had heard Bill Garr's call of the stretch run on his late-afternoon radio show over KIEV. Pacific Prince had apparently led all the way around the course and won easily by a couple of lengths. He paid $29.80 to win.

— 6 —
Choices

Two weeks after our one night together, Allyson was summoned to a fiercely illuminated, wood-paneled courtroom on the seventh floor of the Criminal Courts building in downtown Los Angeles. She arrived promptly at nine, but, because the calendar was crowded, as usual, she sat there for two days on a wooden bench. She was not allowed to read or even to go to the bathroom without permission, until presiding Judge John Michael Barret dismissed everyone, usually well before five o'clock.

It occurred to Allyson, as she sat there hour after hour, that one of the reasons for such a backlog of cases was that so little real work ever seemed to get done. Most of the time was spent waiting for someone, usually a lawyer or a witness, to show up, while the working day itself was short and interrupted by a lunch break that often lasted nearly two hours. Judge Barret, a mild-looking, plump, fifty-two-year-old Reagan appointee, was considered a tough judge, according to Jamie Horton. He tried to keep things moving by at least hanging on to his defendants, but to Allyson it seemed as if she had already begun to serve a sentence without having been convicted of anything.

She was struck, too, by how few white people found themselves in her position. In fact, all of the other defend-

ants she saw were black or Hispanic. The whites who sauntered in and out of the courtroom were all part of the legal
power structure, and they assumed, without exception, that
she, too, was an attorney. Several of them asked her what
case she was handling. "When they found out I was a defendant," she told me over the phone, "they backed away
from me as if I'd blown my nose on my sleeve."

Midway through her third morning in the room, the
bailiff took advantage of a break in the proceedings to
strike up a conversation with her. He was a good-looking,
dark-haired young man named Gomez, impressive in his
khaki uniform and gold badge, with a big bunch of keys
and a gun dangling from his belt. His eyes feasted on her
as he talked.

"Hi," he said. "You look like a very nice lady."

"That's very kind of you," Allyson answered.

"I guess this isn't any of my business," the man continued, "but you've been here a couple of days now and you
must have noticed about this judge."

"What about him?"

"He's pretty tough."

"He is?"

"Sure. We haven't had a Not Guilty verdict in here in
over six months."

"I didn't know that."

"No, you wouldn't," Gomez said, shaking his head sympathetically. "That's why maybe I thought I ought to warn
you."

"About what?"

"If you go to trial," Gomez said, "I suppose you could
be sent up to Sybill Brand for ninety days and have to pay
a big fine."

"Sybill Brand?" Allyson asked, startled.

"The women's county jail," Gomez explained. "That could
happen, ma'am."

Amazed, Allyson stared at him. "What are you trying to tell me?"

"Nothing, ma'am. Just passing the time of day," And he sauntered casually back to his post, as the judge emerged from his chambers.

Allyson reported this conversation to Jamie Horton, who shook her head and told her that the man had been way out of line. "I could make a lot of trouble for him," she said. "Let me know if it happens again."

Late that afternoon, Judge Barret finally got around to Allyson. He declared that, due to her previous unsullied record, he would be happy to discuss her case in chambers. Jamie Horton squeezed Allyson's arm reassuringly and disappeared into the judge's private office, accompanied by Jed Waters, the dapper-looking trial deputy assigned to the courtroom.

Twenty minutes later, Jamie was able to inform Allyson out in the corridor that both the judge and the prosecutor were ready to accept a plea-bargain. "If you plead guilty to trespassing, which is a lesser charge," Jamie explained, "Judge Barret will probably fine you no more than a couple of hundred dollars and put you on probation for a period of between eighteen to twenty-four months."

"My God," Allyson said. "Probation?"

"It sounds worse than it is," the lawyer explained. "Once it's over, you won't have a record or anything."

"But that's two years..."

"Waters thinks he has a case strong enough for him to prosecute, if you refuse," Jamie Horton said. "I know they'd favor the plea-bargain."

"It's crazy," Allyson began. "I didn't trespass—"

"Look, Allyson, most of these judges favor a disposition in these cases," the lawyer said. "If everyone insisted on a trial, the whole system would collapse."

"What do you think I should do?"

"I don't know," Jamie Horton admitted. "I don't think you're guilty, and there's no absolute guarantee that you won't have to go to jail." She paused and resumed, measuring her words as carefully now as if each were a speck of gold dust. "This judge has a reputation as an incarcerator. On the other hand, if you insist on a jury trial and you lose, he could throw the book at you."

"Jesus Christ." Allyson steadied herself against the wall with one hand. "I can't believe this is happening to me."

The lawyer put a consoling hand on her arm. "Allyson, I can't tell you what to do," she said. "If you decide for a trial, I'll give it everything I have. Look, we have the weekend at least. Why don't you talk it over with your husband? We don't have to make a decision right this minute."

The morning after Allyson's hearing, I dropped into her office, which occupied a top corner suite in a small, two-story building on Gardner, about half a block north of Sunset. I had made an appointment there with Ed Hamner, partly because she had told me what a wonderful doctor he was, but mostly because I wanted to see her. We had only spoken on the phone since our one night together, and I was sure she was avoiding me. I knew her well enough by this time to know why, but I also wanted her to realize that I cared about her and that I didn't intend to just let her disappear from my life. I have no aversion to casual sex, but nothing I felt about Allyson Meade could be defined as casual.

I was one of three people in the waiting room when she appeared in the doorway to usher me inside. "Mr. Anderson?" she said, in her friendliest professional voice. "This way, please." I followed her into an examining room, and she shut the door behind us. "What are you doing here?" she asked.

"You told me he was a good doctor," I said. "I need a checkup."

"Why?"

"I'm not sleeping too well."

She avoided my eyes and looked at my hand. "I see the cast is off."

"You're terrifically observant."

"Lou, I can't see you now. Surely you understand—"

"I understand that I like you very much and that I don't want you to run away from me."

"Julian and I are trying to work things out—"

"Fine. Terrific. I still think we can be friends."

"No, I don't think so."

"Why not?"

"Lou, I can't discuss this with you here."

"Where, then?"

"I don't know. Now please sit down over there," she said, once again the professional nurse, "and take your shoes off. I want to weigh you and take your blood pressure and temperature."

She was obviously upset, so I meekly allowed her to go through these routine procedures without putting any more pressure on her. She worked swiftly and efficiently, with the sort of delicate grace I had come to admire in her. Before she could thrust a thermometer into my mouth, however, I gently took her wrist. "Allyson, I really want to talk to you."

"I can't, Lou," she said. "I need—I'm—oh, hell . . ."

To my amazement, I could tell she was close to tears. "Hey," I assured her, "it's all right. I just wanted you to know—"

She brushed my assurances aside. "Put this under your tongue and keep it there," she said, aiming the thermometer at me. "I have to go." And she walked quickly out the door.

I sat there for four or five minutes, feeling increasingly

foolish and frustrated, the little glass tube embedded between my teeth and under my tongue. I was still trying to think of some way to reach her, when she walked briskly in again, this time leaving the door into the corridor open. She took the thermometer out of my mouth and read it.

"Am I dying?"

"Not just yet," she said, "but if you keep pulling shit like this, you will be." She headed for the door again. "Doctor will be with you in a minute," she informed me, and disappeared.

No sooner had she gone than Freddie Chambers popped his head around the corner. "Shifty," he said, grinning, "Ally told me you were here. What's the matter with you?"

"Nothing, Freddie, just a checkup. What about you?"

He held up a plastic cup. "I'm supposed to piss into this thing," he declared. "Want to do it for me?"

"I don't think it would be appropriate," I said. "What's the deal?"

"Ah, I've been having trouble with my stomach," he said. "Too much high life, I guess."

"Celebrating? You must be winning."

"Are you kidding? Me? Nah. I don't even go out there any more. But I'm having a lot of fun." He beamed roguishly at me. "You know I'm seeing Boom Boom, don't you? I let her run my bets, and at night we have a good time."

"Freddie, that's an expensive celebration. No wonder your stomach's shot."

"Yeah, but so what? I deserve it. You know what they say."

"What do they say?"

"A Boom Boom in the hand is better than a bird in the bush."

"I hadn't heard that one, Freddie."

"She's a nice kid," he said. "We're having a good time, that's all." He glanced behind him. "Listen, I gotta go fill this thing, or Ally'll throw me out."

"Freddie, wait for me, " I told him, "or I'll wait for you.
I want to ask you a couple of things."

"Like what?"

"The lady here."

"Oh." He nodded. "Sure. I'll meet you in the hamburger
joint across the street, on the corner of Sunset." He looked
down at his plastic cup. "What if I just filled this with ginger
ale and drank it in front of them? Wouldn't that blow their
minds?"

Ed Hamner loomed up in the hallway behind him. "Come
on, Freddie," he said, "I hold you personally responsible.
I have a nurse back there crying by the X-ray machine.
What's going on here?" He shambled into the room and
shut the door behind him. "What *is* going on?" he asked
me.

"I don't know. Is Allyson upset?"

Hamner regarded me with a certain weariness, too disgusted by my evasiveness to want to grapple with me over
it and clearly annoyed by having his routine working day
complicated by some undercurrent of a plot he hadn't quite
fathomed. "Listen, Lou, I'm just going to say this one thing
to you, and then I'll drop it, okay? It's none of my business."

"Fair enough. Shoot."

"She's in enough trouble now," he said. "Don't put any
pressure on her."

"I'll try not to. But her husband's a prick."

"You know it and I know it," Ed Hamner said, "but
Allyson isn't sure of it yet. She doesn't need complications
in her life at the moment. She's been through a lot."

"I hear you," I said. "Anything else I ought to know?"

Ed smiled a little wickedly. "You could start betting on
her horses," he said. "You'd get rich."

"She dreamt any more winners since the last one?"

"We're waiting, I can tell you that," he said, sitting down

facing me with the clipboard on his lap. "Now let's get a history on you."

After I'd provided a detailed rundown of all the minor ailments I'd had during my life, any one of which would have killed me a century earlier, I thrust my healing finger under his eyes. "Well," he said, looking at it dubiously, "it's not my field. What did your orthopedist tell you?"

"The guy at the hospital said to immerse it in warm water several times a day for three or four weeks and flex it, exercise it as much as possible," I told him. "It seems to be getting better."

"It will, and that's the correct therapy." He stared down at the still swollen pinkie. "It would have been better if you hadn't broken the knuckle."

"That's what he said, and it worries me."

"It won't ever be quite the same," he said. "How much do you use it?"

"Enough. Tell me this—if I was Horowitz, would I ever play as well again?"

"Probably not, but only Horowitz would know the difference."

"I suppose that's reassuring."

"Yes, it should be."

I didn't see Allyson again that day; she lingered out of sight till I had gone. I went across the street to the hamburger joint to wait for Freddie, who showed up ten minutes later with a look of mild disapproval on his face. "What are you doing to my girl?" he asked.

"Why?"

"She's pretty shook up. She's terrific at covering up, but I know her. What did you do to her, you bastard?"

"Nothing, Freddie," I assured him. "I really, really like her. And I think she's married to a sonofabitch who's playing around on her."

Freddie looked uncomfortable and sighed. "Yeah, you're

right. Julian was always a player," he said. "Even during the Cerberus days, he always had something going."

"Why does she put up with it?"

"I don't think she knew. Ally was a very naïve girl in many ways. Tough and smart, too, Shifty, but just off the farm, as far as Julian was concerned." Freddie paused, as if to sort his thoughts out more carefully. "I mean, here's a guy who's been around all over the world and comes from money. Hell, he was like a god to her at first. You got to remember, she had nothing going for her at the time she met him. She was blind about him from the first day."

"You make him sound like a devious, two-timing schemer," I said. "I thought you were a friend of his."

"Me?" Freddie looked astonished. "Who told you that?"

"Allyson said you're the only one of his old artists he still sees," I explained. "She says you're in the gallery from time to time."

"That's strictly business," Freddie said. "I work for Julian."

"Doing what?"

"This and that." Freddie looked away from me; he seemed anxious to change the subject. "Restoration, mostly."

"Restoration? Of what? Paintings?"

"Yeah." Freddie exhaled, as if to blow the subject away. "Look, let's not talk about what I do. It's just work. Julian pays good money."

"So that's where you're getting all this loot to blow at the track," I observed. "And now you've got Boom Boom to help you spend it. He must pay terrific money. I never knew restoration was such a good racket."

"It's not a racket, Shifty. It's a skill, a very difficult skill, pal." He sat back in his seat and folded his arms across his stomach. He looked suddenly like a smug little Oriental potentate. "Julian needs me. I'm the best there is. And he pays me. It's just that simple."

"Until a couple of weeks ago, I didn't even know you were an artist," I told him. "Allyson said you painted beautiful, very unusual still lifes."

Freddie nodded unhappily. "Yeah, only nobody bought them."

"I'd like to see them sometime."

Freddie shrugged and again looked away from me, as if embarrassed by such obviously unaccustomed interest in his work. "I guess. If I still have any."

"So you don't paint anymore?"

The question seemed to galvanize him, as if I had jolted him with a cattle prod. "That's what you think!" he said. "I still paint, all right!"

"I'd like to see your work."

"No, I don't think so, kid," he said, getting up and dropping change on the table to pay for his coffee. "I don't show my stuff anymore."

"I thought you just said—"

"I was bullshitting. I don't want to, Shifty." He leaned toward me, his face set and angry. "Nobody, I mean nobody ever liked my work well enough to lay out one dime for it," he said. "For a lot of years, you know what I did?"

"I have no idea, Freddie."

"I turned out shit," he informed me. "I painted two, three, four canvases a week—clowns, flowers, little kids with red cheeks and big saucer eyes, seascapes, cheery old folks with dogs. Shit, man, just plain shit. They paid me twenty-five to fifty bucks a painting, and I sold them in carloads to a guy who decorated fleabag motels and poisonous chain restaurants. I got so I hated every goddamn moment at my easel."

"Yes, but what about the good work?"

"I told you—it didn't sell."

"What about now?"

"Now?" He paused and sucked in a big breath. "Now?

I'm the best there is at what I do," he said fiercely. "Nobody can do what I do better than me, Shifty. That's why Julian needs me. And he pays me top dollar, pal."

"You mean a lot of these old paintings he sells need to be cleaned up, huh? I don't know much about the art world, really. It sounds interesting."

"Well, I don't really want to talk about it, Shifty." And to my surprise he suddenly bolted out the door without another word. My God, I thought, somebody sure stuck it into you, you poor bastard, and I'm glad you're making somebody pay you for what you do, especially Julian Meade. But I found myself wondering, too, what kind of work in the art world, however skillful, could carry a hard knocker like Freddie through a losing season at the track, with Boom Boom and her dynamite legs sitting on his back like a hundred and thirty pounds of lead on a crippled plater.

"Why don't you pay the two dollars?" Julian Meade said, as he dropped two ice cubes into his Scotch and added soda.

"What does that mean?" Allyson asked.

"It's the punch line to an old vaudeville sketch," he explained. "A man refuses to cough up for what he considers an unjust parking violation and he winds up in the gas chamber."

She sipped her wine and studied his back as he fussed over his drink. "So you think I ought to admit to something I didn't do?"

"No, I don't mean that," he answered, turning now to confront her. She could see that he was annoyed. "Look, Allyson, I figure you just got caught up in the system. It's gone too far."

"Tell me about the system."

"Okay. The thing you have to understand is that justice has nothing to do with anything. There's no justice, obviously, in any arrangement in which guilt and innocence have become irrelevant. Plea-bargaining is a convenience, that's all."

"For whom?"

"For everybody. It's a way of handling a lot of cases involving mostly poor people in trouble."

"We're not poor," she said. "The sole reason, Julian, is speeding things up, is that it?"

"Precisely."

They stared at each other in silence. "You must think I meant to steal that bag," she said, at last. "You do, don't you?"

Exasperated, he fell into a chair across from her. "Christ, all I meant was, it's easier to compromise, that's all."

"I'm sorry to inconvenience you, Julian."

"Me? It's you I'm worried about."

"Poor Julian," she said, "you have so much on your mind."

"Now what the hell does that mean?" he asked angrily, but she had anticipated this reaction and was already on her way out of the room.

"I'm going out," she called back.

"Where to?"

"I don't know. To get some air. I need to think this through."

She got into her car and drove out along the boulevards toward the beach. She parked finally at the end of Wilshire and sat for a long time on a bench along a path on the palisades high above the ocean, silvered in the glow of a three-quarter moon. It was a warm night for this late in the year, with a light Santa Ana wind rustling the palm fronds above her head, and she thought she might just stay there until dawn. When two young studs in motorcycle gear came by, however, and tried clumsily to strike up a conversation with her, she went back to her car, turned the radio on to a soft-rock station, and drove slowly home.

Julian was slumped in front of their TV set, his eyes focused morosely on the harmless shenanigans of an old movie about Hollywood fringe people sharing a house in Malibu or somewhere. She paused by his chair. "I'm going to sleep in the guest bedroom," she said quietly. He did not answer, so she walked past him, got her things out of their bedroom, and took a sleeping pill.

While she was lying there in the darkness of the little room, staring out the window at the fat oleander bushes lining their driveway and waiting for the pill to take hold, she had a vision. Or it may actually have been a dream; she couldn't be sure. In any case, it involved a horse called Choosing. She saw him being loaded into a starting gate for a race to be run down the hillside turf course at Santa Anita. Choosing broke last from the number two hole, then went wide on the turn and won easily.

She called me up at home the next morning to tell me about it. "I know the horse," I told her, "but he's not entered at Hollywood."

"No, of course not," she said. "I saw him at Santa Anita."

"I'll watch for him," I told her. "How are you?"

"I'm all right," she said. "I moved out last night."

"Of the house?"

"No, the bedroom."

"Can we have lunch?"

"No, I have to go to court."

"Want me to come with you?"

"No, really. I'm all right."

"Then how about a drink or dinner?"

"Dinner I can't, but a drink—I may need one. Okay."

"I'll meet you at Saratoga West at—when? Six?"

"When's the last race go off?"

"It's Monday, Allyson. I only go to the track when it's open."

She laughed. "At six, then."

"It's nice to hear you laugh," I said. "I was getting worried about you."

"You don't have to worry about me, Lou," she said. "You're a horseplayer. You have your own worries, I know all about that."

Judge Barret evidently found it hard to believe that his sensible offer had been refused. After Jamie Horton had informed him of her client's decision to ask for a jury trial, he peered over his rimless half-lenses at Allyson, who was sitting quietly in the front row of benches facing him. "I would like to urge your client to reconsider," he said. "If she wishes to do so at any time before the jury is selected, my chambers remain open."

Jed Waters, standing next to Jamie in front of the judge, informed the lawyer that he had thoroughly acquainted himself with the case. He had interviewed Harold Grant, as well as the two police officers who had answered the call. "I'm going to prosecute your client as a savvy shoplifter." He did not raise his voice or even glance at Allyson, but he clearly intended to be overheard. Allyson felt as if a stake had been driven into the pit of her stomach. Jamie saw her go pale and asked the judge for a recess, so that she could confer one more time with her client.

Out in the corridor a few minutes later, Allyson leaned back against the wall and began to cry. She couldn't help herself, but it made her angry, too. She had begun to understand what she was up against. Jamie Horton leaned in toward her, her face full of concern and sympathy, but helpless to aid her. And what could she do? Allyson asked herself. Jamie was obviously a competent counsel, but they were playing in a game with rules devised by a Mad Hatter. "I'll accept the plea-bargain," Jamie said. "I think we'd better, don't you?"

Allyson shut her eyes. She found she could not blot out the vision of Jed Waters, the handsome prosecutor, who, she had learned earlier from the chatty bailiff, was working on a string of fourteen or fifteen consecutive convictions. Young, tall, personable, supremely confident, attired in tailormade three-piece suits, he was obviously a comer. He was being groomed, Gomez had also confided, for the U.S. Attorney's office. He reminded Allyson of Julian, as he had appeared in her eyes when she first met him.

"All right," Allyson heard Jamie say. "I'll tell the judge we've changed our minds."

"No." Allyson pushed herself away from the wall and blinked angrily at her lawyer. "No, I haven't," she said. "I didn't take that bag on purpose and I'm not going to back down, damn them."

Jamie Horton gazed thoughtfully at her client. "Allyson, if you lose," she said softly, "this judge might throw the book at you."

"My whole life seems to have become an inconvenience to men," Allyson said. "Screw them."

"What?"

"I want to tell my story to a jury," she said. "I have a right to do that, don't I?"

When Jamie told Judge Barret that her client had not changed her mind, the jurist ignored Allyson, as if she had ceased to exist except as an abstract phenomenon. He summoned the lawyers to his bench. "We'll set it on the calendar for two weeks from Monday," he said. "Is that agreeable with the parties?"

"Your Honor," Jed Waters objected, "that is Christmas week."

"This court is open, as far as I know," the judge told him. "Monday isn't Christmas Day, is it?"

"No, sir," the prosecutor replied, "but my chief witness, Harold Grant, is absent due to a death in the family. I have reason to believe he will not return until after the first of the year. I would like to move to continue to a later date."

"That's fine," Judge Barret said. "How about four weeks from Monday?"

"No objection, Your Honor," Jamie said.

"Mark that down for the appropriate date," the judge instructed the clerk, "so the people will be ready to present their case at that time."

Allyson caught Gomez staring at her with what she interpreted to be an expression of mingled awe and pity. She resisted an impulse to tell him to go and sit on his big gun and simply smiled sweetly at him. He shook his head and turned away from her. In his eyes, she was clearly a lost, crazy lady.

7

Christmas Lights

The Christmas holidays have never been my idea of a good time. Usually, I manage to get myself employed somewhere, either at the Magic Castle in Hollywood or on a cruise ship, but this year I was trapped. In addition to the warm-water therapy on my finger, I had begun to shuffle cards and work on my repertoire, but I was several weeks away, at least, from being able to perform. There was some pain in the joint and the knuckle was still swollen; it was a frustrating, anxious time for me. I didn't want to be reduced in rank among my fellow close-up artists, so I was not about to risk appearing anywhere yet. I worked every morning at my magic for several hours and got so I could execute some of my moves with a passable degree of skill, but there were many, especially the ones involving coins and other small objects, that were still chancy, if not beyond me. The slowness of my progress worried me and also began to affect my action at the track. I started to lose again, and despite the arrival of a couple of unemployment checks, I was down to a reserve of about five hundred dollars coming into the last few days of the Hollywood fall meet.

Allyson was my only consolation during this fairly grim period for me. Despite the fact that she had plenty of worries of her own and a home life that had become very nearly intolerable, she spent a lot of time cheering me up. She filled my apartment with plants, until I protested that I was in danger of being suffocated by the hothouse atmosphere. "Don't be silly," she said. "Plants create oxygen, they don't suck it out of the air. You don't know anything, do you?"

"Not much," I confessed. "But how in the hell am I supposed to work here? I can't even see my posters and stuff anymore."

"I've put them where they'll dress up the place, not hide anything," she retorted. "This room was a monk's cell until I did something about it."

"Are any of these growing things of yours carnivorous?" I asked. "I mean, I wouldn't want to be swallowed up and digested one night just to keep your ferns happy."

"They're not ferns."

"Well, whatever they are. If they're green, they're ferns. If they've got flowers growing out of them, they're roses. And don't correct me. I can't stand pushy women."

"You can't stand to live like a human being," she said. "Look at this place. Till you met me it was unlivable."

"I lived here," I said. "I liked it."

"You're a stubborn, ignorant man, which, I guess, is a redundancy," she informed me, "like all those redneck good ole boys I grew up with."

"I'll bet they didn't have cute little plants cluttering up their premises," I said. "Next thing you know, you'll start sewing curtains or something."

"I've been thinking about it," she admitted. "Don't tempt me, Lou."

"I'll tempt you all I want."

"Seriously, you don't like the plants?"

"They're okay," I said. "At least they don't bark or have to be walked at night. And they don't go to the bathroom on the rug."

"And they're beautiful. You do have to talk to them,"

she advised me. "They get lonely."

"I draw the line at conversation with flowers," I said. "That's your department."

"You hate me," she said.

"That is a damn lie and you know it."

I was in love with her, no doubt about it. We spent as much time together as we could, which meant Wednesday, Saturday, and Sunday afternoons at the track and several evenings a week either out to dinner or at my place. She usually went home by eleven o'clock, often to an empty house, as Julian was almost always out somewhere and sometimes did not come back for days. They had had one conversation, really, since the night Allyson had moved into the guest bedroom, but it had been coldly acrimonious and inconclusive. She had admitted to him that she was seeing another man, which seemed to relieve him, as if a burden of guilt had been lifted off his back. They had not pursued the topic, but had agreed, at least, to let the holidays pass before trying to make some decision about their future together, if any. Allyson wanted to get through her trial before having to deal with her broken marriage and, she told me, the whole question appeared to be only mildly bothersome to her husband, who seemed to have slipped into another world and another life without even the echo of a regret for the old one.

"I think he's happy I'm seeing you," she said. "I didn't tell him who you are or anything about you, but then I know he doesn't care. He's got Linda now and her racing stable and all that money, so what can I mean to him?"

I was happy for myself. I was having a love affair with a woman I really cared about and so far without any of the responsibilities such a relationship could impose. I would worry about all that later, I told myself, when Allyson and her husband decided to separate formally. Until then I was safe. She sensed what I was thinking and one night, after we had made love and were lying in bed sipping cold white wine, she challenged me on it. "What are you so afraid of?" she asked.

"Afraid? What are you talking about?"

"If I showed up here one night with a suitcase in my hand, you'd probably panic."

"No, I wouldn't. You'd be welcome, honest."

"As a visitor, okay. But not if I moved in."

"How do you know?"

"I know. You didn't get your nickname just from what you do with cards."

I started to argue with her, but she cut me off in mid-protest. "Don't worry, Lou," she said. "I'm not making any demands on you. I know you're glad to see me, but you're just as happy when I leave."

"Not true," I said, meaning it. "I really enjoy your company, Allyson. Don't you know that?"

She didn't answer, but looked around the premises instead. Yes, the plants she had imported into my quarters had improved the look of the place; they had added a feminine touch, toned down the self-centered masculinity of this studio flat. But to a woman this room I lived in must have seemed hostile territory, almost beyond civilizing. The blowups of horses running across one wall, the posters of magicians doing their miraculous stuff, the stacks of old *Racing Forms* and programs from recently concluded race meets, the shelves of books on magic and gambling at the track—all must have struck her as alien, the appurtenances of a life both limited and obsessed. And yet the room did reflect me accurately, I had to admit. I had not come to this place by accident, but out of choice.

"Hey," I said, leaning over to pick up a deck of cards I had left on the night table and quickly shuffling it, sending the little boards skimming from hand to hand with the old practiced ease outsiders found so astonishing. "Pick a card,"

I said, fanning the deck out toward her. "Come on."

"No, I don't want tricks, Lou." She took another sip of her wine and looked at me over the rim of her glass. "It's nice," she said, "it's just nice being here, with you. I don't want to ruin it."

"You couldn't do that." I put the cards away and leaned over to kiss her. "And you can even leave your toothbrush."

"You must have been a lonely kid," she said later, just before she began to dress.

"Why do you say that?"

"Because I was, too. I recognize the symptoms."

"Yeah, I guess I was. Nobody in my family gave a damn about what I liked."

"Magic and horses?"

"The horses came later. Magic, music, the theater, dance— all those pursuits were unpopular around the Anderson household. My dad owned a liquor store on the north shore of Long Island, near Oyster Bay. What my folks liked were picnics, cookouts, movies, fishing, all the right masculine sports, like baseball, basketball, and football."

"Were you an only child?"

"No, I have an older brother. He went into the army, became a career military man. He's a top sergeant somewhere and the hell with him."

"You didn't get along, huh?"

"I despised him as much as he did me," I confessed. "He thought I was a fag because I liked what I liked and I thought football was a moron's game. He used to improve my morale by beating me up a couple of times a month. I hope he's happy in his hog heaven somewhere."

"I can see you, all right," she said, "holed up in some room, practicing your magic for hours, probably with the radio on."

"You got it," I told her, "a very accurate picture. Plus one added factor."

"What's that?"

"I had acid eczema as a kid," I said. "It was some sort of chemical imbalance or something. It broke out on my face and on the insides of my arms. When it got real bad, it would cover half my body. I had it a lot until I was well into my late teens, then it began to clear up and now I hardly ever get an outbreak, usually only minor stuff. Anyway, when it was healing, I looked like a leprosy victim. You can imagine how popular I was with girls and how the condition contributed to my self-confidence."

"And so you took refuge in illusions. You know something?"

"What?"

"I've watched you when you're practicing or when you're in the middle of a trick, and you look very different."

"In what way?"

"There's something a little out of this world about you," she said. "You look—well, beautiful."

"Hey, Allyson—"

"No, I mean it. You do. Does that embarrass you?"

I thought about it and shook my head. "Coming from you, no."

Christmas Eve fell on a Monday that year. Allyson's office closed at three o'clock, and she came by my place. We then drove together to an empty lot off Wilshire, a few blocks east of La Brea, where the Weasel, a horse degenerate I knew, was hustling Christmas trees in order to put together a stake for Santa Anita. The Weasel's real name was Mort Something-or-other, but everybody I knew called him the Weasel, because he had a sly, underhanded manner at the track; if he wanted to get a bet down, for instance, and it looked like he might be shut out, he could slither into a gap at the speed of light and have his money in action before a serious protest could get organized. Once some irate citizen had taken a swing at him; the Weasel had slipped under it, grabbed his assailant's testicles, and twisted until the man had dropped, writhing, to the ground. By the time the security guards had shown up, the Weasel had skipped away. He was always in some sort of trouble, but he managed, like most of his kind, to remain in action, which was his way of staying alive. The Weasel had a lot of fast moves and a dangerous bite.

Allyson and I had decided not to give each other presents, but to spend some money on a feast, which Allyson would cook that night at my place. I had bought a thirty-five-dollar bottle of Bordeaux to celebrate, and at the last minute Allyson had insisted on a tree. "We don't have to decorate it or anything," she said, "but it would be nice to have it there. You know, the spirit and all like that." I had remembered that the Weasel had this lot on Wilshire every year, and so I suggested we go there and pick out what we wanted.

"Shifty, I didn't know you was into the holiday shit," the Weasel said, when he spotted us. "You want a tree? Take one. I'll let you have anything you want for ten bucks and a winner on opening day." He smiled his crooked little yellow smile at Allyson, who was already surveying the choices left to us. "You got anything you like?"

"Tree-wise?"

"Nah. Who gives a shit about trees? No, I meant opening day."

"I haven't seen the entries," I informed him. "How'd you do at Hollywood?"

"Terrible," the Weasel confided. "I hate that fuckin' place. It ain't a racetrack, it's a goddamn supermarket. Anyway, I been sellin' this shit here for the last two weeks, so I don't even know who's running no more." He cocked his head toward Allyson, who had moved away from us. "Who's the pewzy?"

"Weasel, that is not what you call pewzy," I said. "Can't you tell class in life either?"

"I didn't think you was into broads," he said. "Women at the fuckin' track—death, man, it's like death." He pondered the problem briefly. "Pewzy, it's like you need it from time to time, I guess, but you know what?" He held up his right hand and wiggled his fingers at me. "See these? They don't say I love you."

"A cancerous approach to life, Weasel."

"And it don't cost no money, either," he continued. "Good pewzy is all in the mind, man."

Allyson rejoined us, holding a small white pine she had salvaged from the remnants of the Weasel's depleted stock, and she insisted on paying for it, which clearly astonished him. As he pocketed her ten-dollar bill, he grinned at me and shrugged, as if to admit he might have been slightly out of line. He tried to avoid even looking at Allyson. "So you going opening day?" he asked me.

"We'll be there, Weasel," I said. "I never miss opening day at Santa Anita, unless I'm working."

"Working? It's hard enough pickin' winners without working," the Weasel said. "Once I get through here tonight with these fuckin' trees, I'm back at the *Form* tomorrow and the track on Wednesday. I'm gonna bury 'em this meet, I can feel it."

"Merry Christmas," Allyson said. "And thank you."

The Weasel looked at her as if she had dropped in front of him from outer space, then abruptly scurried away from us to take care of a couple of other late shoppers, who had appeared at the other end of his lot.

Allyson watched him go. "That is a sad little man," she said. "What does he do when he isn't selling trees?"

"He survives," I explained. "When he taps out at the track, he disappears for a while, until he can reassemble a bankroll somehow. I don't know how he does it. I don't know how most of them do it. But they manage."

"I don't think he really understands about the spirit of Christmas, do you?"

"The only thing the Weasel understands is getting a bet down," I said. "If Christmas were an overlay at two to one or better, with one of Santa's elves up and in a good post position, the Weasel would get down on it. Guys like the Weasel were around Bethlehem hustling action on camel racing the night the star rose in the East."

Allyson laughed. "Nothing's sacred, is it?"

"Not at the track," I said, "unless it's a piece of privileged information nobody else knows about, like a fast workout the clockers missed or the fact that some horse stopped running in his previous race because his saddle slipped. That kind of knowledge *is* sacred. My friend Jay Fox has devoted his entire life to ferreting out tidbits like that in order to linger at the feast. The reason Judas sold Jesus out for twenty pieces of silver is that he was tapped out and needed the money to get back in action, any horseplayer can tell you that. But Christmas? In L.A., Christmas is the day before Santa Anita opens."

We drove slowly back along the boulevard toward my apartment. The city seemed to be emptying out, with last-minute shoppers hurrying in and out of the stores and homeward-bound workers already pouring out of the office towers near La Brea. Everywhere Christmas lights twinkled in the early dusk, and tinselly decorations graced doorways, windows, and street lamps.

"Park over here," Allyson said, as I waited for a light to change.

"What's the matter?"

"It's early and there's something I want to show you."

"What is it?"

"Never mind. But it has to do with Christmas."

"Oh, Allyson—"

"You can park at the corner, right there," she said. "It's in the museum."

I had been looking forward to getting home and the start of our romantic celebration, the first such Christmas Eve I could recall in several years, since a nice woman named Dawn Caputo and I had split up, but I could tell Allyson was serious about whatever it was she wanted to show me, so I obediently pulled over and parked. We were just up the street from the Los Angeles County Art Museum, which I had probably passed a thousand times without ever visiting. I couldn't imagine that this was where Allyson intended to take me, but I quickly found out it was. No sooner had I parked and stepped out of the car than she took my hand and pointed us in the direction of the museum entrance.

"Allyson, are you sure I really need this cultural moment?" I asked.

"I've been thinking about this all day," she said. "I just want you to see it."

"First plants and now art. You're trying to move me up in class."

"You bet. Come on."

The museum was still open, but there were very few people about. The staff seemed itchy to get home, and I felt a bit guilty about being one of the few visitors in the building; it seemed an imposition, even if the place was public property and partly paid for with tax dollars.

"Where are we going?" I demanded. "What's so terrific?"

"You'll see. Have you ever been in here before?"

"No."

"I thought not. Okay now, just be patient."

She obviously knew exactly where we were headed. We walked through the ground-floor lobby and up the stairs, then right along a corridor lined by a temporary display of drawings by some Italian Renaissance master—all cherubs, winged angels, and Virgins in various stages of completion.

"I hope it's not this guy," I said.

"Who?"

"The artist. I've never been a fan of Renaissance art," I explained. "It's all the same—big brown paintings about brown people in brown situations. I mean, once you've seen one Virgin and Child, you've seen all you need to see."

"Lou, you're very sweet and all like that," Allyson said, "but you don't know shit-all about art."

"I know what I don't like."

She didn't answer me, but suddenly tugged me around the corner into a large room at the very end of the hall and said, "There!"

I stood transfixed. Facing us and dominating one whole wall was a large, ornately framed portrait of an old, bearded man seated in a straightbacked wooden chair and staring directly at us. His face was full of kindness and great wisdom, the features of a man who had lived long and well and understood too much to be arrogant about his knowledge. I had no idea who he was or what he represented, apart from himself, but he seemed to loom out of the wall, as if he were a living presence. There were other paintings in the room, I realized, but I saw only this one; the others simply fell into the background. I remembered having taken an art course in high school in which the teacher spoke all the time about what he called "the inner life of a painting," and I had never really understood what he meant. But the old man in this picture had it; there was some sort of an energy build-up going on inside that frame that made it seem as if the old man would speak to us.

I walked slowly toward it and became aware now of the precision of detail in the picture; every wrinkle of the old man's face, every fold of his garments, the lace of his collar, the nails on his fingers, the wisps of hair behind his ears— every particular was as clear, as precise as a highlighted photograph. This old man was a living presence. I had seen the work of only one other artist I could compare to him and that was Rembrandt.

"Who is this?" I asked.

"I thought you'd like it," Allyson said. "I wanted you to see it."

"It's incredible."

"I don't know why, but this picture just seems like Christmas to me," she said. "I've come here a dozen times to look at it since Julian got it."

"Julian? Julian bought this painting?"

"It was the first acquisition he ever made for the museum," she explained. "Actually, he bought it in Europe at an auction in London for Bernard Halsey five years ago. Halsey donated it to the museum last year. This room is the Halsey Gallery, in case you didn't know, but this is the only Donabella in it."

I peered down at the name of the artist, then stepped back to admire his work again. "This guy is some kind of painter," I said. "I'd never even heard of him."

Allyson slipped her arm through mine. "Isn't it terrific?" she said. "I'm just crazy about it. It's a *Lazarus*, but it's supposed to be a portrait of the artist's father, one of the last he ever painted. He died very young, in his thirties. That's why there's so little of his work available. But I wanted you to see this tonight. I mean, there's something about this painting. . . . I've only had one experience like this with a work of art anywhere, and that was the year Julian took me to Italy and we went to see Michelangelo's *David* in Florence. It just stunned me, exactly like this old man."

"The life in this painting . . ." I said. "Nobody paints like this anymore."

"You're wrong, Shifty," a voice behind me declared. "You don't know anything."

I turned around to find myself facing Freddie Chambers, who must have come in after us, as I had seen no one else in the gallery while we had been there. "Freddie!" Allyson exclaimed. "How nice to see you! What are you doing here?"

Freddie stared past us at the Donabella. "It's a great goddamn picture, isn't it?" he said. "Look at that old sonofabitch! It says it all, doesn't it?"

"Yeah, it does," I agreed.

Freddie brushed past us and, hands on his hips, confronted the canvas. He seemed defiant, as if challenging the picture to speak to him. "I love you, you old coot," he said. "You're the best of the lot."

"What do you mean, Freddie?" I asked.

Freddie didn't answer. He stood immobile before the canvas for a minute or so, then suddenly whirled about and walked swiftly past us. He seemed upset and angry; in fact, I was fairly sure that he had tears in his eyes. "The dirty bastard," he mumbled, and disappeared out into the corridor.

Allyson started after him. "Freddie—"

I grabbed her arm and detained her. "Let him go," I said. "He's really upset about something, but I think he'd rather be by himself."

"It's funny, isn't it? I mean, him being here tonight and all."

"Freddie's been full of surprises lately," I said. "You think maybe Julian had him work on this painting?"

"He may have. I know that two or three of the Donabellas needed restoration, but Julian never mentioned this one." She took my arm again. "Ready to go now, sweetheart?"

"Yeah. Thanks for bringing me here," I said. "It's quite an experience."

We took one long last look at the picture, then walked silently hand in hand out of the museum. We drove away through the glittery Christmas lights of L.A. and went home to celebrate with each other what had always been for me, until I had met Allyson, one of the loneliest times of the year.

Allyson went back to work on Wednesday morning, but we met again at Santa Anita that afternoon. I wasted no time getting to the doctors' box, which at this track was located in the first row of the grandstand, at about the sixteenth pole. I found her, as usual, after the first race, flanked by Ed and Charlie. They were all flushed with anticipatory excitement. I leaned into the box and jabbed my opening-day program at her. "Allyson, I have to warn you," I said. "Jay Fox doesn't think your horse here has much of a chance. And neither do I."

She smiled sweetly at me. "I'm sorry to hear that," she said. "Please don't tell me why."

"The horse can't lose," Ed declared. "I'm wheeling him up and back."

"I like him, too," Charlie said. "Want to book our action?"

"I'm not that crazy," I answered. "I've seen Allyson's dreams at work."

Will Thompson, the gambling sawbones, came shambling down the aisle toward us, his face already a study in confusion and incipient disaster. "Here comes our main problem," Ed said. "If Will bets on him, the horse could break a leg."

Choosing, Allyson's latest dream horse, had popped up on the opening-day card. He was entered in the fifth race, at six and a half furlongs on the hillside turf course, exactly as she had envisioned it. Unfortunately, he didn't appear to have much of a chance. He was a four-year-old just up from the claiming ranks and going against decent allowance horses for the first time. He had never run on grass before, and his favorite distance was a mile; he had won twice last year in nine starts on the dirt by making one late run from eight or more lengths off the pace. The only rational reason to bet on him here was his price; he was listed at twelve to one in the morning line, with a decent journeyman jock named Bobby Siegel up.

"And there is one other thing," I told Allyson. "Didn't you see the number two on the horse?"

"Yes, that's right."

"Well, he's in the seven hole," I pointed out. "How do you account for that?"

"I don't know. I'm only going to bet two dollars."

"Don't worry about it," Ed said. "I know the reason." He looked at me and cocked a thumb in her direction. "Don't you know she's nearsighted? To her most twos look like sevens and vice versa."

That must have been it. *Of course.* I didn't even consult Jay Fox again or glance at my *Form.* I simply went to the windows this time and bet twenty dollars to win and place on the horse. Then I sat back and waited for the race to go off, content to bask, as I always do, in the glow of a new Santa Anita racing season.

It was no contest. Choosing went off an underlay, at five to one, broke last, looped the field on the turn and won going away, paying $12.40. To everyone except Will Thompson, who had decided at the last minute to key the favorite, which ran last. With that race, Allyson made a true believer out of me, in more ways than one.

8

Atmosphere

The alarm went off at five a.m., and by ten after I had the coffee machine plugged in and was standing in front of my bathroom mirror, shaving. The call was for seven o'clock on location at Hollywood Park, of all places, which, under normal conditions, was only about a half-hour drive from my apartment. I was allowing myself plenty of time, however, because I am never late for a job. This one wasn't much, but it was work, and I was glad to get it. If I was lucky, I might even be able to make the second half of the card at Santa Anita, I reasoned, even though my agent, Happy Hal Mancuso, had told me over the phone that the stint might work out into a two-day gig. "It's *Malone*. You know the show?" he had asked me.

"No," I confessed.

"Randall West is the star of it," Happy explained. "He plays an insurance investigator named Malone. Randy's a real pain in the ass to work with. He's a cokehead, he's always late, and he screws around on set a lot, so they're usually a day or two off, which could be good for you. The studio hates him, everybody hates him, but they're making so much money with this show they put up with his crap. The boobs out there in TV land think he's adorable, so what can you do? Money is money."

"A philosophical insight I approve of," I said. "What's the part, Hal? Do I have any magic?"

"No. You play a horse owner who's sitting in a box right behind where Malone is, and you see something in the race that tips him off to some sort of scam that's going on. Then you have a quick two-scene with him, when he turns to ask you what you meant. It's right up your alley, Shifty. You have exactly four lines."

"Terrific. Think I can handle it?"

"I hope so. You're a great magician, but as an actor, John Gielgud you are not."

"How good do I have to be for four lines?"

"That's my point, Shifty," the agent said. "You need the bread, don't you? I can get you four hundred a day, mainly because the casting director's a friend of mine."

"I don't know," I said. "I'm doing very well at the track. Best first week of any meet I ever had."

"You are diseased—"

"Hey, just kidding, Hal," I said quickly. "Of course I'll take it. And thanks."

"You need gray slacks and a dark blazer, off-white shirt and tie," Hal instructed me. "And be on time. How's your hand?"

"It's coming along," I said. "A couple of more weeks and I'll go up to the Castle one night and give it a try."

"Good." And he hung up. He wasn't known as Happy Hal because he was the soul of geniality, but basically he was a pretty good man. He was a small independent agent, who booked mainly nightclub and variety acts, and he cared about his clients. I had been with him for about a year now and he had found me work, which is all anyone can ask of an agent, after all.

I arrived at Hollywood Park twenty minutes early and had no trouble finding the *Malone* company, whose trailers and equipment trucks were parked behind the grandstand near the finish line. It was a cold, misty morning and the empty stands loomed gloomily over the infield and the dirt-brown main track, where a couple of dozen Thoroughbreds were working or galloping past the box section where the *Malone* crew was setting up for the day's shooting. With Santa Anita now open, only a few hundred horses, the overflow, were still stabled here, but they would be invisible by nine o'clock, and the *Malone* unit would be able to film uninterruptedly until evening, if necessary.

I checked in with the first assistant director, a weary-looking middle-aged black named Bill Otis, who seemed worried about how things were going, even this early. "I hope everybody's on time today," he confided. "We have a big cast and forty-five extras to deal with."

"I thought you called them atmosphere now."

"I don't care what they call themselves," he said, "to me they're extras."

I walked back under the grandstand to get myself a cup of coffee and bumped into Marty Joyce, who was all dressed up in a three-piece suit and looked almost respectable. "Hey, Shifty, I didn't know you worked extra," he said. "Since when?"

"Since never," I corrected him. "I have two scenes, one with West. I play a horse owner. What are you?"

"Strictly atmosphere. How you been going?"

"It's been an okay meet so far, but it's early."

"Yeah. I don't mind missing the first couple of weeks of any meet," he said, "till the form establishes itself, you know what I mean? So I trot out the old wardrobe and call up Central Casting. It's an easy dollar. Last week I was a doctor for two days on a soap and yesterday I was a juror and next week sometime I'm a stockbroker. Some of these jobs are crazy. I once worked as a mole person in a sci-fi flick and a guy who turns into a chicken. And you don't have to do anything, you know? You just kick back and relax."

It was becoming perfectly clear to me by this time that it would be a while before anyone started working today. The crew had been setting up upstairs, but no one had yet seen either Randall West or the director, an old hand named Herman Tisdale, and, according to Marty, the prop truck was lost or tied up in traffic somewhere. One of the A.D.s, a young guy with a droopy mustache, had also been complaining that the call sheet and pay vouchers for atmosphere hadn't arrived either. "Look at this scene," Marty said, indicating the sixty or seventy people milling about under the stands. "It's just like the army. You hurry, hurry, hurry, and wait."

"Hi!" a familiar voice chirped behind us. "I know you guys from somewhere."

I turned around to find myself confronted by Boom Boom Hogan, looking astonishingly ripe in a nurse's uniform designed to accentuate her already formidable assets.

"Boom Boom, what are you doing here?"

"Same thing you are, Shifty," she said. "Making a buck."

"I thought you and Freddie—"

"Oh, sure, but he's crazy, you know? I mean, he goes through money like it's confetti or something. He's real nice, but—"

"Where are the phones?" Marty asked.

"Over there," Boom Boom said, indicating a bank of six pay phones in a corner. "The one at the far end is out of order."

"Thanks," Marty said. "I gotta go call in. I got nothing for tomorrow." He departed, the change jingling in his pockets, to contact Central and the other casting agencies, and he was soon joined by a group of other extras, all equipped with enough coins to keep themselves in action.

"Isn't that a gas?" Boom Boom commented. "I mean, how can you work atmosphere without any change? And I never remember to bring any. People just call *me*, I don't know why."

"I know why. But you're a nurse on this show? How come?"

"Who knows? Somebody faints and they want me to come running up the aisle. It's a bit and I get more money. Only I think this horny asshole West wants to get into my pants."

"I guess that happens a lot."

"Yeah, it does," she agreed sadly. "You know, Shifty, when I first got to Hollywood, before I met anybody, I had no money at all. I lived on a cup of coffee a day and I ate at parties. Then I worked as a topless waitress in a club and I toured as a Polynesian dancer and I'm Polish-Irish, right? Then I made a whole bunch of independent garbage movies, where I had to run around with my tits bouncing and get raped and stuff, and I had some crazy jobs, like packing insects in this pet store. Then I met this producer guy who was married and he got me into the union and so now, if I need the bread and the horses are losing, well, I do this. But you know, it's funny."

"What is?"

"Being atmosphere. It's like you're the lowest of the low. I mean, working topless, with people who offered me money to fuck them, I got more respect. Here you're treated like a lump of shit."

"You and Freddie split up?"

"Not exactly," she said, "but he's a wild man. He can't win for losing. It's like he has a compulsion to blow his wad out there. I can't take it, Shifty."

"Has he gone through all his money?"

"I don't know. Most of it. He keeps saying it doesn't matter, but it does. I mean, I'm not into poverty, Shifty."

Our conversation was interrupted by the A.D. with the

droopy mustache, who suddenly came bouncing down the escalator and sang out, "Atmosphere, please!" Twenty minutes later, Bill Otis called the actors and we all trooped upstairs, where he quickly assigned us our places. Two men in baggy brown ushers' uniforms stood at the top of the aisles; the other extras were scattered about the boxes surrounding the one to be occupied by Randall West and the actors playing the first scene directly with him. I was assigned to a spot directly behind him and told to speak my first line to a young couple in the box with me. "Hey," one of the kids said, "this is all right. We might get a silent bit."

"No chance," Otis told him. "Today you are strictly background." He turned to address the assembled company. "Ladies and gentlemen, you are watching a horse race," he explained through a megaphone, as two crew members passed out old pari-mutuel tickets, programs, tout sheets, and *Racing Forms*. "You'll see the horses as they turn into the stretch. I am the horses. When I come running down this aisle over here, you all stand up and shout and cheer. As the horses hit the finish line, some of you are winners, some of you are losers. Talk it up, throw tickets away, consult your programs. Then some of you go up the aisles, others sit down again. Just don't get in the way of the actors. Anderson?"

"Yes?"

"You stand up, turn to the couple you're with, and shout your line. You want to try it?"

"Sure." I stood up. "It's a disgrace!" I shouted. "That horse has been doped!"

"Fine," Otis said. "Only be a little more frantic about it, like you've just lost a big bet on it. Okay?"

"Sure." I sat down again.

"Where's the nurse?" Otis asked.

Boom Boom appeared, looking like a bowl of ripe fruit on legs.

"Okay," Otis said. "Now, honey, as soon as Anderson here yells his line, Pembroke faints and you come running up the aisle."

"Who's Pembroke?" Boom Boom asked.

"He's sitting in the box with Mr. West," Otis explained. "But don't worry about it. The minute you hear Anderson, you come running up the aisle. Got that?"

"Yeah," Boom Boom said. "Sure."

Marty Joyce, who was sitting several rows behind me, stood up. "Excuse me!" he called out.

"Yeah? What is it?" Otis asked.

"What about binoculars?"

"What about them?"

"Whoever heard of a horse race without binoculars?"

"The prop truck didn't make it," the droopy mustache shouted. "We dug up all this other stuff on the spot. Fake it."

"How? By peering through my fingers?" Marty asked.

Otis laughed. "You're all farsighted!" he bellowed.

Marty sat down and some old geezer directly behind me snorted contemptuously. "Typical of TV," he observed. "In the old days, the prop truck would have made it. And look at this crowd—forty-five of us, including the ushers. What kind of authentic atmosphere is that? De Mille would have had thousands."

Randall West, looking tanned and ageless in a sculpted toupée, dark slacks, and light-blue sports jacket, appeared, along with Doug Pembroke, a regular on the show, and two other male actors. They sat down in their box and Tisdale, a gray-haired veteran who looked as if he were barely surviving the ravages of a very complicated night, leaned in to give them their instructions. What he said was inaudible to me, but West and the actors nodded, after which Otis raised his megaphone. "Let's try it now!" he shouted.

We rehearsed the scene twice, with Boom Boom stealing it each time. Randall West focused his cobra eyes on her and, after the second rehearsal, he got up and walked over to her. I couldn't hear what he said, but she simply looked back at him with big saucer eyes and a slight half-smile on her face. After the star came back to his seat, looking enormously pleased with himself, Tisdale blew his nose into a huge red handkerchief and gasped hoarsely, "Okay, the next one's a take."

"Atmosphere, pay attention!" Otis shouted. "Now watch me, please, and let's have a lot of excitement this time!"

Tisdale turned out to be a one-take director, which in television is a definite plus. "All right, atmosphere, please everybody shift over to the left!" Otis cried. "We're shooting this way now!"

It would be another half-hour at least before they set up the next camera angle, so I went into the aisle to chat with Boom Boom, who had perched herself on a railing, her long legs dangling like carnal bait. Randall West had disappeared toward his trailer, after casting a long, hungry glance at her.

"Looks like you made a conquest," I observed.

"That turkey," Boom Boom said. "I know him. He just wants a quick blow job between takes."

"Graciously put, Boom Boom."

"You're a class act, Shifty," she said. "You don't know what it's like to live in a dungheap. Guys like this West, they're human cockroaches. I only go out with the A team."

"Like Freddie."

"Yeah, he's nice." A frown troubled her otherwise serene features. "Only he's so crazy, Lou," she said. "I mean, he spends money—he *throws* it away, like it's gonna dirty him or something. You know, three days ago he told me he was down to his last few thou. I tried to get him to cut down on his bets and he just laughed at me. He said the BW would take care of him."

"The BW?"

"Yeah, that's what I asked him. But he wouldn't tell me what BW stood for. All he kept saying was that the BW would take care of him. I kept after him. So then he told me that BW stood for Beautiful Woman. So I told him no way. See, I thought he meant me. I don't take care of people, Shifty. People take care of me now."

"But he didn't mean you."

"Oh, no. He just laughed and laughed when I told him that. Like I cracked the greatest joke in the world, you know? I mean, Freddie's very sweet and generous, but he's crazy."

"So who did he mean?"

"I don't know. He wouldn't tell me. He just keeps laughing and winking. The BW will take care of him. Okay, so let her. I don't give a shit, so long as I don't have to meet her. And then there's this room."

"What room?"

"It's a room Freddie's got somewhere, very secret and all, where he goes a lot. He won't tell me where it is."

"Maybe that's where she lives."

"The BW? In a single room? I don't think so. I mean, if the chick is some old rich bag, then she wouldn't be in some room somewhere, would she?"

"I wouldn't think so."

Our conversation was interrupted by the droopy mustache, who came hurrying up to us from under the stands. "Hey, honey," he said to Boom Boom, "he's been waiting for you. You better go see him."

Boom Boom gazed serenely at him. "Listen," she said very sweetly, "tell him I'm busy talking to my friend, okay?"

The mustache wilted. "He's not going to like it."

"Say, that's too bad," Boom Boom said. "He could try the beast with five fingers."

The A.D. departed, looking a little pale, and Marty Joyce joined us. "What a crock!" he said. "Imagine, shooting a racetrack scene without binocs. Hell, that's like playing baseball without bats. It's dumb."

"What do you care, Marty?" Boom Boom answered. "It's TV shit. You take the money and run."

Bill Otis called a lunch break before we could shoot the second scene, which meant they were going to be running very late. West had not returned from his trailer, and there had been a series of hurried conferences between the A.Ds and Tisdale, who by this time looked ready for an intravenous injection. I noticed that during these conferences glances were periodically cast toward Boom Boom, who appeared to be oblivious to the possibility that she might be the cause of the delay. I was happy enough, because I was scheduled to stay on the payroll through my second scene and a possible close-up. If West was throwing one of his celebrated tantrums, we might all get two days out of this fiasco.

While we were standing in line at the chow wagon, which Marty referred to as the roach coach, the droopy mustache came over and confronted Boom Boom again. "Mr. West insists on seeing you," he said, his eyes as furtive as those of a small rodent sneaking across open terrain. "Mr. Tisdale would appreciate it, too, if you would do that."

"I don't do two jobs for the price of one," Boom Boom said.

"Then pick up your pay voucher," the A.D. told her. "You're off the show."

"Boy, are you a sad sort," Boom Boom told him. "What did you do before show business? Shovel elephant shit?"

Pale and sweaty, the A.D. scurried away from her. "They fired you?" Marty asked. "What a crock!"

"Hey, guys, it's cool," Boom Boom said. "They got to pay me, right? And nobody's gonna make any waves for me either. I'll see you at the races." And with a little flick of fingers she moved away from us, as unconcerned and sure of herself as Cleopatra newly unrolled from her rug.

Shooting was delayed for two more hours, until a presumably more compliant substitute for Boom Boom could be found, and the company was not reassembled in the grandstand box seats until midafternoon, by which time Tisdale had become too feeble to move and sat slumped to one side, while Bill Otis did all the work. The young couple in my box couldn't believe their luck, since it had become clear by now that we'd all be working two days. "It's incredible," the woman said, "that it could take them so long."

"This is nothing," the old geezer in back of us commented, "this is standard. Once, on *Spartacus,* I hung on a cross for three months."

_ 9 _

Winds

The Sunday before Allyson's trial date, we drove out to Santa Anita in the early morning to watch the workouts. She had been sleeping badly for several days, and I'm basically an early riser, so it was no real hardship for us to be out on the freeway by six a.m. Besides, we had an excuse for going there that early, as if I needed one. The doctors owned a three-year-old California-bred filly named Lost Lady, who was scheduled to go four furlongs in preparation for the first race of her life. She had been prepping for four months, under the tutelage of one Boris Ignatiev, a trainer I had never heard of. He was the grandson of a White Russian cavalry officer, Allyson informed me, and had been a patient in their office ever since his arrival in America from France five years ago. It was he who had persuaded Ed and Charlie to buy the horse—for fourteen thousand dollars, at a public sale six months earlier—and turn her over to him.

"What qualifications does he have?" I asked in the car. "I mean, besides having been a patient of yours?"

"I don't know," Allyson said. "I think he knows horses. He told me his grandfather commanded a troop of Cossacks."

"Terrific. That and a sharp saber will get you a dead

peasant. But can he train racehorses?"

Allyson giggled. "He says he can. I think he has a couple of horses of his own. He's just really getting into it, Ed told me. He was in the wholesale flower business."

"Oh, God. I'll ask Jay about him."

"He says this filly is fast, honey."

"How fast?"

"I don't know. I think Ed said that she worked one-twelve and something last week."

"For six furlongs that would be fast," I conceded. "What did you dream about her?"

"Nothing yet."

"I wouldn't let them put her in a race until you do."

"Now you're just being silly and all."

By the time we arrived at the track, the sun was peeking over the corner of the grandstand roof and beginning to burn off the early-morning mist, through which the horses seemed to glide along the white inside rail like soft-footed phantoms, their riders hunched down low and clucking to them, bodies flattened to complement the long, ground-eating strides of their mounts. Closer to us, by the outer rail, the animals just out for a gallop or coming back from a workout moved past more slowly, heads bowed against the tug of the bit, necks lathered, manes tossing, the riders tall in the saddle or standing high in the stirrups, as they chatted and joked with each other. In the clear, cool air, the green, flower-strewn infield and turf course gleamed, and the slopes of Old Baldy and the Sierra Madre mountains in the background framed the whole spectacle, one which has never failed to move me. I had to tear myself away from it to get us some coffee at Clockers Corner, the public patio area at the head of the stretch, and when I rejoined Allyson at the gap, where the horses come and go from the stable area to the track, I found her no longer alone.

"Lou, this is Boris," Allyson said, introducing me to a

short, stout man of about forty, with a round, puffy face hidden by a full black beard and a great mop of busy hair that threatened to tumble down over a pair of sharp, beady brown eyes. "Boris, my friend Lou Anderson." She turned to me. "We missed Lost Lady. She worked very early."

"You come back and see her," Boris told her. "I have to look at one more horse here, but you know where is the barn, right?"

"Oh, yes, that'll be nice."

"How did she do?" I asked.

He looked at me suspiciously, as if I had inquired into the solvency of his bank account. "The clockers have written her in forty-seven and two," he said. "I have caught her faster than that." He grinned, a flash of white teeth through the hair like a laser beam, then glanced nervously out at the track to locate his other horse and departed. "We get rich," he called back.

We stayed by the gap to watch the action long after we had finished our coffees, while the fascinating comings and goings, the real life of the track, continued around us. Trainers, grooms, hot-walkers, exercise riders, veterinarians, owners milled about us in the early-morning chill, while high above us, in their booth on the grandstand roof, the clockers with their stopwatches caught and noted down the number of ticks it took each working animal to negotiate his prescribed distance. It was here, and at this time of day, that the crucial preliminary figurings were carried out. And it was on the slender threads of such chancy calculations, so subject to error, whim, and misinterpretation, that the professional players hung their hopes for the betting coups intended to enrich them. The prospect was mind-boggling.

Ten feet away from us, an old man in a long, flapping overcoat argued over a phone line in the guardhouse with the clockers on the roof. He was unhappy because they had caught one of his horses in an impressive training move, five furlongs in 59.2 seconds. "I had him in a minute flat," the old trainer insisted. "You guys can't clock a horse up there. You missed him six lengths." He slammed the receiver down and walked away, unhappy over the knowledge that what he thought was the wrong figure would now pop up in the *Form* before his horse ran in a race, thus helping to shorten the odds on him. I thought of Jay Fox, already up and focused on his complicated calculations, completely dependent on such uncertain statistics, and I actually felt sorry for him. But only briefly. What the hell, he was doing what he loved, wasn't he? Why should I feel sorry for him? During one long bad streak a few years ago he had been forced for several weeks to take a job as a shoe salesman. That was when I should have felt sorry for him. There is nothing sadder, after all, than the spectacle of a free spirit suddenly chained to an oar. Was I going to give up magic and horses to go to work in a bank? Not likely.

It was about nine o'clock by the time we finally walked back into the stable area, and the heavy work of the day was winding down. A few horses were still being hot-walked or washed and groomed, but a hush, broken only by distant traffic noises and the snorting and coughing of the animals themselves, had begun to fall over the backstage world of the Thoroughbred. We strolled past the track kitchen, then turned left and up between two rows of long, low green barns until we reached the four stalls assigned to Ignatiev. They were at the very end of a stable occupied on both sides by the horses of Mel Ducato, one of the more successful younger trainers on the grounds.

"That's funny," Allyson said.

"What is?"

"This is Mel Ducato's shed row."

"What about it?"

"He trains for Julian and his lady friend."

"A nice coincidence."

"Isn't it?"

Lost Lady was in the end stall. She was a little bit of a thing, fragile-looking, but with a strong rear end and an air of quiet confidence about her. She ignored us and concentrated on her feed, her dark-bay coat gleaming in the soft light. "I'm impressed," I said. "Maybe she *can* run."

"Oh, she can run, yes," Boris said, coming up behind us out of the tack room. "Maybe I find race for her next week. She is ready."

"Open maidens?" I asked.

The trainer shrugged. "Maybe I put her in claimer," he said. "Her breeding is not fancy, you know. I think eventually she go long, however. I don't know. I decide in two days, when the new condition book is coming out." Boris winked at me. "You keep quiet, huh? When I run this filly, we going to cash big ticket. One more blow-out and then— bam!" He slammed his big hands gleefully together.

"My lips are sealed, Boris."

Allyson had wandered away from us. She was looking for a carrot for Lost Lady and had spotted a burlap sack full of them a few stalls away. As she leaned over to grab a handful, a big gray horse in the bin directly behind her whinnied and began bobbing his head violently up and down. Allyson turned to look at him. "Hello there," she said softly. "What is it? You want a carrot? I'll bet you do." The horse continued to nod fiercely at her, then turned his head sideways and contemplated her out of a wild, distrustful eye. "Well," she said, "you're just a little crazy, aren't you?" The horse pinned his ears back and continued to bob up and down.

"You not go close, Allyson," Boris warned her. "That old horse is mean."

Allyson ignored him. She began talking to the horse in a soft, low, caressing tone, commiserating with him on all the iniquities of the world. Then, without pausing, she walked up to him, fed him a carrot and patted him on the neck. The animal chewed the delicacy up a bit at a time, like an old man with dentures eating peanut brittle, then suddenly broke away and whirled to the back of his stall, his rump thrust toward her. Allyson did not move; she continued to talk to the horse, until he again turned toward her and daintily went to work on his second carrot, with Allyson once more patting away at his neck. By the end of the third tidbit, she had worked her way up to his ears and was scratching away behind them, then running her fingers lightly over his forehead and face, the stream of consoling words flowing ceaselessly out of her. By the time the horse had stopped eating, he appeared to be totally enthralled by whatever it was she was saying to him, like a patient in a hypnotist's office.

"What the hell are you doing?" the voice interrupted her.

"Just giving him a couple of carrots," Allyson explained. "He wanted one, so I gave it to him."

I recognized Mel Ducato. He had come around the corner of the barn and spotted her. "You got to be nuts, lady," he said, walking up to her. "That old sucker could take your arm off."

"I guess he would, if you were mean to him. But he likes me," she said.

The trainer stared glumly at her. He was in his late thirties, I knew, but seemed younger, with black eyes, curly brown hair, and a long, slightly pendulous lower lip—the sullen good looks of a New York sidewalk dude. "What do you know about horses?" he asked. "I got a groom in the hospital because of this animal. Bit him and took a chunk out of him. You're gonna tell me he likes you? He don't like anyone."

"Oh, he likes me all right," Allyson said. "I think his back hurts."

"What?"

"I said I think his back hurts. Have you tried any heat up there?"

Ducato stared dourly at her, an expression I had come to know well. Since coming out from New York a few years earlier, where he had been one of the hotshot young trainers on the way up, he had established himself as one of the leading horsemen in the West, always in the top five or six in the trainer standings. At first most of his horses had been cheap or ailing animals he had claimed for various small investors and managed almost always to win with, but lately he had been making noises about moving up in class. "I'm tired of these cheap pigs," was the gracious way he had recently put it to a reporter for *Sports Illustrated*. "I'm tired of cheap owners. I want to work with good horses for people who are willing to spend money for the best. I'm a winner. And I can make a winner out of anybody." Shortly after that interview, he had become the trainer for the Halsey string, all high-priced allowance and stakes horses, but evidently this coup hadn't improved his disposition. I couldn't recall ever having seen him smile, even in the winner's circle.

"I know this horse," Boris said, as we joined Allyson and Ducato. "This is Prairie Winds, no?"

"Yeah," Ducato answered, with a barely perceptible nod of the head, his sullen gaze still focused on Allyson. "So what do you know about horses' backs, huh?"

"I just think it hurts," she insisted. "He's an old horse, isn't he? Like old people, they develop aches. I have a feeling, that's all."

"What a bunch of shit," the trainer said. "He's just a mean old gelding who'd as soon tear your head off as breathe. The guy I claimed him for wanted a horse to have some fun with. Some fun."

"I know this horse," I said. "He used to be a good one."

"A long time ago," the trainer said. "He's lost his last eight starts and he don't even come close. He don't want to run, and he's getting worse. You stay away from him, lady. I don't want no more people in the hospital. Especially dumb women."

Allyson's face flushed with anger and her jaw set. "You stupid man," she said. "You think you know everything, and you're angry because you think this horse should run his balls off for you."

"He's already done that for someone else," I said. "He's a gelding."

Allyson ignored the interruption. "You don't know how to treat him, you don't know what's wrong with him, and you don't even want to listen," she continued. "The horse is mean because he's hurting, and you're too dumb to figure out what it is and too pigheaded to even consider anyone else's opinion."

To my surprise, Ducato seemed to be enjoying this outburst, as if he derived pleasure from opposition. Allyson under a full head of steam was an attractive force of nature, and I could see the appreciation of it in his eyes. He reached out and took her arm. "Hey, honey, what's your name?" he asked.

"What do you want, big man, to get your little penis wet?" she snapped. "I don't have my tweezers with me. And take your hands off me."

"Holy shit—" the trainer began.

"I want to know what you're going to do with this horse," she said. "You don't deserve a horse like this."

"You want him? You can have him. He's running today. You can claim him for ten thousand dollars."

"I don't have an owner's license."

"That's too bad, honey. Because if he doesn't win today, he's going down to Caliente."

"Aw," Boris said, "that's wrong. What you want ship

nice old horse like this to Mexico for?"

"Because he can't win here," Ducato snapped. "I don't keep the losers around."

"No, you wouldn't," Allyson said. "I'll tell you what. I'll buy him from you now. I'll give you a check for ten thousand and you turn him over to Boris after the race today."

"How do I know your check's any good?"

"You can't even tell class when you see it, can you?" Allyson said. "How are you going to train stakes horses?"

"Lady, you're full of shit, you know that?"

"Probably, but I'll be fine. You're better than any laxative. My name's Meade, Mrs. Julian Meade." Ducato's eyes opened wide in amazement. "Yes, that's the one," Allyson confirmed.

"He was just here."

"With the glamorous blond bombshell, I'm sure." She opened her purse to make certain that she had her checkbook, then snapped it shut again. "I'll leave the check with Boris. You turn the horse over to him after the race."

"What if he is claimed?" Boris asked.

"No chance," Ducato declared. "Not the way he's been going lately. And people don't like to claim off me." He smirked, which was the closest I had ever seen him come to a smile. "And I'll tell you what—I'll throw in half of whatever share of the purse he wins, how's that?"

"An offer I can't refuse," Allyson said. She turned to Boris, who seemed more than a bit dazed by the turn events had taken. "Boris, Prairie Winds is no longer in Mr. Ducato's barn. He's in ours, beginning this afternoon."

"Your husband know about this?" Ducato asked.

"He will, soon enough," she said. "Is he here?"

"I saw him at the cafeteria."

"Then I'll tell him. But don't worry, I don't need his approval. My check is good, with or without it."

Ducato looked very pleased with himself. "I'll call you," he said.

"What about?"

"Like maybe you'd like to go out sometime. You and Julian are split, aren't you?"

"Don't you have any pride?" Allyson asked him. "And don't you see I'm with somebody?"

The trainer ignored me. "He don't own you, does he? Just thought I'd ask." And he walked indifferently away from us. At the end of the shed row, he looked back. "And stay away from the horse. He ain't yours yet. After today, I don't care if he tears your arm off." He disappeared around the corner of the barn.

"That's a sweet guy," I observed. "You certainly know how to make friends, Allyson."

"I got to find stall for this horse," Boris said glumly. "You sure you want him? He is eight years old now."

"Yes, I want him. And work on his back, Boris," she said. "I know that's where he's hurting."

"How do you know?" I asked.

She looked at me and smiled. "He told me," she said. "What did you think we were doing there? Just passing the time of day?"

We didn't find Julian in the cafeteria, so we drove out of the track grounds and into Pasadena, where I knew a nice restaurant for brunch. While we were waiting for our eggs Benedict, Allyson called the Turf Club and arranged for passes; I consulted Jay Fox on the phone about Prairie Winds. "You're not going to bet on him?" Jay asked me. "He has no chance today, the way he's going."

"A friend of mine wants to buy him," I explained. "Didn't he used to be a good horse?"

"Oh, yeah, until a couple of years ago," Jay said. "He was a real hard knocker. Look at his record—twenty-four wins in seventy-four starts. But he hasn't won a race in two years. He was out all last year with some kind of injury; then, after he came back, he couldn't run. He just kept getting worse. When Ducato claimed him at Hollywood Park last spring, I thought he'd be able to turn him around. He's just the kind of horse Ducato moves up. He took him for sixteen thousand, I think. Well, he's just gotten worse. He's one of Ducato's few real failures. Now he's in for ten, the bottom of the barrel. I wouldn't touch him. Who's your friend?"

"The lady I'm seeing."

"The dreamer?" Jay laughed. "Try to talk her out of it."

"She says his back hurts."

"How does she know?"

"She talked to the horse this morning, in his stall."

"Yeah? Shifty, are you kidding?"

"Why would I kid you? I was there."

"Shifty, the more you tell me about this broad, the crazier I think she is," he said. "Lose her. I'll see you at the races." And he hung up on me again.

I reported the gist of this conversation to Allyson, who didn't seem in the least put off by it. In fact, Jay's statistics were a source of comfort and reassurance to her. "I knew it," she said. "I knew he was a good horse. There's just something about that old boy. I mean, he's ornery and feisty and all like that, but he's in pain. Your friend Jay says he can run, too. What we have to do then is get Boris to make him well. And I'll help him."

"Have you ever owned a racehorse before?"

She shook her head. "No."

"They're expensive and frustrating and as delicate as fine porcelain," I warned her. "Do you think you're ready for this?"

She nodded, her jaw again set in that stubborn attitude I had learned to recognize. "I think it's about time I spent some of Julian's money," she said. "He's got a whole bunch of horses and that blond bitch goddess besides. All I want is Windy."

"Who's Windy?"

"Prairie Winds, but that's so formal," she said. "He won't mind if I call him Windy, do you think?"

"Why should he mind? He's only a horse. And it's a cute name."

"I'm glad you like it," she said. "Of course, if he objects to it, I'll call him something else."

"How would he object to it?"

"They have ways. Animals can talk, you know. It's just that most people aren't listening."

We arrived back at the track about an hour before post time, picked up our passes, and went directly to the Turf Club. Julian Meade and Linda Halsey were sipping Bloody Marys at an outside table directly over the finish line, and they were not enchanted to see us. Julian, his face a mask of confusion and suspicion, started to rise out of his chair, but Allyson stopped him. "It's all right, Julian," she said, "you don't have to get up. This won't take long. I want you to meet my friend, Lou Anderson. He's a magician."

"Allyson, what the hell is this?" Julian asked.

"I don't think I want any part of this," Linda Halsey said, rising to her feet. She had a nice contralto that was being partly blocked by the potato she was apparently storing up behind her nasal passages.

"Perhaps I could help you disappear," I said. "Usually, I only work with small objects. You'd be a real challenge."

"Julian, I don't find this amusing," she intoned between clenched teeth. "I'll be in the bar." And she quickly moved away from us.

"She has great tits," Allyson said. "You must be very happy, Julian. I never had any to speak of."

Julian Meade looked like a man who was being forced

to perform a monkey dance in his underwear in public. "Allyson, this isn't like you," he said. "If you want to talk, let's do it in private."

"I'm for that," I agreed. "Maybe I'll go keep Miss Halsey company."

"Stay here. This isn't going to take long," Allyson declared. "Julian, I'm buying a horse. I've written a check for ten thousand dollars made out to Boris Ignatiev. He's a trainer, if you don't know. There will be some other expenses—taxes and stuff. Please make sure that the check clears. I wanted to tell you about it, so you wouldn't think I was raiding the bank account or something."

"Ally, I wouldn't think that. I—"

"Good. I have to go to the Racing Office to get my owner's license now. I'm sorry to have upset Linda. But she looks like she could use a good shaking up."

"I'd rather not discuss that with you, especially now," Julian said.

"I can understand that. That's all I had to tell you."

"What is this horse you're buying?"

"Prairie Winds. He's in the ninth today."

"That broken-down old thing?" Julian said. "Who talked you into that? Him?" He indicated me with a nod of his head, but his eyes remained focused on her.

"Oh, no, it was my own decision," she said. "You know what, Julian? I'm making a lot of my own decisions now and I'm enjoying it. That's got to be a shock, coming from a little old country girl like me."

"Well, it's been very pleasant meeting you," I said, as Allyson and I departed. "I wouldn't bet against Prairie Winds the next time he runs, if I were you." He didn't answer, but then I couldn't really blame him.

Allyson spent the next few races downstairs, applying for her official papers, while I sat down to study the *Form*. I could find nothing I liked, so I dropped by Jay's box after the third race to see if he had come up with anything. I was too late. He had hit the double for over four hundred dollars and was sitting on his winnings until the seventh, when he had an eight-to-one shot he was going to anchor in Exactas. I decided I would wait with him, so we spent a pleasant hour talking horses, while the brain drains, who fed like jackals on his expertise, trooped by one by one in search of help. As I was getting ready to rejoin Allyson, just before the sixth race, Jay asked me who would be training Prairie Winds. "Ignatiev?" he echoed my answer. "I don't know about him."

"I don't either."

"He's only run a few horses," Jay said, picking up one of his bulky black notebooks and flipping through it. "Yeah, here he is," he continued, his forefinger jabbing at the page in front of him. "Say, he's not bad. He only ran five horses at Hollywood and won with two of them, both maidens first time out. And at nice prices. It's too little to go on, of course, but I'm going to keep my eye on him."

"His grandfather was a Cossack and he himself was in the flower business," I told him. "He has a three-year-old filly for the doctors."

"Nothing significant there, Shifty. But if you hear anything useful, you know where to find me."

"Yeah, and you'll spill your guts to Pinhead and Who-doyalike and Action Jackson and anyone else who massages your ego," I said, only half in jest.

"It's a two-way street," he said. "I get little perks, you see, like parking stickers and free rides on Pick Six tickets. You know how it works. What do I get from you?"

"Friendship and admiration."

"Nice, Shifty, but not bankable. And anyway, it doesn't matter what I tell them. They're losers. They don't know how to use the information I give them." He smiled, looking suddenly like a crafty old tomcat sitting on a fence in the moonlight. "By the way, did you hear about Freddie?"

"No, what?"

"He got mugged the other night. They beat the shit out of him."

"Where?"

"Somewhere near his place, I guess. He's in Cedars Sinai."

"Is he okay?"

"I'm not sure. I heard about it yesterday from Marty, who got it from Freddie's girlfriend."

"Boom Boom?"

"Yeah. I guess he's going to live."

I went back to the Turf Club, but I didn't find either Allyson or Boom Boom, so I sat down in the doctors' box. We all cashed tickets on Jay's selection in the seventh, after which Allyson finally rejoined us. "What a mess," she said. "There were twelve people ahead of me. I guess everyone wants to own a horse these days. But I thought I'd better get it done." She flashed us her new owner's license, a little plastic card with her picture in color up in one corner.

"You look like a criminal," I quipped. And then I told her about Freddie.

"I'll find out if he's all right," she said. "How terrible, poor Freddie."

"Listen, it'll cost him less in the hospital than at the track," I told her. "He's saving money."

"That's not funny."

"I thought it was," Ed Hamner said. "He's all right, Allyson. I saw him this morning. They beat him about the head and took his cash. Freddie doesn't remember much else, or he doesn't want to talk about it."

"Just his head?"

"Yeah. They did a pretty good job on him. They roughed him up, all right. One of them must have had a club or a baseball bat."

"I wonder if Freddie owes some bookie," I speculated.

"I know he bets on everything."

"Say, what about Prairie Winds?" Charlie Tanana asked, his nose buried in the *Form*.

"Tell your friend Thompson not to bet on him," I suggested. "Maybe he'll win."

"I don't think so," Allyson said. "His back hurts. But Boris will fix that."

We all waited around for the ninth to watch Prairie Winds show brief lick, then come in a poor eighth, beaten twenty lengths in a field of twelve. He looked old and arthritic, the pale, shambling shadow of a once competitive racehorse. Nobody said anything afterward, but Allyson seemed undismayed. "Poor old Windy," she commented. "He wants to run so bad, but he's in such pain. He'll feel better soon."

"I'm going to wait until you dream about him," I said. "Right, guys?"

"Right," Ed and Charlie chorused in unison.

I think we all pretended to a confidence none of us felt. I looked at Allyson, as Prairie Winds came lumbering painfully back toward the stands. Her face was aglow with love and compassion. I felt sorry for her, but then I still didn't know any better.

10

Trials

It took over three hours to select the jury to try Allyson, with Jamie Horton using her ten peremptory challenges to eliminate anyone who had worked in a store, in security, or in a bank, and anyone who had had anything to do with a shoplifter. Jed Waters concentrated mainly on dismissing people who obviously had fixed ideas about shoplifting in general or who might assume that such an appealing, well-dressed person as this defendant couldn't have stolen anything. Judge John Michael Barret seemed to have lost interest in the proceedings. From where she sat at the defendant's table, all Allyson could see of him were his forehead, his carefully combed graying blond hair, and the shine of his rimless eyeglasses, like small twin reflectors aimed blindly at the room.

"It gave me a spooky feeling," she told me. "Like there wasn't a real person up there, but a wax dummy of one. The only time he moved was to go back and forth to his chambers. He never looked at me once. I just know he's going to send me to jail if I lose."

I had asked her if she wanted me to come with her, but she had said no. "I might want you there tomorrow," she said, "if you want to come."

"Sure I do."

"Well, that would be nice."

"Allyson, they don't send people to jail for first offenses involving fifteen-dollar handbags," I assured her.

"I hope not," she said. "But I don't think this judge likes me."

"He's a judge," I said. "Unless he's an outright psycho, he's supposed to be above like and dislike."

"In some ways, sweetheart, you're real innocent," Allyson said. "I come from a part of the country where justice is what the damn judge says it is."

"God's country."

"You know it. And God in the Panhandle, honey, is a hangin' fool."

"Well, this is L.A. It's all singing and dancing out here."

"They educated you pretty damn dumb out there on Long Island," she said, in her finest flat nasal drawl. "Shitfire, honey, we'd as soon lock you up as talk to you west of the Mississippi, don't you know that? It's not all Hollywood."

"I just love it when you talk Panhandle to me."

"If this jury votes me guilty, sweetheart, you're going to see what Panhandle justice is," she said. "Maybe I should have listened to Julian. Maybe I should have paid the two dollars."

"There's still time, isn't there?"

"I don't think so. Not now. This judge could stick it to me anyway."

It was midafternoon by the time the last juror had been chosen, and Judge Barret let everyone go for the day. The trial would begin at nine the following morning, with Harold Grant, back from his vacation and family troubles in Georgia, scheduled to take the stand first. Jed Waters looked supremely confident, Allyson thought, and she found herself wondering how she would adjust to life in a cell, even if for only a few weeks. She shut her eyes and had what she realized later was an anxiety attack. She felt unconnected to anything and weightless, as if at any moment she would float up through the ceiling and out into the smoggy blue sky over the city. It was Jamie Horton who brought her back to earth. "Allyson? Allyson? Are you all right?"

Allyson opened her eyes to find herself confronted by the lawyer's worried face peering into hers; Jamie had her hand on her shoulder.

"Yes, I'm all right."

"You're very pale."

"I forgot to eat anything," Allyson said. "I'll be all right."

"You're sure?"

"Yes, thanks. I'm fine now."

"You want me to drive you home?"

"No, I'll be fine." She rose to her feet, as the room emptied around her. "I'll grab a sandwich in the cafeteria. I'll be okay, really." And she made herself walk firmly and quickly out of the courtroom, with Jamie holding her by the arm. On the way out, they passed the bailiff, whose black eyes seemed to be empty of compassion now and full of a mean-spirited satisfaction. At least so it seemed to Allyson, who had to resist an impulse to kick him as they brushed past him. "I really don't like that man," Allyson said, as they emerged into the corridor.

"Don't worry," Jamie told her, "I've already spoken to him once. One more peep out of him and I'll have his ass."

"How you do talk, Miz Horton," Allyson said, with a giggle. "I declare, I do think I've corrupted you."

I went to see Freddie Chambers that afternoon at Cedars Sinai, a hospital in West Hollywood constructed on the Pentagon theory of inaccessibility and so huge that it took me four elevator rides, seven wrong turnings, two orderlies, several perambulating patients, and, finally, a kindly, middle-aged black nurse to lead me to him. "And how am I going to get out of here?" I asked her, as she guided me down two seemingly endless corridors and around two more corners, then at last pointed to an end room where, presumably, old Freddie lay mending. "I forgot to drop bread crumbs behind me."

"Aw, don't worry about it," she said. "If you can't find your own way out, just sit down in the first empty wheelchair you see and somebody'll get you out to the parking lot. We don't want no healthy people in this place. You don't get outta here by nightfall, we goin' to make you a patient and then you ain't never gonna get out."

"I like your spirit."

"Yeah," she said, "I'm about the only good news on this floor. You stay healthy, hear?"

I left this cheerful healer and sauntered casually toward Freddie's room. From about ten feet away, I could hear a spirited discussion going on through the half-open door. "Freddie, this is absurd," a man's voice said. "You don't believe that."

Whatever it was Freddie didn't believe, I couldn't make out his answer, but I stopped just outside the door and listened anyway. "I tell you you've got it all wrong," the voice resumed. "You got hit by a couple of muggers. I don't know who did it. Does it make any sense at all? Why? What would be the point?"

Freddie mumbled something in reply.

"That is preposterous," the voice continued. "You got hit on the head because that is where people get hit with clubs. Be sensible, Freddie. This isn't going to get you anyplace."

Again I missed Freddie's reply, but I gathered that he wasn't being sensible. I also now knew who his visitor was and I waited to hear more. "Obviously, the beating you got has scrambled your brains," Julian Meade declared. "If you want to believe it, then do so. But I think you're being a bit paranoid, Freddie. Nobody wants to hurt you. And as soon as you're feeling better, we'll get together and talk, I promise you. All right?"

Freddie's hoarse answer, unmistakable in its hostility, propelled Julian Meade out into the corridor, where he came face to face with me. "What are you doing here?" he asked, his face flushed with exasperation.

"I'm a friend of Freddie's," I said. "What did you do, have him beaten up? Does he owe you money?"

"Are you mad? How dare you make such an accusation?" He pulled the door of Freddie's room shut behind him, his face dark with anger; apparently I had unwittingly jangled a very delicate nerve. "I don't know who you are—"

"Anderson, Lou Anderson," I said. "I'm Allyson's magician friend."

"Don't be stupid. Of course I know your name."

"Oh, I thought you might have forgotten. You were a bit put off yesterday."

I had an uncomfortable feeling he might be angry enough to take a swing at me, so I stayed up on the balls of my feet, ready to duck or run, whichever might be called for. Julian Meade outweighed me by forty pounds and looked in excellent condition, the sort of man any Nautilus would be proud to flaunt in an ad on middle-aged fitness. I have never been fit, and my physique can be charitably described as wiry.

Julian Meade, however, stepped back. He looked at me long and searchingly, as if attempting unexpectedly to come to some definitive conclusion about me. "I suppose you know that Chambers works for me," he said, having apparently made up his mind not to dismantle me. "I think this beating he's received has unhinged his reason. He thinks I had something to do with it."

"Why would he think that?"

"I don't know. I've been trying to reason with him. I pay

him very well for what he does, and he's worth it, of course."
He was suddenly making a serious effort to be ingratiating,
I realized. It surprised me almost as much as his previous
instant hostility. "Perhaps you can talk to him," he said. "I
gather you're a close friend."

"We're friends."

"Yes, I see." He hesitated again, unsure of himself and
wrestling with some obviously troublesome problem. "Well,
anyway, I guess there's nothing more to be said on the
subject, is there?"

"I don't know. Is there?"

"No, I guess not."

"What does Freddie do for you, exactly?"

"A good deal of restoration, mostly. He's absolutely tops
in his field."

"I'd heard that."

"Yes. Well..." Julian Meade hesitated again. "Look,
Mr. Anderson, whatever he says—please take it with a grain
of salt."

"You mean, if he says you had him beaten up."

"That, too. Yes, of course. You see... well, Freddie's
had a lot of disappointment in his life. He was a very fine
painter on his own, you know."

"So Allyson told me."

"His failure has embittered him. Sometimes I think it's
unhinged him. He blames me. But it's not my fault, you
see. I simply couldn't sell his work."

"Why not?"

"I really don't know. We've talked about it a lot. I suppose Allyson told you that, too." He sighed and ran a hand
over his face, as if to clear it of cobwebs. "His work was
really very beautiful. It was very precise and very delicate,
quite unique. But he kept painting the same things over
and over again—bottles, ashtrays, salt shakers, silverware,
glasses, just a lot of small objects on a table. I gave him a

one-man show and we didn't sell one picture. Hardly anybody even came to see it. I suppose that's when he gave up."

"And became embittered."

"Yes. I couldn't carry him, you see. I was trying to run a gallery to make some money. Several of my other artists sold well, a couple have since become famous—Abstract Expressionists, of course." He glanced sharply at me. "You do know something about art, I gather?"

I smiled. "Sure. I know what I like."

"You and millions of others," Julian Meade commented drily. "Well, it's been a pleasure talking to you." He nodded affably enough and started to move past me.

"I'd like to see some of Freddie's paintings sometime," I said.

"Then you must ask him."

"I did. He doesn't want any part of that."

"You see what I mean?" Julian Meade declared, with a quick, dismissing wave of one hand. "He's given up. And he thinks it's my fault. Please bear that in mind. Without me, you know, he'd have starved to death. I'd appreciate it if you'd remind him of that." And he walked briskly, confidently away from me.

I went in to see Freddie. At first I wasn't sure he was in the room, until I spotted his pale blue eyes peering at me from inside his bandaged head; they looked like agates embedded in vanilla icing. "Boy, you look terrible," I said. "You could be the star of *The Mummy's Curse.*"

"What's that?" he whispered in a hoarse, broken voice.

"A horror movie, Freddie. What did they do, hit your windpipe?"

"Yeah," he said. "I'm not supposed to talk much."

"Still hurts?"

He nodded.

"What else did they do to you?"

"Head, nose, cheekbone. Luckily my jaw's okay," he croaked. "Two ribs cracked. My hands are fine. They didn't touch those. They wouldn't." He waved both of them feebly at me.

"Julian says you think he did it."

"Yeah."

"Why would he do that, Freddie?"

The little man didn't answer; he simply lay there staring at me from within his gauze cocoon, as if trying to make up his mind about something. "Listen, is there anything I can do for you, Freddie?" I asked. "How long you going to be here?"

"Maybe a week." His right hand went protectively to his throat.

"I'm making you talk too much," I said. "I'll go soon, but just nod yes or no when you can, okay?" He nodded. "Do you need anything?"

"No," he answered, his lips forming the word inaudibly. He beckoned me closer and I leaned over the bed. "Listen, they're trying to kill me," he whispered.

"Who's they, Freddie? Who'd want to kill you?"

"It's okay," he said. "I still have the BW."

"Boom Boom?"

The blue eyes opened wide and he started to laugh, but stopped because it was causing him pain. "Forget it," he croaked. "No, listen—" He tried to sit up, then half turned, a hand groping in the drawer of his nightstand. "Pencil . . ."

I produced a ballpoint and a piece of paper and handed them to him. Lying on his back, he laboriously scribbled an address for me. Then he wrote underneath, "Boom Boom has key."

"What am I supposed to do with this, Freddie?" I asked.

"Go there. Package in closet. Take it and keep it for me, okay?" he rasped. "Keep it till I ask for it."

"Sure. No problem." I stood up to go. "So what is it?"

"Can't tell you. Better you don't know. Don't open it. Just keep it. I'll pay you."

"Come on, Freddie, I don't want your money. It's not drugs, is it?"

He shook his head. "No drugs. But it's better you don't know, okay?"

"So don't worry about it. And listen, you'll be fine soon. Everyone at the track's been asking about you. I tell them not to worry, that you're probably losing less money in here," I told him. "Oh, I'm sorry, I don't want to make you laugh." I started for the door. "And Allyson sends her best. She couldn't come with me today."

"Tell her to watch out," Freddie said.

"For what? Julian? They hardly even see each other, Freddie."

He lay back on his pillows and stared at me. "Don't forget," he whispered. "The BW . . ."

I waited long enough to see if he would pursue the topic, but he seemed exhausted and simply waved feebly at me. "Thanks, Shifty," he whispered, "thanks for coming. Play a couple of good horses for me. And don't worry." He kept his eyes focused on me as I let myself out.

Allyson's trial was put off one more day because the judge had a political function he suddenly had to attend in Sacramento, so I was unable to be with her. Happy Hal Mancuso had come up with another TV job, this one as a magic-working bartender in a two-hour pilot for a series featuring a troupe of odious crime-solving teenagers. During breaks in the shooting on the Burbank lot, I tried to find out several times how things were going, but nobody in Jamie Horton's law office had heard anything. So it wasn't until evening, shortly after I had returned home, that I heard what had happened from Allyson herself. She called me just as I was again reaching for the telephone, this time to contact her at home. "Lou," she said, "it's fine, I'm all right. They acquitted me."

To her great surprise, she had turned out to be a strong witness, whom not even Jed Waters could shake. She told her story calmly, straightforwardly, with a wealth of significant details. Jamie brought out the fact that, by leaving the price tag on the handle of the bag in plain view, as Grant himself had been forced to confirm, Allyson had obviously not been trying to hide the object. Jamie had also produced the receipts and price tags for everything Allyson said she had bought that day. By the time she had completed her testimony, Allyson could tell that her own lawyer at least was satisfied. This provided a small measure of consolation and, in fact, had kept her going, calmly and without fuss. "I looked at the jury," she said, "and they didn't scare me. They were caught up in this Mad Hatter's game, just as I was."

In contrast to her low-pitched, self-effacing voice clicking off small facts and explanations, the prosecutor hammered loudly at her credibility. Although Allyson had been prepared for it, she found herself marveling at the weight of professional hostility this man lavished on her. How could he do it? she wondered. The man knew nothing more about her than what he had managed to glean from a couple of hours of testimony by other total strangers. She listened to his depiction of her as a canny thief as if he were describing a character out of a book or a movie, someone completely unknown to her.

When the jury withdrew to consider the verdict, she had risen and walked out of the courtroom past the prosecutor, as if he had actually ceased to exist in any physical sense. Nothing he had said earlier about her mattered, she felt, because she understood now that he had no abiding belief in what he did, merely the simpleminded desire to advance himself in the public view. He was a careerist, nothing more.

In the coffee shop, Jamie told her that a quick verdict often meant one for the prosecution, so they were both startled when the bailiff summoned them back to court in less than an hour. Allyson sat beside Jamie, holding her hand, as the foreman rose to speak. He was a small, round man whose glasses kept sliding off the bridge of his nose and whose thick, oily-looking hair, slicked straight back, was salted with dandruff flakes. He cleared his throat before he spoke, and he avoided Allyson's blank stare. "We find the defendant not guilty," he barked, as if expecting the judge to contradict him.

Allyson broke into tears. Astonished, Judge Barret leaned toward her. "Mrs. Meade," he said, "based on the verdict the jury brought in, you should be all smiles."

She fled. She ran down the hall toward the elevators, her one fixed idea being to escape not only from what they had put her through in these cold, impersonal surroundings, but, she explained, from what she had suddenly found to be the inexplicable complexity of her whole life.

"Where are you now?" I asked.

"The Beverly Wilshire Hotel," she said. "I took a room here."

"You did? What for?"

"I don't know. I wanted to, I guess."

"Do you want me to come over?"

"No, I don't think so," she said hesitantly. "I don't know, Lou, I don't know what I want right now. Don't be mad."

"I'm not mad. How long are you planning on staying?"

"I don't know that, either. Tonight, at least. Maybe a few days. I don't want to go home."

"You could come here."

"No, I couldn't. There isn't room. And you don't want me there."

"Allyson, that's not fair. I—"

"Lou, please. Don't push me. Not tonight. I just want to

be by myself, all right? I—I have some thinking to do."

"Is it okay if I send you up a bottle of champagne or something?"

She laughed. "I've done that," she said. "I have some very nice white wine right here in an ice bucket beside me. And I have this beautiful view right over the swimming pool. I'm going to have some supper sent up and I'm going right to sleep. I have all the drugs I need."

"Allyson, I really miss you. And congratulations."

"You know what?" she said. "Now that it's all over, I'm beginning to wonder if I didn't mean to steal that bag."

"Why would you do that?"

"I was unhappy and all. Maybe I should discuss it with Dr. Ravick."

"Who's that?"

"Ellen Ravick, my therapist."

"How about me? Aren't I good therapy?"

"Yes. Yes, you are. And I'm going to dream about you tonight, sweetheart."

"A good dirty one, I hope."

She didn't dream about me at all. She dreamed instead about Lost Lady. She was at the track and standing in the winner's circle, right next to the horse, and with Ed and Charlie beside her. At the last second, Ellen Ravick, a plump little person in Bermuda shorts, came running up and wedged herself between them. There was nothing in the dream about the race itself, but no one, Allyson remembered, was smiling.

— II —

Sympathy

Three days after the trial, Allyson moved out of her house into a small, furnished one-bedroom apartment in West Los Angeles. It was on the top floor of a nondescript four-story building on a dead-end street that backed up against the hospital grounds of the Veterans Administration. The flat had a terrace with a decent view over an expanse of lawn and trees, and the only noise came from the distant, steady hum of traffic on the San Diego Freeway, a few blocks away. "After a while you don't even hear it anymore," she told me, when I went up to see the place the day she moved in. "It's like the ocean, or like when you put your ear up to a big conch."

I didn't answer. I looked around at her belongings, most of them still in cartons, her clothes scattered over the bed and the couch, and I felt sorry for her. "I don't get it," I said. "I don't understand."

"What?"

"Why you did this?"

"I had to," she explained. "I couldn't live with Julian anymore."

"That I can grasp," I said. "But this?"

"I'll fix it up. It'll be nice, you'll see," she said. "And

that way I won't have to come to you all the time. I won't be in the way."

I sat down on one of the boxes and tried to explain how I felt to her. "Don't you see, Allyson? He's got the house and everything in it. What have you got? Nothing."

"It's what I had when Julian married me."

"That's really not an answer. You have ten years of your life invested in your marriage."

"Nine."

"Okay, nine. They're worth something."

"You sound like a lawyer, sweetheart."

"I think you're going to need one."

"I don't want anything of his," she said. "You know what I had when I married him? A dining-room table and four chairs and my bed. Everything else Julian gave me."

"Wait a minute, wait a minute. You also gave him a piece of your life and you made a home for him."

"He didn't need me, Lou. He didn't need anyone. I found that out after I married him." She sighed, pushed her clothes aside, and sank into the couch. "I am pooped. I've been up since six this morning with this move."

"What kind of a career would he have had without you?" I asked. "I mean, the gallery and his art business, all that?"

"He'd have made it faster without me," she said. "He'd have dropped the Cerberus two years earlier than he did. He kept it going only because he knew I was proud of him and believed in it, even if I didn't like most of the art he was showing. But it turned out that Julian's real talent in the art world is for making money. He's a terrific wheeler-dealer. I'm not sure he knew it about himself, but I did, right after the Cerberus folded. I mean, you should have seen him when he was on the staff at the museum. The deals he put through, the way he charmed everyone—it was incredible. I saw a whole new Julian, one I hadn't really known before at all. He could really maneuver people with money around. He should never have gotten married at all. I was a handicap to him—the cute little wife who worked as a nurse in a doctors' office. That wasn't the image Julian wanted to get across, once he began to really move in the art world."

"When you had the Cerberus, what about then? I mean, didn't he maneuver then?"

"We had a couple of rich clients, people who bought modern art as an investment, yes. And we even had one guy who bought paintings by one of our artists because he actually liked them." She laughed. "But it was small potatoes, honey. The really rich folks want to spend for the already established artists. Big, big bucks. Julian suddenly found himself in a world where he could get clients to lay out millions for pictures and statues. And he found himself going to auctions all over the world where that kind of money routinely changed hands. So if he could do it for a museum, why not for himself? All he needed was one big collector, and he found him."

"Bernard Halsey."

"That's right. And with Bernard Halsey you get Linda Halsey."

"And the horses."

"And the expensive horses." She sighed. "Of course Julian didn't know anything about Thoroughbreds, or even goats or any kind of animal life, till he met her. That all came with the new territory. I lost Julian a long time ago, but now I don't think I ever had him. Maybe if we'd had children, it might have been different, but I don't think so."

"You're still entitled to more than this," I said, waving my hand at the room. "There is community property in California."

"Oh, I know, honey. We'll settle it all later, I'm sure.

Julian's not too bad about things like that. Mainly, he doesn't want to be bothered."

"Do you own that house?"

"Julian bought it three years ago."

"Then half of it is yours. And what about the gallery?"

"That's his."

"No, it's not, Allyson. You have an equity in it. Don't be a jerk."

"I don't want any part of the gallery. That's his life, not mine."

"And what about the artwork? Don't you have a right to some of the pictures?"

"No. Maybe one or two of the things from the Cerberus. But I wouldn't want most of those." She laughed again. "I mean, our most successful artist was Leconte. You know, the guy who paints those huge black-and-white abstractions. I mean, I wouldn't want them on my walls, even assuming I could fit one in here. It would be like living with a huge railroad map in front of your eyes all the time. Or Morrison, the guy who used to hammer nails into pieces of driftwood. Thousands and thousands of nails. My God, would you want that on your wall? Or those big metal hoops Waxle made. Who wants to live in a garage?"

"But what about the stuff he's selling now? That's beautiful work."

"He doesn't own most of those, Lou. Those are things he buys at auction or takes on consignment for clients, and he has to sell them. Julian's not a collector himself. He's a dealer, that's all. He's been making a lot of money, but it flows out pretty fast. Much of his capital is in the stable now."

"His own or Linda's?"

"I don't know. Both, I guess. Some he owns in partnership, some he has shares in. I just don't know." She paused, as if trying to get her bearings in that regard for the very first time. "He has his own breeding operation, which is called the Masters, after the gallery. And he has investments in Halsey Enterprises, which owns the Halsey racing interests. It's really pretty complicated and I've never asked him about it."

"Why not?"

"It's his money."

"It's your money, too, Allyson."

"I just don't see it that way. Our marriage was pretty much over by then." She ran a hand over her eyes. "Oh, dear, I'm suddenly so tired."

"Want to go out for a bite to eat? It's nearly seven."

"Yes, that would be nice." She got up and headed for the bathroom. "I'll just wash up. We'll go somewhere in the neighborhood, all right?"

"Sure. Fine. Listen, Julian must have made a lot of money to be investing in all these racehorses," I said, pursuing her down the hallway. "I mean, why horses, especially?"

"Because Linda loves horses, that's why. And I guess Julian loves Linda."

"Well, some of that loot belongs to you."

"That's the way you see it, sweetheart, but it's not the way I see it." She shut the bathroom door firmly in my face. "Pour yourself a glass of wine," she called out. "There's some in the icebox."

Later, over the sushi in a Japanese restaurant on Santa Monica Boulevard, I returned to the attack; I was determined not to let her throw nine years' worth of what I saw as financial equity out the window with the corpse of her marriage. "I think you've got to get a financial statement from Julian and a fair settlement," I insisted. "Why don't you talk to Jamie Horton about it?"

"I guess," she agreed vaguely.

"Come on, you must know Julian's rich," I said. "The

house, the business, all this money poured into horses—I mean, you've seen your tax returns."

"We file separately," she said.

"You do? How come?"

"We always wanted to keep our finances separate. It was my idea originally. I didn't want to feel like a chattel."

"Boy, he knew a good thing when he saw it, didn't he?"

"Don't be mean, Lou," she said. "There were a few good years with Julian."

"Well, it's your business."

"Yes, I guess it is." She paused thoughtfully. "I guess it's hard to make you understand."

"Don't try. I've about given up. By the way, what about this guy Halsey?"

"Never met him. The one time we were invited to his house for dinner, I was sick and couldn't go." She smiled ruefully. "I think that must have been the night he and Linda found true love."

"I've only seen pictures of him," I said. "He does look like what he's supposed to be—a ruthless s.o.b."

"He's pretty much a recluse now. Julian told me a year ago he hardly ever goes out anymore. Just sits up there in his big mansion up the coast and looks at his million-dollar pictures. On open-house days, when the public shows up, he stays upstairs, in his private apartment. He must be quite a character, huh?"

"I guess so. I'd like to see that collection."

"We'll go some Wednesday afternoon, when I'm off. You have to call up ahead and make an appointment. They'll only take so many visitors a day."

"What, and give up the track?"

"You can do it one day, if you try," she said. "Go cold turkey."

"The sacrifices men make for women..."

"Some *men,*" she said. "Some women..."

* * *

That weekend I went back to work at the Magic Castle, where I concentrated mainly on the basics. My great strength as a magician has always been with cards, so I started out in the close-up room there with a few relatively simple moves, like the Giant Card Fan and rolling the deck over, first face down and then face up. They aren't too hard to do, but they get people interested. Then I performed some stunts involving dealing from the bottom, the middle, and second from the top, after which I casually shuffled the deck with one hand and broke into a little three-card monte, the old swifter-than-the-eye gambling game that never fails to draw attention.

I had about twenty-five people in the room by this time, including a sprinkling of my fellow artists, who were eager to see what kind of form I was in. I don't think I disappointed them, but I stuck pretty much to routine. During the three-card monte, none of the amateurs who played with me could isolate the black card from the two red ones in eight attempts, so I knew I was doing all right, and my confidence grew as the act progressed. By the end of my first half-hour, I was into Cups and Balls and some of my other moves involving coins, but none of the really complicated ones. I was leery of failure and didn't quite trust my mending finger to work well enough. Still, I was pleased with myself and, after my second session, during which I gave my fans one of my favorites, Ring-on-a-Stick, I went to the downstairs bar for a brandy.

"Hey, Shifty," I heard a familiar voice call out, "what are you doing here?"

Boom Boom, looking absolutely sensational in a red satin skirt slit up to her hipbone and a sequined black blouse slashed nearly to her navel, was sitting at a corner table with a deeply tanned, gray-haired, middle-aged man who looked vaguely familiar. I took my drink over. "So what are you doing here?" Boom Boom asked.

"It's my home grounds," I explained. "I'm a magician, Boom Boom, remember?"

"Oh, yeah," she said, "I always forget. The only time I ever see you is at the track. Gee, I really love this place, it's so crazy. It was somebody's old mansion, I guess. I'd always heard about it, but I never knew what it was—all this Victorian shit and all. It's fantastic!"

"I'm glad you like it. I'm working this weekend, trying to get my act together, as the cliché goes." I held out my hand to the man at the table. "Hello, my name's Lou Anderson, better known as Shifty. I'm a magician."

"Well, of course, dear boy, I know you," the man said. "Please sit down. My name's Doug Pembroke. We recently worked on a *Malone* together."

"Of course. I'm sorry, I should have recognized you."

"Not at all," he answered, in his impeccable upper-class English accent, "no reason why you should. We're all out of context here, I gather. At least in relation to each other."

"Dougie called me the day after I got fired off the show," Boom Boom explained. "He was so nice."

"Randall was a bit of a swine, I'm afraid," Pembroke said. "He does that sort of thing all the time. Usually, of course, he gets his way."

"Dougie thought what I did was wonderful," Boom Boom interjected, "so he asked me out."

"Yes, it was a quite remarkable exception to the general rule," the actor continued. "I thought it deserved at least a good dinner and a show somewhere, so here we are."

"Picking up the succulent crumbs from Randy's table," I couldn't help observing.

"Oh, goodness no, you mustn't think that," Pembroke assured me. "I'm of quite the other persuasion, dear boy. I'd rather fancy you, if you weren't a bit long in the tooth. No, no—" he waved his hands deprecatingly about in front of his face—"a quite horrid idea, actually. You see, I admired what Miss Hogan did. I've worked with that stinker on this show for three years, and it's the first time I've ever seen him humiliated. I loved it. This evening is in the nature of an appreciation. I'm a member here. I thought Miss Hogan might enjoy it."

"He won't call me anything but Miss Hogan."

"Well, Boom Boom—not quite my sort of name, you know. Shall I call you Fifi? I rather like that one."

"My real name's Lucille, but nobody calls me that and don't you do it either," Boom Boom warned him. "I mean, I'll belt you right in the mouth."

"I shan't risk it," Pembroke informed her. "I've only just had my teeth recapped by an outrageously expensive dental embezzler and I haven't the least desire to have it done all over again. I've been hit there quite a lot, most recently in the men's room of the Bonaventure. A most unfortunate misinterpretation on my part. The chap at the next urinal smiled at me, so naturally I reached over and gave it a gentle honk. Well, it was most assuredly the wrong thing to do."

"Dougie's gay," Boom Boom explained.

"Saying that Dougie's gay, my darling, to a man as obviously sophisticated as this prestidigitator," the actor said, "is akin to informing Galileo that the earth orbits round the sun."

"I don't understand half of what he says," Boom Boom declared, "but he's so cute I don't give a fuck. Excuse me a minute." She got up and headed out toward the rest rooms, an exit so voluptuously executed that it froze the action at the bar and caused the bartender to drop a full jigger of tequila.

"Thank God she didn't come into the close-up room when I was working," I said. "Who would have looked at what I was doing?"

"Who indeed?" Pembroke agreed. "A remarkable natural

manifestation. I can quite appreciate the effect, even though I am happily immune to it. Randall the rotter, of course, was absolutely shattered. He expected to wallow in those goodies like a hippopotamus in a mudbank. You remember how difficult he was?"

"I certainly do. I got an extra day's work out of it."

"Sometimes I wonder what I'm doing on that show," Pembroke mused. "I'm supposed to play the loyal Dr. Watson to his Neanderthal Holmes, but actually I find him loathsome. I don't wish to be a snob, you know, but I was once quite a good actor, classically trained and all that. Still, one can't complain—pots of money in this television trash, you know."

For the next fifteen minutes, the actor entertained me with hair-raising tales of Randall West's public and private peccadillos, most of them involving drugs and kinky sexual scenes. He was halfway through an account of an orgy involving six naked high-school cheerleaders in a hot tub full of Brandy Alexanders, when Boom Boom returned. Her progress through the premises again did not go unnoticed, but she seemed unaware, as usual, of the havoc she was causing. A tall, pale blond man, wearing dark glasses, got up from the bar and stepped into her path.

"What's your problem?" she asked him.

"No problem," he said, smiling and stepping aside.

She brushed past him, and he must have allowed his hand to stray against her thigh. "Asshole," she said. "You ought to be ashamed of yourself."

The pale man watched her rejoin us, then, still smiling, he sauntered casually out of the room.

"I know that guy from somewhere," I said. "You ever seen him before?"

"Nah, just some weirdo," Boom Boom observed. "You get these creeps everywhere."

"You can't really blame him," Pembroke said. "You're

not exactly the Flying Nun, you know."

I suddenly remembered where I'd seen the stranger. "He knows Freddie," I said. "He was chasing him at the track one day. You sure you don't know him?"

"Why would I know him?"

Boom Boom sat down, still looking faintly annoyed. "I want to see some magic," she said. "Shifty, do us a trick."

I contemplated following the man, but then thought better of it. What did I have to ask him, after all?

"I'll show you a move," I told her, "but on one condition."

"What's that?"

"That you never, ever come into a room I'm working looking like that."

"Looking like what? What's the matter with what I got on?"

"It's what you haven't got on that's the matter," I explained. "It looks great, but there isn't enough of it."

"A bit hard to upstage," Pembroke said. "It's like working with animals, you know. They're always masturbating or licking their genitals. One tends to be distracted."

"Hey now," Boom Boom said, "what the hell do you mean by that? I'm not some animal—"

"No, no, of course not," the actor reassured her. "I don't mean to imply that *you* go about doing those nasty things, my sweet. But you *are* a distraction, you see—a veritable force of nature, as it were."

Boom Boom looked puzzled, but I came quickly to the rescue; I had seen her in full eruption, and I didn't want to risk a scene on the premises where I try to earn part of my living. "Look," I said, "let me show you something!"

I performed my version of the Sympathetic Coins, with a ring I borrowed from Boom Boom and six half-dollars, beginning with three in each hand; I also held the ring in my right one. I asked Pembroke to grab my wrists, then passed the three coins from right to left, leaving the ring in place. After that, I made the ring disappear. Then I pulled a sealed envelope out of my jacket pocket and handed it to Boom Boom. She tore it open and found the ring. "That's fantastic!" she squealed. "How did you do that, Shifty?"

"Like anything else, it takes practice," I told her. "Actually, I didn't originate this one. There's a guy in Vegas named Jimmy Grippo who does it better than anyone. He uses silver dollars."

"I say, quite remarkable," Pembroke observed. "Sympathetic Coins, you called it?"

"Yes, that's the name of the illusion."

"It was smashing, dear boy."

"Do another one, Shifty," Boom Boom urged me. "Come on."

I begged off. I was tired, my pinkie was a little sore and I was afraid of failure. But I suggested they take in a couple of attractions on the premises. "There are other magicians on the grounds," I said, "and they're pretty good. You're wasting your evening in here."

"Quite right," Pembroke agreed. "We'll finish our drinks and move on. Care to join us?"

"No, thanks. I'm beat. I'm going to go home." I stood up to leave. "By the way, how's Freddie?" I asked.

"Who's seen him?" she answered. "I guess he'll call when he gets out of the hospital."

"You haven't been to see him?"

Boom Boom looked uncomfortable. "Oh, Shifty, those places just depress me, you know? I'll see him when he's okay."

"Listen, he gave me an address to go to. I got to pick up something for him and he said you have the key. Maybe I should get it from you."

"Oh, sure. He left it for me in an envelope. I'll bring it to the track tomorrow. You going to be there?"

"Yes. The doctors have their filly running."

"What filly?"

"Lost Lady. She's a first-time starter."

"Is she going to win?"

"I'll tell you tomorrow, when I see you."

"Am I missing something?" Pembroke asked.

"Do you bet on horses?"

"Never," he said. "Only on love, and that's risky enough."

"Oh, Dougie, you're so cute," Boom Boom said, leaning over to give him a kiss. "What a shame you don't like girls."

"I've tried to, my dear," the actor confessed, "but it confuses my genes. And actually I prefer being gay. I've always abhorred tits and tots."

I left them laughing and hugging each other and went upstairs. I was feeling elated at my success and had to force myself not to call Allyson. She had wanted to come, of course, but I had been too nervous and unsure of myself to let her. Now I felt a need to share my small triumph, but it was too late, nearly midnight. So I drove home by myself, fell into bed, and immediately went to sleep without even glancing at *The Racing Form.*

The ringing of the telephone woke me up. I hate late-night calls, because they often portend disaster. This time, however, my caller chose not to speak to me at first. I heard him breathing at the other end of the line. "Pervert," I mumbled and started to hang up.

"I wouldn't do it," a male voice whispered.

"What?"

"You heard me," the voice continued. "I wouldn't become involved."

"Mister, I think you've got the wrong number."

I slammed the receiver down. Luckily, the man did not call back, and I quickly fell asleep again. I don't remember looking at my watch, but it must have been very late, perhaps between three and four a.m.

Lost Lady

"What is the point?" the Weasel asked. "I mean, you got a first-time starter here who's supposed to be able to run and you want to cash a bet on the pig and you put up this bum Clayton. I mean, what is it with this trainer Ignatz? He got a death wish or something?"

"Weasel, the trainer's name is Ignatiev," I said. "That's Russian."

"I don't give a fuck what he is," the Weasel said. "He could be Armenian, who gives a shit? What I'm talking about is you got a filly with speed, if the works mean anything, and this Commie bastard you got training the animal puts up Clayton."

"What's the matter with Clayton?" I asked. "He gets his share of winners. He's always in the top ten, isn't he?"

"Shifty, you got to be kidding," the Weasel countered. "The guy wins races, sure, but not this kind of race. He comes from behind. Now you got a little filly here that I hear can run some and you send her going short and you draw the rail. You don't want Wib Clayton up on your horse."

"Why not, Weasel?" I asked, knowing pretty well what his answer would be.

"Two reasons. One, half the time he don't get horses out

of the gate," the Weasel explained. "Two, he don't think good. He makes all kinds of mistakes. I mean, they don't call this bum the Brain on account of he discovered the Theory of Relativity. You understand what I'm saying?"

"Listen, Weasel, it's all in the luck of the draw," I told him. "We drew the one hole, and that's that. Anyway, she ought to beat this field, even if she breaks last. Who calls him the Brain?"

"Some guys I know. I mean, if Clayton was retired, he could make a good living sittin' on some ventriloquist's knee, you know what I'm saying?"

"I guess so, Weasel," I said, "only there isn't much I can do about it." I started to leave. "I have to get downstairs."

The Weasel followed me to the escalator. "You gonna bet her anyway?"

"Yeah, I think so. I like her chances in this field."

The Weasel looked miserable. "I hope the price gets knocked down," he said. "That way *I* don't have to bet her, see?"

"She'll be under her morning line," I said, "but we ought to get five to two."

"Yeah. Shit. The fuckin' Brain on the rail. We all got to be crazy." The Weasel watched me step on the escalator taking me down toward the paddock and stayed behind, his face a study in gloom. If I hadn't been so nervous myself about Lost Lady's chances, I would have enjoyed the Weasel's dilemma. But I knew perfectly well what the problem was.

Boris had entered Lost Lady in a maiden claiming race for three-year-old fillies at six furlongs. He had put her in for a tag of thirty-two thousand dollars, which meant he was going for a win first crack out of the box against mediocre horses that had never won a race. The doctors figured to bank a decent purse and also to cash a bet. That was the up side. The down side was that they had drawn a poor position on the rail, where young, inexperienced horses tend to react poorly to all the dirt that inevitably gets kicked into their faces and take back, unless they can break very quickly out of the starting gate and get the lead by the time they reach the turn. Wib Clayton, as the Weasel had so colorfully pointed out, was not noted for getting horses alertly out of the stall; he was a strong finisher, but from the inside post he'd have to be lucky to come from behind. Lost Lady risked being shuffled back and blocked or would have to come very wide around horses, which figured to cost her several lengths.

Also, it had obviously become no secret around the track that the filly had some ability, which meant that the doctors might lose her to anyone with the cash to buy her out of the race. That was the trouble with claiming races, but I couldn't fault Boris's decision to enter her in one. In a straight maiden event, Lost Lady would probably have found herself competing against several monsters and wound up no better than third, at best. She had some ability, all right, but not the kind of talent to throw up against top horses owned by the biggest stables. Racing is a game in which the sound thing to do is to enter your animal where it belongs, against horses it can compete against; all the rest is vanity and foolishness. But so far today, I had to admit that the Weasel had a point; we had not been lucky.

I arrived at the paddock a minute or two before Allyson and the doctors, who had come straight to the track from the office and looked it. Allyson was in her blue-and-white nurse's uniform, and Charlie Tanana had a stethoscope stuffed into his left jacket pocket. "We had a little crisis," Ed explained. "A cardiac arrest right in our waiting room. I didn't think we'd make it."

"Did the patient make it?" I asked.

"He's all right," Allyson said. "We pounded on his chest, got his heart going again, and he's now in intensive care and stable."

"We've been trying to talk the idiot into a bypass for two years," Charlie explained, "but the guy doesn't believe in surgery and put himself on some kind of macrobiotic diet he got from a swami. Some people don't deserve to live."

"Especially when you have a horse entered in the fourth," I observed.

"And that isn't all that happened," Ed said. "Your pal Freddie Chambers tried to walk out of Cedars this morning."

"What do you mean, walk out?"

"Just exactly that."

"Freddie got up, got dressed, and just started out," Allyson confirmed. "Luckily, somebody saw him and they got him back to bed."

"He was screaming about people coming to kill him or something," Ed continued. "He's got a nice concussion and he's a little nuts. Anyway, he shouldn't be walking around."

"He was pretty paranoid when I saw him," I said. "My guess is he's hurting for money."

Our conversation was interrupted by the arrival of the horses. Boris himself led in Lost Lady before turning her over to his groom and it was immediately clear to me that he was worried. The filly looked wonderful, with a gleaming coat and on edge, her ears pricked, every inch of her ready to run, but the trainer was sunk in gloom. He was dressed funereally in a dark blue, lumpy woolen suit that made him look like a hairy bolster, from which a pair of despairing eyes peered out in misery. He came shambling toward us, shaking his head. "I don't know, I don't know," he pronounced. "Is not good."

"What's not good?" Ed asked. "She looks terrific."

"Oh, she run good," Boris said. "If this boy get her out, she win."

"So what's the problem?" Charlie wanted to know. "She's three to one on the board."

"There was four trainers looking at her in there," Boris explained, cocking a stubby thumb back toward the receiving barn. "I think we lose her."

"So we lose her," Ed said. "We win the purse, we cash some tickets, and we pick up thirty-two grand on the claim. We do better than double our money for the year with her. What's so bad?"

"Oh, I'm sorry," Allyson said to the trainer. "I know you don't want to lose her."

"Good filly," Boris mumbled into his beard. "I make mistake. I never should put her in this race."

"It'll be all right," Allyson assured him. "Maybe no one will take her."

"She isn't that royally bred," I said, trying to be encouraging. "I mean, right now she's not worth much as a possible broodmare. Maybe Allyson's right, Boris. Maybe nobody will take her."

"I don't know," Boris said. "I make mistake."

The trainer's dark forebodings were interrupted by the arrival of the jockeys, who fanned briskly out into the ring from their quarters behind the saddling stalls. Wib Clayton, looking like a small fudge sundae in the doctors' brown-and-white silks, came striding confidently toward us, whip tucked under his left arm. His face was ruddy-cheeked, with hazel eyes set closely together over a long, pointed nose. "Hi," he said, smiling mainly at Allyson. "How ya doin'?"

Boris loomed over him like a bear over a berry patch. "Listen," he said, "this filly ready now. She going to run good. You get her out of gate and go. Not much speed in this race."

"Sure, sure," the jockey said, smiling and nodding, his eyes still fixed lustfully on Allyson. "I got ya. Don't you worry, folks, I'll get her to runnin'."

Something about his self-assurance made me want to kick him. I wondered if he had heard a word of Boris's instructions; he hadn't even glanced at the horse. She was directly behind us, up on her dancing feet, her head bobbing excitedly up and down against the groom's tight hold on her.

"Listen," Boris said, "I work her out of gate and she break good. If she don't like the dirt in her face, let her relax, don't push."

"Sure, sure," the Brain answered. "No sweat. I got ya."

"She's five to two now," Ed said, glancing up at the odds as they blinked at us from the tote board. "I'm going to bet five hundred on her."

"Me, too," said Charlie.

"Where's Thompson?" I asked. "I didn't think he'd miss this."

"He can't make it today," Charlie said, "but he sent out three hundred to bet on her."

"That worries me," I said.

"No worry," Ed declared. "Lost Lady is a winner."

"Riders up!" the paddock judge called out.

Boris lumbered awkwardly to his horse's side and gave Clayton a leg up into the saddle. The jockey grinned and cocked his whip jauntily in our direction, his gaze still focused on Allyson. "He must have a thing about nurses," I said. "Either that or you're his type."

Allyson didn't answer; her face was solemn and her hands, I noticed, were trembling slightly. "Come on," I said, taking her arm as we followed the horses out of the paddock back toward our box, "it'll be all right. Just because you dreamed trouble doesn't mean it will happen. Not *all* dreams come true, Allyson."

"Mine do," she said, as if she had decided to steel herself for the worst. "I just hope nothing happens to her."

A small, plump woman in a brown tweed suit was waiting

for us at the top of the escalator. "Allyson!" she exclaimed, obviously excited. "Some friends brought me out for the day. I never dreamed you and the doctors would have a horse running! Does she have a chance? I want to bet two dollars on her!"

"You can bet on her," Allyson told her. "She's supposed to win."

"Oh, that's wonderful!" the woman said, clapping her pudgy little hands together. "Are Ed and Charlie here?"

"Yes, they went off to bet on her." Allyson turned toward me, her face now pale with fear.

"Don't tell me," I said. "You're the famous Dr. Ravick."

"How did you know?"

"Telepathy," I said. "I'm a magician. My name's Lou Anderson, I'm a friend of Allyson's."

"What's the matter, darling?" the therapist said to Allyson. "You look strange."

"She dreamt you'd be here," I explained.

"Those dreams again, Allyson. I think you'd better come and see me."

"Yes, I'll call you," Allyson said. "Look, you'd better go make your bet. Come down to the winner's circle, if she wins."

"Oh, I'd love to! How do I do that?"

"Ask any usher," I instructed her. "They'll tell you. But don't bet more than two dollars."

"Oh, I won't," she replied. "That's my absolute limit on any gambling event." She patted Allyson on the arm and left us.

"You all right?" I asked.

"I'll be fine," Allyson said, "Don't worry."

"I'm going to bet on her myself. Want to come?"

"No," she answered, shaking her head. "Don't bet a lot, Lou."

"Twenty dollars. I'm going to risk a little that you might

be wrong," I said. "Nobody's right all the time, even you. What did she mean about your going to see her?"

"The last time I had these prophetic dreams, about three years ago, was when my marriage was beginning to fall apart," Allyson explained. "I went to see her and, after a few sessions with her, they stopped."

"Well, my God, don't go now," I said. "You've been dreaming winners."

"Not this time, Lou. Go make your bet. I'll see you in the box."

"Listen, you're wrong," I told her. "You saw Ravick in Bermuda shorts. She's not wearing Bermuda shorts."

She didn't answer, so I hurried away toward the windows and got in line, with about five minutes to go before post time. I had to bet on the horse, because she figured to win and the price was right, but, out of respect for Allyson's clairvoyance, I was not going to risk the hundred dollars I had originally intended to wager. In any case, the line was moving very slowly and I was in danger of being shut out, which I wouldn't have minded in the least. I glanced at the board and saw that the price on the filly had dropped to two to one. If she went any lower, I promised myself, I wouldn't risk even my twenty on her; no first-time starter, especially a green three-year-old filly on the rail, is worth risking money on at low odds.

"Shifty!" the voice called out. "I've been looking for you!" Boom Boom Hogan had spotted me in the line and came hurrying over from her post at the corner of a nearby grandstand bar. She was wearing tight slacks and a silk turtleneck, one of her few PG outfits. "She's gonna win, isn't she?"

"I don't know," I said. "I wouldn't bet much."

"I put fifty on her. You said she'd run good."

"Yeah, I think she will." I glanced beyond Boom Boom to where I thought I recognized a familiar figure from the night before. "My God, you're still with Pembroke? What did you do, make a convert?"

"Oh, God, no," she said. "But it was so late and he just wanted company. He was too loaded to drive. Anyway, it was real lucky I went home with him, Shifty. Somebody broke into my apartment last night."

"You're kidding? They stole something?"

"They tore the place up real good, the bastards," she said. "I found out when Dougie drove me home this morning. Somehow they got in by jimmying the lock, and they just tore the place all up. Slashed the chairs and the bed and everything."

"What did they take?"

"Some of my jewelry, that's all, but it's mostly junk," she said. "The good stuff I keep in my box at the bank. I got a TV and a Betamax and a stereo, and they didn't touch any of that. Or my furs and stuff. It's funny, it's like they were looking for something. Drugs, maybe—I don't know. Anyway, isn't it lucky I wasn't there?"

"You bet."

"And they were real quiet," she continued. "I live in this condo-apartment building on Orange Grove, and there's always people coming and going at all hours in the neighborhood. Nobody saw or heard anything. Anyway, the cops came and took a report, which is just a waste of time, and I had to call up and get the lock changed. But the place is a mess, so Dougie said I could stay with him for a few days. He has this really gorgeous home up on Mulholland. It's got this incredible view over the whole Valley. Isn't that sweet of him?"

"It certainly is. Excuse me a second." I had reached the head of the line by this time, and I bought my twenty-dollar ticket on Lost Lady.

"You want to join us?" Boom Boom asked, as I stepped away from the window.

"No, Boom Boom, I'm with some friends. Say hello to Doug for me."

"He's right over there," she said. "Come say hello yourself."

"The horses are approaching the starting gate!" the announcer intoned.

"I can't." I waved at Doug, who waved back and raised a drink on high. Then I started toward our box.

"Hey, wait," she said, "I almost forgot." She opened her purse and produced a small, white envelope bound up by a rubber band. "Freddie's key. I had it in my bag all the time." She handed it to me.

"Has he called you?"

"No. Isn't he still in the hospital?"

"I think so. He tried to walk out of there this morning."

"No kidding? Well, I won't be home. If you hear from him or you talk to him, tell him where I am. Dougie's in the phone book, under Douglas Wilson. That's his middle name. Is Freddie okay?"

"I don't know," I said. "He's got a good paranoia going. I think he must be broke."

"Oh, for sure. You know Freddie," she said. "But he'll be back. He gets money, lots of it, from somewhere."

"It is now post time!" the announcer declared.

"I'll see you, Boom Boom," I said, hurrying away from her. "Aren't you going to watch the race?"

"We watch them on the monitor," Boom Boom called after me. "Dougie doesn't care about the races. He likes the bar action."

I got back to the box just as the horses were being loaded into the starting gate. Lost Lady's price had dipped to nine to five, and Boris was a study in black, even though he had a battered pair of enormous submarine commander's binoculars trained on his animal. Ed and Charlie were also focused on the start, but Allyson was not; she was sitting with her hands tightly clenched in her lap, her face white. I wanted to say something comforting to her, but as I leaned forward, the announcer barked, "They're off!"

"Shit!" Ed exclaimed.

"Did you see that?" Charlie shouted. "He took up!"

The Brain had just given us one of his patented poor starts. Unprepared, he had been sitting back on his horse, so that when the stall gate sprang open, he had been forced to jerk hard on the reins, causing the filly to toss her head up and almost rear. She lost half a dozen lengths within the first fifty yards and by the time Clayton had her straightened out, she was next to last and pinned along the rail.

"I kill him," Boris growled. "I kill that sonbitch!"

As the horses neared the turn, Lost Lady began to make up ground, but she was still eight or nine lengths off the lead and trapped along the inside. When the front speed began to tire and stop in front of her, she would have no place to go. "The Weasel was right," I mumbled. "The guy's a disaster."

Suddenly, however, as the field neared the three-eighths pole, Lost Lady began to turn it on. Clayton was now showing what he *could* do; he was crouched up behind the filly's neck, driving hard as he steered her through horses. By the time the three front-runners had reached the head of the stretch, Lost Lady was tucked in directly behind them, no more than two lengths back. "Jesus Christ!" I heard myself shouting. "Look at her run! She's going to win anyway!" We all rose to our feet as one and began screaming encouragement.

The trouble was she had no place to go; the three leaders were in too tight for Lost Lady to get through, and Clayton could not risk swinging her to the outside this late in the race without losing too much ground, perhaps causing her to check again, even break stride. I prayed for a hole to open up, but it didn't seem likely. A hundred yards from the finish line I would have been happy to sell my ticket at face value.

Clayton, however, had a lot of horse under him. He reached back and stung her twice with the whip, and the filly made her own hole. She came surging through between the leaders with one last, tremendous move that thrust her to the wire half a length in front. "Oh, God!" Ed shouted. "Did you see that? She did it! She did it!" He and Charlie began bouncing up and down in each other's arms.

Boris, Allyson, and I knew better. The trainer had lowered his glasses and was staring stonily straight ahead. Allyson had not moved an inch; her eyes were closed and I suspected she was praying. In winning the race, Lost Lady had knocked one of the two horses beside her almost sideways in her explosive charge. I held my breath and watched the board.

Sure enough, within a few seconds the lighted numbers of the first three horses began to blink and the announcer's voice confirmed my worst fears. "Your attention, please." it declared, in a tone of incipient doom. "There will be a stewards' inquiry into the running of this race! Please hold all tickets!"

"They won't take her down," Charlie said confidently. "Those horses in front of her were tiring. How else was she going to get through?"

No one answered. I took Allyson's hand, and we all threaded our way silently down through the crowd toward the winners' circle. On the way, Dr. Ravick, her face alight with innocent joy, fell in with us. "Isn't it wonderful!" she exclaimed, waving her two-dollar ticket at us. "I didn't see how she could win!"

"And neither did the stewards," I said, but the good doctor had no idea what I was talking about. Blessed are the ignorant, especially at the track.

"I think it's just grand," she said, squeezing Allyson's

arm and beaming, apparently oblivious even of her former patient's distress. Some therapist, I thought, some insight. She looked, I realized with a start, like a plump little man in Bermuda shorts.

I glanced at Allyson. "It's okay, honey," I said. "It'll be all right, you'll see."

It wasn't all right at all. No sooner had we had our picture taken in the winner's circle, with Boris standing glumly by the horse's head and the rest of us strung out beyond him in a semicircle, than the lights on the board stopped blinking. "Your attention, please!" the voice of doom boomed over our heads. "By order of the stewards, number one, Lost Lady, has been disqualified for interference in the stretch and placed third!" The crowd roared, as the board now showed our horse in third place. To make matters worse, once Clayton had vaulted lightly from the saddle, a uniformed attendant attached a red tag to Lost Lady's bridle and led her away. "Two claims for her," Boris said. "Mitchum got her."

"Goddamn," Ed said, "this just isn't our day."

"That chemist will break her down in six months," Charlie predicted gloomily.

"What happened?" Ellen Ravick asked. "Didn't she win the race?"

Nobody had the heart to enlighten her. Clayton now walked cheerfully up to the trainer. "Sorry," he said. "The hole closed up on me."

"Sure," Boris told him. "You could win by ten."

"Next time for sure," the jockey said, apparently oblivious of the fact that we had just lost the horse.

"They don't call him the Brain for nothing," I observed.

But Allyson wasn't listening; she was in tears. She put her head down and walked quickly away from us. Something in her attitude—the set of her shoulders, perhaps, or the determined stride with which she cut through the crowd—

made me pause and I let her go. I thought I'd catch up with her upstairs, but she didn't come back to the box and I didn't see her again that afternoon.

She telephoned me that night at home. "I'm sorry, Lou," she said. "I couldn't stay."

"Where'd you go? I've been calling you all evening."

"I went to the barn to see Windy. I wanted to be by myself. I'm sorry."

"It's okay," I lied. "How'd you get home?"

"Boris drove me. He was so upset."

"Yeah, I can imagine."

"He really loved that little filly. She had so much heart."

"It was his fault. He picked the race and he put the Brain up."

"That's a little unfair. Lou."

"Is it?"

"I think you're just angry at me."

"Maybe I am. I was worried about you. So were Ed and Charlie. Nobody knew where the hell you'd gone."

"Sometimes I just need to be by myself."

"Yes, so I've noticed." I took a deep breath and tried to cool myself down. After all, I didn't own this woman, did I? I was behaving like a jealous husband. Me, the perennial bachelor and loner. "So how's Windy?" I asked.

"He's so much better," she said. "Boris has been putting damp heat on his back, and he's really improved. He must have had a really sore muscle back there. He's coming along so well now. Boris is also feeding him vitamins and supplements and his coat is all shiny."

"Who, Boris?"

She laughed. "No, silly. Windy."

"When's he going to run?"

"Oh, I don't know. Not for a week or two, at least. The horse'll let us know."

"Is he still talking to you?"

"Oh, yes, all the time. He's so feisty. But he likes me. I make him his coffee now and we drink it together."

"The horse drinks coffee?"

"Oh, yes, he loves it. With lots of cream and sugar. He just slurps it up from my hand."

"Boy, you're weird. Just don't give it to him on race days. Listen, do you want me to come over?"

"No, not tonight. Please try to understand."

"I am."

"I'll call you in the morning from the office, all right?"

"Sure."

"Good night, Lou. Thanks for being so sweet today." And she hung up, as if I meant nothing more to her than any other good friend. Well, perhaps that was all I was, I realized.

I was too agitated to sleep, so I sat down at the kitchen table and worked for a couple of hours on my moves. I was almost all the way back, I felt, and it was simply a question now of continued practice and refining some of the more difficult effects, especially the ones involving my injured finger. By eleven o'clock, I was tired out and ready for bed. I got up, turned on the TV for the late news, and went into the bathroom to brush my teeth.

I had barely finished rinsing my mouth, when I heard a reporter on screen say, "No one knows how the fire started, but it has been contained and firemen expect to have some answers soon." I came back and lay down on the bed in time to see the earnest, sweating face of the reporter, with a background shot of a large private house reduced to a smouldering ruin around which a team of firefighters still swarmed, equipped with hoses and axes. "It's lucky there was no wind tonight, or it could have spread very quickly," the reporter continued, "with disastrous results for this whole area. As one neighbor down the road put it, it looked like

Valhalla burning up here. From the top of Mulholland Drive, this is Bob Tracy for Channel Two News."

I punched the set off, rolled over on my side and went almost immediately to sleep.

– 13 –

Killings

The address Freddie had given me turned out to be in
East L.A., in an area of factory buildings and warehouses
near the Santa Fe railroad yard. Even at midmorning, with
people in the streets, this section, like much of downtown,
had a shabby, abandoned look, as if a previous civilization
had passed by, leaving in its wake these ugly relics of a
lost prosperity. It was a breezy day, presaging the onset of
a possible Santa Ana wind, and papers and bits of refuse
blew along the sidewalks; pedestrians hunched up against
the blast, and the air was coldly clear, accentuating the
shabbiness of the surroundings. I parked at the corner of
Freddie's block, between an empty moving van and a battered pickup truck, in which three scrawny Mexican teenagers sat huddling together for warmth and staring at me
out of curious, mildly fearful eyes, and I walked down the
street, scanning the façades of a row of commercial structures for the right number.

Freddie's building turned out to be a small, rickety-
looking, four-story abandoned factory sandwiched between
a defunct bakery and a storage warehouse. Like some other
structures in the area, it had been converted into artists'
studios, whose names appeared, neatly stenciled, by the
entrance. Freddie's was not among them, but I guessed that

his place must be on the top floor, the only loft apparently unoccupied. The front door was open and I walked up a slightly lopsided flight of stairs until I reached the landing and found myself facing a closed door. I inserted Freddie's key and turned it five or six times to the right to unlock an iron bolt, then opened the door and walked in.

The room was huge, occupying almost the whole top floor of the building and with a slanted skylight that flooded the premises with sunshine. It was also as empty as a skating rink, except for one corner where Freddie, or somebody, had put up overlapping plywood partitions. Behind them were a single bed, a caved-in armchair, several packing boxes, a couple of orange crates stuffed with tattered paperback books, and a tiny kitchen range, with a couple of electric burners. There were also paper plates, plastic coffee cups, an old-fashioned percolator, and a cabinet full of canned goods. A tiny icebox contained a carton of festering milk, two eggs, and a blob of rancid butter. The bed had been slept in, but not recently; the sheets were gray and coffee-stained, and the pillow had fallen to the floor, where it languished surrounded by crumbs and bits of social debris. A wooden easel leaned against the wall and dust lay over everything. Obviously, no one had used this area in several weeks.

Beyond the partitioned alcove, in the very far corner of the room, was an improvised bathroom containing a toilet and a small sink, both badly in need of cleaning, and next to it, built out from the wall, was a plain wooden closet. I walked over to it and opened the door. At first I thought it was completely empty, except for a half-dozen or so naked wire hangers, but then I noticed two folded olive-green army blankets in one corner. Lying between them, carefully wrapped in thick, brown corrugated paper and tied up with twine, was a flat parcel about two and a half feet square. It was quite heavy for its size, but lighter than a book might have been, and I guessed it was a picture of some sort. I tucked it under my arm and took another long look around the room. I saw nothing of significance, except possibly for a pocket-sized brown notebook lying on the floor beside one of the orange crates. I picked it up, flipped it open, and saw that it contained some telephone numbers and a few hastily scrawled notations. To this day I don't know why I kept it, but I did. I thrust it into my pocket and left, with the heavy wrapped parcel still under my arm.

On my way down the stairs, I met one of the other tenants coming up. He was a husky, balding young man of about thirty, carrying a couple of bags full of groceries. He was dressed in jeans and a paint-stained T-shirt, so I guessed he was also an artist. "Thanks," he said, as I stepped aside to let him squeeze past me on the narrow staircase.

"Sure. Say, do you live here?" I asked.

"Yeah, sure do."

"Listen, I'm looking for Freddie Chambers. Do you know him?"

"No, I don't think so."

"The little bearded guy on the top floor."

"Oh, him. Camerini. Yeah, but I haven't seen him in months. I thought maybe he'd left town again."

"No, he's around. By the way, do you know his work?"

"No, he won't let anybody see it." The young man grinned and leaned back against the wall. "He's a funny guy. I once went up to his place to borrow some olive oil, and he wouldn't let me in. I mean, he kept me standing outside the door, which he bolted, until he came back with the oil. I figured he was working on something, but what the hell, I didn't care what he was doing. I wasn't about to copy him or anything, you know?"

"This was his studio, I gather."

"He used to work up there, but he'd also be gone for long stretches. I've been here about three years now, and he was already up there when I came. He didn't live there. He just went up there to paint. Lately, though, I haven't seen him around. I thought he gave up or moved out or something."

"Why would he give up?"

"Well, he got some Mexicans over with a truck one day, not long after I moved in here, and they took all this stuff out. Stacks and stacks of paintings, you've never seen anything like it. There was a lot of garbage. It was a factory up there."

"And you haven't seen him for a while?"

"No. I don't know why, but I got the feeling he wasn't doing much anymore. You a friend of his?"

"Yeah. If you see him, tell him I was around, okay?"

"Sure thing. What's your name?"

"Anderson, Lou Anderson. Shifty to my friends."

"Well, okay. I'll see you."

"Yeah, thanks. Need some help with those bags?"

"No, it's okay. My girlfriend's home, and she'll get the door."

Out in the street, the Mexican kids were still sitting in the pickup, but nobody else was around. I stashed the parcel under some beach towels in the back of my car, the same old battered Datsun 310 I had been married to now for five years, and drove into midtown, on my way toward a freeway. A couple of blocks off Main, I spotted a parking space by a meter, pulled in, and called Allyson from a public phone on the corner.

"Where are you?" she asked.

I told her, as well as all about my visit to Freddie's studio. "I don't think he's been there for quite a while," I concluded.

"Yes, well, Dr. Hamner just called us from the hospital," she said. "Freddie walked out of there again last night, but this time he made it."

"He did? Where'd he go?"

"Nobody knows. Ed is furious. The idea that a patient can just get up and leave makes him real mad. I mean, Freddie was still all bandaged up and all like that."

"I guess we'll be hearing from him," I told her. "I've got his picture, or whatever it is."

"You haven't opened it?"

"No. Freddie insisted I'd be better off not knowing what it is," I explained. "He just asked me to hold it for him."

"I don't like that," she said, after a second's pause. "Let's find out what's in it."

"I'll come over tonight and we'll open it together."

"All right. Are you going to the track?"

"Did the sun rise this morning?"

"I had a dream last night."

"Ah. What did you dream?"

"Luis Pelé was helping me with my laundry."

"Helping with your laundry?"

"Yes. We were in the laundry room of my building, and he was helping me take my laundry out of the dryer and folding it for me."

"Sounds a little kinky."

"Doesn't it? I don't know what it means."

"Neither do I, but I'll think about it."

"We're going to be working late tonight," she said, "so I probably won't get home till after six."

"Shall I bring something?"

"We're having steak and corn. We'll barbecue on the terrace, all right?"

"Sounds wonderful. I'll bring the wine."

"Lou?"

"Yeah?"

"Please be careful."

"Of what?"

"I don't know. I have a feeling, that's all."

It wasn't until I was halfway out to Santa Anita that I

figured out what her dream meant. Luis Pelé happened to be my favorite jockey. He was a veteran Latin American rider whom the Weasel called Muscles, because he was such a strong finisher that he could almost quite literally carry a tiring or quitting horse over the finish line. He was always among the top three or four in the local jockey standings, and he rarely made mistakes. Whatever his mount had to give in a race, Luis Pelé would extract it and more. And I had never seen him stiff a horse or fail to take the necessary, often dangerous chances that sometimes have to be taken in order to win. Now, as I sped along the freeway toward my daily rendezvous with the worshipers of the Dummy God, I had a revelation. Luis Pelé at Allyson's side in the laundry room clearly meant that he was helping her to clean up. I began to hum to myself in anticipation of a killing.

Almost the first person I saw at the track was Jay Fox. The handicapper was strolling in from the parking lot with his black notebooks under one arm and a pair of large binoculars hanging off his other shoulder. He seemed at ease, at peace with himself and the world, so I knew he must have been having a good meet.

"Shifty, I've been trying to get hold of you," he said, as I fell into step beside him. "Where you been?"

"Around, Jay. How are you doing?"

"Very well," And he filled me in. He was putting in daily Pick Six tickets for two plungers, who were footing all the expenses and paying him a commission of twenty-five percent of any profits. So far Jay had banked over eleven hundred dollars on that action. The betting syndicate he wagered for, also on commission, was solidly in the black to the tune of about six thousand dollars, which meant another twelve hundred or so for him. All tax free and at no personal risk to himself. Even better, he confided, his own private action had been paying off, at over two thousand dollars, and the meeting was still in its infancy. "I'm on a reign of terror," he said cheerfully, as we headed up the escalator toward the grandstand boxes. "But I've been doing a little research I want to tell you about."

I followed him to his seat and waited out the parade of mendicants, who now came trooping by to find out what his action would be. Mercifully, he didn't have much to impart, since he had decided to bet only the eighth and ninth races and to put in two small Pick Six tickets, for a total of a hundred and twenty-eight dollars. His conservative play, I could tell, disappointed his more fervent admirers, two of whom, Action Jackson and Pinhead, had information to report.

"The Mitchum horse is a lock in the first," Action Jackson confided. "I got it from Clayton's agent. Can't lose. I'm gonna wheel him in the double."

"Great," Jay said, munching on an imaginary canary, "You do that, Jackson."

"You ain't gonna bet him?"

"Nope."

Action Jackson looked momentarily stricken, like a greedy child denied a promised candy bar, but he rallied. "I'm still gonna bet him," he said defiantly.

"Good," Jay answered. "Go get 'em."

The brain drain hesitated, then shrugged and rushed away to buy his double wheel. "It's hopeless," I said.

Jay smiled benignly, St. Francis presiding protectively over the little furry animals. "I can lead them to salvation," he said softly, "but I can't actually save them."

"What about the Mitchum horse? He looks in form."

"Clayton on the rail in a sprint?"

"A clear case of *dejà* screwed," I agreed. "Say no more."

"Besides which, the horse has had so many needles stuck into him they ought to give Mitchum a license to practice acupuncture."

"I was going to put him up for the Nobel Prize in chemistry."

Pinhead turned out to be more persistent. He had heard about a mare in the fifth race trained by Mel Ducato that was supposed to be what we used to call a mortal lock. The horse showed a series of bad races in the *Form,* but she had recently been claimed by Ducato, freshened for a couple of months, put back into training and entered against a much weaker field than she had been facing. "They had her down at San Luis Rey," Pinhead said, naming the training facility down south where ailing horses were often sent to be restored to health away from the daily grind of the track itself. "You know they don't have the top clockers down there. A guy who works for the Buckingham string told me they missed two of her best moves. The horse is sharp, real sharp. She's going to horrify this field, and she's ten to one in the line." He leaned in close to Jay's ear. "She'll go off at no less than six to one."

"Yes, I considered her," Jay said, "but there are too many negative factors. I'm going to pass."

Pinhead looked quickly around to make sure he couldn't be overheard. "One eleven flat out of the gate," he murmured out of the side of his mouth. "Forty-six and two blowout. How does that grab you?"

"Pretty impressive," Jay admitted. "I'm still passing."

Pinhead looked distressed. He obviously believed that if he could persuade a pro like the old Fox to risk money on his tip, it would confirm the value of the information he had been given. He had a paranoid's view of the universe as a sphere of activity where nothing was as it seemed and no one could survive without somehow being included among the small, inner brotherhood of cognoscenti, who presumably made the rules and fixed the game of life to make winners of themselves. Jay's indifference to his information and his trust in his own expertise, hard earned over a period of two decades at the betting windows, disturbed Pinhead; it made him feel he was standing forever outside the charmed circle, denied access to an ultra-exclusive fraternity. He had, after all, never been known even to glance at a *Racing Form* himself.

"Jay, you've got to believe me," he pleaded. "This is real information."

"I believe you."

"I'm sure as hell going to bet on her."

"I'll be rooting for you all the way."

Shaking his head and muttering to himself, Pinhead shuffled morosely away from us. I couldn't feel sorry for him; we were, after all, basically in competition with each other. "The horse will probably either win or run last," I observed. "That's usually Ducato's style."

"There's no edge in that kind of action," Jay said. "It's all guesswork and faith. At the track I don't trust anyone except myself."

"Want to hear another horse story?"

"Not especially. I want you to listen to me," he said. "I've been doing a little homework." He reached for one of his notebooks.

"On what?"

"On Prairie Winds. How's he doing, by the way?"

"Much better, according to Allyson. She's been going out to see him almost every morning. Boris knows what he's about, even though I haven't the faintest idea how selling flowers wholesale qualifies you to train horses."

"His percentages are okay," Jay informed me. "He did a nice job bringing that maiden up to her first race."

"Lost Lady? Yes, he did."

"Now let me tell you what I found out about Prairie

Winds," he said. "I've been doing some research."

"Shoot."

"Well, after you told me that lady of yours was going to claim him, I got to thinking about him," Jay said. "I knew something about the horse, but I couldn't remember what it was. His record the last two years, which is all the *Form* shows, didn't tell me anything. So I went back and looked up his whole career. Shifty, this used to be a nice animal."

"I know that."

"As a four- and five-year-old, he was running in allowance and top claiming races," Jay continued, "and winning more than his share. When he didn't win, it was because a better horse beat him, not because he didn't try. He was always around the money and he was indestructible. He ran fifteen, twenty times a year—about as honest a hard knocker as you could hope to find. He once ran within two lengths of John Henry on the turf, at eighty to one. He had stakes horses behind him in that one."

"What are you saying? We should put him on the turf?" I asked. "He's running too cheap now, and he's too old. They don't write those kinds of races."

"That's not what I'm saying. Let me finish." Jay flipped his notebook open to a chart of a race at Santa Anita run three years earlier. It showed Prairie Winds going wire to wire and winning by eight lengths at a mile and a sixteenth on the main track. "You see that?"

I nodded. "That was three years ago."

"Wait. Here's another one." He riffled through the pages and produced a second chart, this one showing Prairie Winds winning, again on the front end, this time at a mile and one-eighth at Santa Anita. The margin of victory was twelve lengths. "What does that tell you?"

"That he was one hell of a horse."

Jay looked at me in disgust, like a law professor appalled by the ineptitude of a once promising student. "Shifty, you make me sad," he said. "How can you expect to survive out here if you don't know what you're looking at?" He thrust the chart under my nose. "Look again. Look hard this time."

I stared at the figures in silence. At first I still saw nothing, but then it hit me. "The track was off," I said, looking up in time to see Jay's face soften into a huge grin.

"Off? That's a massive understatement," he said. "Three years ago, it rained here for over a month, you remember? From early January to mid-February, damn near every day. During that period Prairie Winds ran twice. The first time the track was muddy, the second time it was heavy, the real sticky stuff. The *Form* puts a little star by his name, indicating that he can run some on a wet surface, but that doesn't begin to tell the story. Only one other time in his whole life has this horse run on a muddy or gooey track, and that was up in Bay Meadows in San Francisco, when he broke his maiden as a three-year-old going long for the first time and in the mud. That day he won by fifteen, eased up. This horse is a mudlark, Shifty. You want an edge on a bet? We got one, man. All we have to do is get this horse sound enough to run some and wait for it to rain."

"Yes, but can we count on that?"

"We've had two fairly dry winters in a row," Jay pointed out. "But it's got to rain sometime. It always does. We wait for it."

"We? I don't own this horse."

"Talk to the lady, Shifty," he urged me. "Tell her the facts of life. We can make a real killing here. Most trainers never bother to look up their horses' past records, especially if they're old claimers like this. They're too lazy and too incompetent. I'll bet not even Ducato knows, or he wouldn't have let this animal get away at this time of year. He was still back in New York when this horse was good. Talk to the lady, Shifty, and keep quiet around here."

"Very interesting, Jay."

"It's more than interesting," he said. "We stand to make big bucks."

"Not if you spill your guts to your syndicate and the brain drains."

"Don't ever underestimate me, Shifty. There are some nuggets of information I share with no one."

The horses for the first race appeared on the track and I stood up to go and make a bet.

"Sit down," Jay said. "There's nothing to risk money on in here."

"I think there is," I declared. "Pelé has a mount."

"That pig? He has one win in thirty-five lifetime starts."

"He'll have two after today."

Jay shrugged and gave up on me. "Go ahead, go throw your money away."

"Jay, let me tell you something," I said. "Pelé is going to win a whole bunch of races today. Don't bet against him."

"I'm not betting at all until the eighth," he answered, "but I'm not betting Pelé's horse in that one."

"Okay, don't say I didn't warn you." I started out of the box.

"Your lady friend been dreaming again?"

I didn't answer him; I didn't want to affront his acknowledged expertise. In fact, I decided that, for both our sakes, I ought to stay away from him the rest of the day. I put ten dollars on the nose of Allyson's dream jockey in the first, then went outside behind the stands and sat on the green bench in the sunshine facing the now empty paddock to listen to the call of the race. Until Allyson had come into my life, I had never bet money on a horse race in such a way before, simply on someone else's dreams or hunches, and suddenly it was making me nervous. At first it had been a lark, but now, I realized, it was becoming a serious matter to me. What if Jay was wrong? What if skill and hard work and painfully acquired knowledge meant nothing? What if it was basically instinct and blind luck? What if some malevolent fate was at work here? I could not, in that case, keep on coming to the track, not as a serious avocation. I was perfectly willing to pit my own skill and experience against anybody else's, even Jay's, but I was not willing to gamble money against primeval forces I didn't understand. I had a lot less faith in logic than the Fox, but I didn't believe in the supernatural either. In my chosen profession, true magic was achieved by dedication and constant practice, not by merely waving a wand about and gazing into crystal balls. For once I found myself hoping Allyson's dream would turn out to be a dud.

It didn't. I sat out there in the sunshine for the next two and a half hours and listened while Luis Pelé won all six of the races he competed in. I parlayed my original ten-spot into eleven hundred and eighty-five dollars, and I walked out of the track before the ninth in a daze. My hands were shaking, and I had to sit for a while in my car, until I felt sure I could concentrate on the mundane routine of the drive home.

As I turned into the Pasadena Freeway heading back toward L.A., I flipped on KNX, the news station, to hear the call of the last race, which is usually broadcast about half an hour after it has been run. Pelé did not have a mount and I had not bet on the race, but I usually listened to it, whether I had seen it or not, simply as a way of passing time. It usually took me about forty minutes to drive home, and the rush-hour traffic could be ferocious. KNX also put out periodic traffic advisories, which could be useful in helping to circumvent the horrendous logjams that occasionally clogged the freeway network.

This time I didn't immediately pay much attention to what the announcer was saying, something about the lack of a motive in what might turn out to be a double murder in a house somewhere in the Hollywood hills. He sounded as assured and blandly serene, as if he were selling toothpaste. "So far the police have no clues," the mellifluous baritone voice continued, "but it has definitely been established that both the victims were dead before the fire was set. Douglas Pembroke was killed by a single shot through the temple, while the still unidentified woman, whose badly burned nude body was found on the floor of the living room, may have been stabbed. It is not known whether she was also sexually molested. The police believe..."

I was shaking and had to keep both hands firmly on the wheel. I swung the car over into the number three lane, slowed down, and turned the volume up.

"...presently no motive for the killings," the voice droned on. "What is clear is that the arson was committed apparently as an attempt to destroy evidence. Mr. Pembroke, who appeared in more than thirty movies and was for several years a featured actor on the ABC *Malone* series, is survived by his mother in London, England." The announcer took a deep breath. "Friends, do you have a problem with your dentures? Decaying bits of food caught up in there? Sore gums? Bad breath..."

I turned the radio off and concentrated on driving.

— 14 —

Paranoia

"What are we going to do?" Allyson asked.

"I don't know," I said. "I don't know what we're involved in yet. I wish I knew where Freddie was."

"You don't think Julian is mixed up in this? He couldn't be."

"You're positive of that?"

"Julian is not a murderer, that much I'm sure of."

"But he may be dealing with people who obviously are capable of almost anything. Freddie definitely seemed to think he was in some sort of danger when I went to see him in the hospital," I reminded her. "And Julian was there just before me."

Allyson shook her head firmly. "It's not Julian, I know that," she insisted.

"Who then?"

"I don't know any more than you do." She paused and took a deep breath, as if gathering her thoughts to try to make some sense of what appeared to be a senseless crime. "Isn't it possible some punk or maniac broke into the house and did this?" she asked. "It happens every day. Pembroke's house was isolated."

"It's possible," I agreed. "Anything is possible in this great crazy country of ours."

She grimaced and sipped her wine. "Are you hungry? Should I put the steaks on?"

"I guess. Otherwise we'll get too drunk to make sense out of anything."

She got up, went to the kitchen and turned on the gas burners under the corn, then came back and put the steaks on over the charcoal grill simmering on the terrace. It was a cold, clammy night, with fog rising off the lawns of the VA and muffling the sound of the freeway. Allyson, fork in hand and dressed only in slacks and a long-sleeved sweater, hugged herself tightly as she stood over the sizzling meat. She looked lost and wistful, and I wanted to take her in my arms. Instead I made myself pick up the late edition of the *Herald-Examiner* I had bought on the way over and once again read through the front-page story.

It didn't tell me much more than I had already gleaned from the fragmented radio account and the early-evening TV news. "I can't imagine why anyone would want to kill Doug Pembroke," the producer of *Malone* had informed the press. "He didn't have an enemy in the world." "It must have been some maniac," Randall West had declared. "Maybe somebody who came looking for the girl and he just got in the way. It's ironic, isn't it?" Ironic because it was well known in the industry, the reporter wrote, that Doug Pembroke wasn't much attracted to girls. "I don't know if he was gay or not," the producer said. "Doug never brought his sex life onto the set. Whatever he did, it was strictly his own business. He was a very private man." The dead woman had been tentatively identified, pending a forensic medical report from the coroner's office, as one Lucille Hogan, "better known as Boom Boom," an actress and dancer whom Pembroke had met during a recent episode of *Malone*. The couple had been seen together at the Magic Castle over the weekend. No word yet on exactly how Miss Hogan had died, but the police believed she had been stabbed at least twice and possibly sexually abused. Pembroke had been killed by a single .22-caliber bullet shot into his temple from close range, probably as he lay sleeping. Whereas there were signs that the woman had put up some resistance, the actor had probably been killed first, before the assault on his overnight guest took place.

"Do you think we should call the police?" Allyson asked. She was standing in the doorway, fork still in hand and gazing at me intently. "It just hit me that maybe we're not doing the right thing."

"What do we have to tell them?"

"I don't know." She shrugged helplessly. "Whatever we know, I guess."

"I'd have to involve Julian."

"Is he involved?"

"Look, we don't know much, Allyson. And frankly, I'm not anxious to draw attention our way. Not if there's someone out there who had a reason to do this. He or they might come looking for us."

"Maybe what they're looking for is right there," she said, pointing with her fork to the parcel I had taken from Freddie's loft and which now lay against the pillows on her couch. "We ought to find out what it is, don't you think?"

"Freddie didn't think so, but I agree. Can we eat first?"

"I insist on that," she said. "I'm not going to have this good dinner totally ruined."

It was pretty much ruined anyway. We became so tense and so curious over the contents of the package that we hardly tasted our feast. In fact, we didn't even finish it. "I don't think I can take this any longer," I said, suddenly rising to my feet. "I'm going to open it."

"Wait, let me do it," she said, heading for the kitchen. "I'll get a knife. You're such an oaf in the house, you'll probably hurt your finger again or cut yourself." It was an effective way to stop me. I waited impatiently for her to open the package, which she managed to do with the infuriatingly deliberate approach of an elderly archaeologist unwrapping a two-thousand-year-old mummy. But it was worth the delay, all right.

"Oh, my God," Allyson said, stepping back. "Jesus..."

She set the contents on a chair facing the sofa and we both sat down to look at it in amazement. What we were confronted by was a small, simply framed oil painting of a child, a young girl of about ten, dressed in a light-blue smock and sitting on a plain wooden chair against a dark-red background. She had a delicate oval face framed by a halo of wispy blond curls. Her cheeks and brow were almost translucently pale and set off by a pair of round, startlingly blue eyes. The child's mouth was small and pursed, as if deliberately set against an almost irresistible impulse to laugh, and she looked uncomfortable on her seat. The artist had caught her inner life, that of an active and probably mischievous little girl, and frozen it in time by constraining her natural outflow of energy into a single, artificial moment, when she had been forced to sit still and be proper and good. It was a remarkable achievement; the figure threatened to bound out of the canvas at us. And yet it had a terrible melancholy about it, as if all that life on display contained a deadly secret, only hinted at in the figure's pallid countenance, the scrawny arms and legs, the feeling of weightlessness in the flesh. Even in my ignorance of art in general, I knew instantly that I was in the presence of a masterpiece.

"It's a Donabella," Allyson said at once. "Where did Freddie get this? It must have been stolen."

"The Beautiful Woman," I murmured.

"What?"

"Freddie's been referring to his BW for weeks," I explained. "When I went to see him at the hospital and before. Boom Boom referred to it. She told me he'd mention the BW to her. Boom Boom thought he was talking about another woman. As long as he had the BW, Freddie maintained he'd be safe. It's his insurance policy."

"Against what?"

"Against what happened to Boom Boom and Pembroke, I guess."

"Then it wasn't a random killing."

"We don't know that, but what if it wasn't? What if somebody is looking for this painting and would do anything to get it back?"

"Like killing people?"

"Suppose it was stolen from somewhere," I speculated. "Suppose it was stolen from somebody dangerous...."

"What do you mean?"

"I mean somebody who isn't the rightful owner either," I continued. "He wants the picture back and he'll do anything to get it."

"Sounds pretty far out to me."

"It does? What is this picture worth, Allyson?"

She looked hard at it and her mouth grew tight; then she glanced up at me and nodded almost imperceptibly, as if to confirm my suspicion. "Julian's last Donabella was sold for two and a half million dollars, but it was a much bigger canvas. It was one of the religious paintings, of which there are ten or eleven. The portraits and the other secular pictures bring a little less, but I don't recall anything going for under a million. I can think of four sales in the past five years, two of them involving Julian's gallery. There aren't that many Donabellas in the world. He's only been recognized as a very great master in the past fifteen or twenty years, you know."

"How come?"

"Julian told me once. I forget all the details, but basically it was because his pictures just hadn't been seen very much · They were in private collections and in a handful of the less important museums, and people just didn't know all that much about them. The experts knew, of course, but the public just hadn't caught up." She stood up and poured us some more wine, then rejoined me on the couch. "Three years ago, Julian's last show at the museum was an exhibit of Donabellas, mostly from the Halsey collection. The only one the museum owns is the one you saw."

"Bernard Halsey..."

She caught the tone of my voice and peered sharply at me. "You don't think he's behind this, do you?"

"I don't know."

"But that's crazy, Lou," she said. "I mean, he's a retired oil billionaire. He can buy whatever he wants. He's got half the Donabellas in the whole world. He's not going to arrange to kill people just to get his hands on this one little picture."

"It doesn't make sense, does it?"

"No, it sure doesn't. There must be something else going on."

"I guess we'll have to wait for Freddie to tell us."

"If he calls you."

"Oh, he'll call me, Allyson," I said. "I mean, I've got his insurance policy, don't I? What else has Freddie got? He's Tap City at the track again, and his girlfriend's dead. He knows, or at least he hopes, that I have his painting. I wonder how he got it?"

"We'll soon find out, I suppose. Honey?"

"Yeah?"

"We've got to call the police."

"No, not yet."

"But it's wrong to keep it. And what are we going to do with it?"

"I haven't quite figured that out," I said. "First we're going to finish this wine while we look at it some more, then we're going into the bedroom to make magic."

"That sounds very nice and all."

"We'll think of something in the morning."

"I'm going to put the chain on the front lock. You can help me move this armchair up against the terrace door."

"Aren't we getting a little paranoid?"

"I don't think so," she said. "Two people are dead already."

Although we did make magic that night, we slept very badly and we were both up just before dawn, Allyson made us some very strong coffee, and we sat in the living room, as we slowly sipped it in silence and stared glumly at our little masterpiece, still perched there on its chair, where we had left it. "I'm not feeling very well," Allyson said. "I think I drank too much wine."

"Mmm."

"What?"

"Me, too."

"More coffee?"

"Mmm."

"Never heard you so talky."

"My tongue has a little sweater on it."

"Any ideas?"

"Not yet."

About three sips into her second cup, however, Allyson rallied; she began briskly to wrap the painting up again.

"What are you doing?"

"I'm going to take it to the office."

"You're what?"

"It's the safest place," she explained. "We have a walk-in closet full of drugs and prescription medicines behind the lab. It's always locked, and only Gerry, the office manager, and I have keys. The offices and the building are locked up at night, and we have a security system. If anybody tries to break in, a bell rings somewhere in West Hollywood and in about three minutes some armed goons are supposed to show up and beat the shit out of you."

"I was thinking about one of those self-service storage places."

"This is safer. And we can get at it anytime."

"What're you going to tell them?" I asked, my mouth still partly paralyzed.

"That it's a picture and that it's worth a couple of thousand dollars, some kind of old racing print I bought to give you on your birthday. When is your birthday?"

"April."

"Good. Anyway, only Gerry needs to know and I'm almost the only one who ever goes in there anyway. It'll be safe, as least for as long as it takes to figure out what we're going to do."

"Makes sense."

"What *are* we going to do?" she asked, as she finished knotting the twine around the package.

"I wish I knew, Allyson. I guess I'm going to wait to hear from Freddie."

"We can't keep it for long," she said. "At some point we're going to have to go to the police."

"I want to talk to Freddie first. I owe him that much, I guess."

"Well, I'll go have a shower," she said, getting up and heading for the bathroom. "I feel like someone has implanted a lead ball at the back of my skull."

I kissed her first. "It was lovely," I said. "You were lovely."

"Mmm..."

Max Silverman, the manager of my building, was sweeping the patio area around the pool, when I showed up there shortly after nine o'clock that morning. He was still in his slippers and bathrobe, a ragged affair that hung lopsidedly down to his bony white ankles, and he hadn't yet put his teeth in, which made him look like a wizened Popeye. He had, however, remembered to slap on his habitual black beret, which sat on his bald skull like a saucer on a volleyball. Max was a friend of mine, a retired violinist who had played for most of the studios and whose favorite topic of conversation was Russian literature. He was a benevolent soul, which helped account for the fact that so few of his landlord's tenants ever moved out. Unlike most L.A. apartment houses, ours had very little turnover, also because the landlord, an ex-actor, didn't believe in gouging his tenants and kept the rents at a reasonable level. Max was one of the reasons I liked living where I was.

"Hello there," he said, as I skirted his position on the way to my flat. "So where you been?"

"Around, Max. How are you?"

"Good. I didn't see you for a coupla days."

"I was staying at my girlfriend's."

"You got a girlfriend now? What is she, a horse?"

"A nurse, Max. Don't you think I need one?"

"You don't, I do. Does she like vicious old men?"

"I'll ask her. But I wouldn't introduce you, you're too much of a threat."

"A *shiksa?*"

"You got it, Max. Pure Irish Catholic on both sides."

"She religious?"

"I don't think so. Not now, anyway."

"That's good. But you know, sooner or later all these *shiksas* find God again. It's a curse they're born with. Can't get away from it."

"Jewish girls are different, Max?"

"You ever hear of a born-again Jew?"

"Listen, Max, I love to talk to you, you know that, but I'm in kind of a hurry."

"Sure, sure, go ahead, who needs you?" I started to move away from him, but he called after me. "Say, there was a guy looking for you."

"Who?"

"Don't know. Never seen him before. He came by last night, around six, six-thirty. I just happened to be coming in myself and I asked him who he was looking for. He was heading for your place."

"Who was he, Max?"

"What's the matter? You're looking a little funny. You didn't pay your bookie?"

"I don't gamble with bookies, Max."

"He didn't leave a name. He said he knew you from Europe. He had some kind of accent, like maybe German."

"I haven't been in Europe in three years. What did he look like?"

"Tall, thin guy. Kind of wasted-looking, with blond hair, about thirty or thirty-five or so."

"Max, you haven't seen me, you understand? And you don't know where I am. You got that?"

"Yeah, I guess. You in some kinda trouble, Shifty?"

"I don't know, Max. It's too complicated to explain right now. But if you see this guy hanging around, call the cops."

"For what? What's he done?"

"Loitering, whatever. If they pick him up, they may find a gun or a knife on him. They'll hold him."

Max leaned heavily on his broom and gazed at me sorrowfully. "I knew it would come to no good, Shifty," he said. "You and the horses. You know what horse sense is, Shifty?"

"Look, Max—"

He waved my protest aside. "Horse sense, kid," he said, "that's what a horse has that keeps him from betting on people."

"Max, this has nothing to do with horses," I tried to tell him. "This is something else. Promise me you'll call the cops."

"Okay, so I promise. Now you watch yourself. You be good."

"You sound like my grandmother, if I had one."

"You need one. You should be reading Tolstoy, not *The Racing Form.*"

"What about Dostoyevski? He was a gambler."

"He didn't lead a long, happy life, Shifty. And you don't write books."

I left him to his sweeping and cautiously proceeded to my apartment, double-locking my door behind me. I popped on the overhead light to make sure everything was all right and was relieved to find the place exactly as I had left it. The red light on my answering machine was blinking, but there were no significant messages, except possibly for three hang-ups that must have occurred sometime the previous afternoon or evening, just before the last call on the tape, which was from Jay and had come in about ten p.m. He wanted me to know that Prairie Winds had been entered in a six-furlong race the following Friday; he had noticed it in the overnights, the mimeographed entry sheets put out two days in advance by the track, and he wanted to know if I had spoken to Allyson yet. "Prairie Winds is not a sprinter," he concluded. "Does your trainer know what he's doing?"

I made myself a pot of coffee, packed a small suitcase with toilet articles and enough clothes to last me a couple of days, then sat down for a few minutes to read the paper and think. The hot coffee helped.

I wasn't sure yet where I was going to stay, but I was convinced I couldn't just sit still and simply wait for the tall, pale blond man to find me. I had no idea yet who he was, but I had a very good idea who might know all about him. Unfortunately, I would not be around if and when Freddie called, in which case I felt reasonably sure that he would come looking for me in one of two places, either at the track or the Magic Castle. I had to disappear from home until I could make contact with him. Or someone. The follow-up story in the Metro section of my *Los Angeles Times* on the Pembroke murder contained some additional information on the cause of Boom Boom's death. She had not been raped, but she had apparently been tortured and stabbed several times. The ultimate cause of her demise, however, had been similar to Pembroke's—a .22-caliber bullet wound in the temple fired at close range.

The longer I sat there and thought about the possible implications and all the various connections a possible killer could make regarding my own role in the whole affair, the more nervous I became. Suddenly, on an impulse, I picked up the phone, got the number from Information, and called the Masters Gallery. After about eight rings, a woman's voice answered. "Yes?"

"Is this the Masters?"

"Yes, but we're not open yet. Please call back after eleven—"

"This is very urgent," I said, interrupting her. "I have to speak to Mr. Julian Meade."

"I'm afraid he won't be in today," the woman informed me. "Could you call back tomorrow?" She had one of those infuriatingly calm, very precise English voices, unruffled, unflappable, the very soul of the vanished Empire.

"You don't seem to understand," I insisted. "This is a very urgent matter. It is absolutely necessary that I reach him as soon as possible."

"Well, I shall certainly tell him when he comes in," she replied, in the same even, measured tone. I could imagine her imperturbably serving tea on the poop deck of the *Titanic,* as the water lapped around her ankles and she led the passengers in a rousing chorus of "Nearer My God to Thee."

"It may be too late," I told her. "The horse may die." I don't know what made me come out with that, but it proved to be an inspired improvisation.

"Oh, I say," she gasped, suddenly as concerned as if I
had announced an IRA assault on the Queen at Buckingham
Palace. "Are you the veterinarian?"

"Yes," I lied. "Now will you please tell me how I can
get in touch with him."

"He's on his way to Santa Anita," she said. "He left
almost half an hour ago. It's not Prince Willy, is it? Mr.
Meade was so looking forward to seeing him run today."

"No, no, it's not Prince Willy," I assured her. "Look, I
can't chat—"

"Are you presently at the racecourse?" she asked. "In case
you miss him and he calls? He may go right to the Turf Club,
you see. He was meeting Miss Halsey there—"

"Don't worry about it, I'll find him."

"But who shall I say—"

I hung up on her before she could ask any more idiotic
questions, picked up my suitcase, and hurried out toward
my car.

Despite the absence of a pass, I had little trouble getting
into the Turf Club. I simply walked up to the upper level
of the grandstand, prudently waited until no one was looking, then quickly vaulted a waist-high locked gate that separated the elite from the common herd. I strolled downstairs
among the chic and wealthy and found Julian Meade sitting
at what I assumed was his usual spot, the same table Allyson
and I had already tracked him to earlier in the meet. Linda
Halsey was there, of course, as well as another elegantly
dressed couple I had never seen before. I decided to wait
until Meade got up to go to the bathroom or the betting
windows, and I went down to the bar, from where I could
keep an eye on the traffic bound for both locations.

Marty Joyce saw me and drifted over. "Hey, Shifty, how
you been? Say, wasn't that terrible about poor old Boom

Boom?" he commented. "Boy, to get herself caught up with a pervert. The guy must have been a killer fruit."

"Who? Pembroke?"

"Sure. He killed her, didn't he?"

"No, he didn't, Marty."

"I figure he killed her or had her killed, and then things got out of control, see?" he said. "The guy he got to do the job then turned on him."

"That's an interesting theory, Marty. I have to think about it."

"Sure, that's the way it was, Shifty. These fags are all alike. They all hate broads."

"I was a friend of Boom Boom's," I said. "I'd rather not talk about it."

"Sure, sure, I understand," he said, frowning and nodding at me like someone playing a bereaved relative in one of those private-eye TV series. "I'll miss her, too. She had a great ass."

"Marty, I can tell you really like women, all right."

"I'm nuts about pussy. Say, you got anything good today?"

"I like Prince Willy in the seventh."

"Yeah? Really? He's got good European form, all those graded races at Ascot and Longchamps," Marty said, "but he hasn't run in this country. I think I'll give him one."

"I figure he's a nice horse," I said. "He's training well and he's on the turf, which he likes. So..."

"Yeah, yeah," Marty agreed, "but—"

"Excuse me, Marty," I said, as I saw Julian Meade descending the main staircase, "there's a guy I have to talk to."

Meade didn't see me and I followed him into the men's room. Except for the attendant, who was up at the other end sweeping out one of the stalls, we were alone, standing next to each other at the urinals.

"We have to stop meeting like this," I murmured. "People will talk."

He glanced at me in amazement, then looked down at himself and tried, quite literally, to shake himself free of me. "Who let you in here?"

"I had to pee. I also need to talk to you, friend."

"I'm not going to talk to you, and I'm certainly not your friend."

"Only the second part of that statement is true," I said.

He zipped up his trousers and walked over to the sinks to wash his hands; I followed him. "I have the BW," I informed him.

"I haven't the faintest idea what you're talking about."

"You don't? I think you do."

"As soon as I finish in here, I'm going to find out if you belong in the Turf Club. My guess is they'll throw you out."

"If you do that, I may just have to go to the police."

"Look, I don't know what your game is," he declared, staring fixedly at me, "but I want no part of it."

"So you really don't know what I mean by the BW?"

"I thought I'd made that clear. Now, if you'll excuse me..." He pushed past me toward the door, and I went after him.

"The BW is what Freddie Chambers called his insurance policy," I explained. "He thought he was in some danger and you were a prime suspect in his mind. But we've already discussed all that."

"Yes, we have," he said, heading now toward the main dining room. "I'm going to find someone in here to talk to about you. I don't like being harassed or threatened."

"I really wouldn't do that," I said. "You see, what Freddie meant by the BW is a very nice small painting, about two and a half feet square, of a ten- or eleven-year-old girl. It's probably about three hundred and fifty years old. I think it's by a man named Giorgio Donabella."

He stopped in his tracks, as if I had jerked him to a halt on a rope. He turned to look at me, and his face was as white as if he had suddenly been drained of blood. "You have it?" he asked, his eyes wide with disbelief.

"Not exactly," I said. "It's in a very safe place."

"Where is it?"

"That's my little secret. Let's just say I made it disappear. I am a magician, you know."

Meade leaned in very close to me and all but spat his words into my face. "You know it's stolen property," he said. "You could go to jail."

"The question is, who owns it?" I said. "What if there's a difference of opinion on that subject? I imagine the police might ask a lot of embarrassing questions."

"Such as?"

"Such as who is this tall, thin, blond guy who seems to be chasing after it as well? Does he work for you?"

Meade looked at me stonily. "How much?" he asked.

"How much what?"

"Don't be stupid, man," he said. "You'd have already gone to the police if you didn't want money. How much do you want?"

"That's up to Freddie."

"What do you mean, it's up to Freddie? He doesn't have it. You do." He sniffed and backed a step or two away from me, as if he risked contamination. "You're obviously negotiating for him. How much?"

"I have no idea where Freddie is," I said. "As you undoubtedly know, he checked himself out of the hospital a few days ago, and I've been waiting to hear from him. I hope nothing has happened to him. I wouldn't want anything to happen to him. Or to me. Or to anyone else you know. Because, in that case, I will go to the police—"

"No, you won't, you little pipsqueak," he snapped. "You'd have done that already. You want to be paid off."

"Or I could just have the picture destroyed..."

He stared at me in what I took to be absolute loathing. I had never had quite that drastic an effect on anyone else before, and it startled me a bit. "You would, wouldn't you?" he finally said. "I really believe you would do that."

"I don't want to do that. It's a very beautiful painting."

"It's just a copy."

"Really? Still, it's very beautiful. So beautiful that you are willing to ransom it and somebody else is willing to kill for it. If anyone is hurt again, I will destroy it. And that includes your wife."

"My wife? Allyson? She has nothing to—"

"There you are," Linda Halsey said, coming up behind him and taking his arm. "We were wondering about you." She suddenly recognized me, and her face turned to pink marble. "Oh, the boring little man," she observed.

"I didn't know I was such a bore," I said, "or quite so little. Actually, I'm five-eleven in my socks and I weigh about a hundred and sixty in my underwear. That makes me too big to be a jockey. Here..." I slipped my empty left hand out of my pocket, flashed it in her face, then produced a tiny bouquet of little pink flowers out of my palm. "With my compliments."

"You are an ass," she said. "Are you coming, Julian?"

She tugged him away, but he resisted. "I want you to call me," he said. "At the gallery, tomorrow morning."

"That depends."

"On what?"

"On Freddie. You see, I really don't want to be involved in all this. I'm just doing this for Freddie because he's a friend of mine and I'm waiting to hear from him. Do you think I will?"

"I have no idea."

"I don't know why, but I find that reassuring."

He didn't answer, but this time he allowed Linda Halsey

204 THE HARD KNOCKER'S LUCK

to lead him away. I smiled and waved to them. "And good luck!" I called out. "I may even bet on your horse today!"

I spent most of the rest of that afternoon wandering around the track between races. I was certain that eventually Freddie would come looking for me there, and I even made inquiries about him, but no one had seen him recently. I checked quickly with Jay, who hadn't seen him either, but who did agree with me about Prince Willy's chances in the seventh. "He's got a lot of class and the works say he's ready to fire," was his estimate. "Ducato never gives his horses a race, he's always trying. This animal should air against this kind of field. If he's six to five or better, I'm going to risk five bills on him."

"Five hundred?"

"You got it, Shifty."

I went down to the paddock twenty minutes before the race and was almost immediately joined at the rail by the Weasel, whose yellow eyes were alive with incipient fury. "You know what I call this kind of race, Shifty?" he said. "The Paranoia Purse."

"Why's that, Weasel?"

"Only six horses in it, right?"

"Right."

"Two of them can't run, right?"

"Right, Weasel."

"Okay, so that leaves us with one horse out of the claiming ranks," he continued. "It has cheap speed and figures to fold at this distance, right?"

"I'm with you so far."

"That gets it down to this Ducato pig from Europe, which is probably in here for a gallop, right?"

"Maybe not, Weasel. That animal is not a pig. But go on."

"Okay, so I figure it's one of these other two horses," the Weasel said, jabbing a spiky forefinger at his program.

"The pig in the one hole is trained by Mitchum, and he's got Bill Scarpe up, who has stiffed more horses out of the gate than any rider in history. The one in the four box is trained by Mitchum's girlfriend, and she's got Hidalgo riding and he ain't known as the Hillside Strangler 'cause he don't take up. So all you gotta do to win the race is figure out which of the two horses they are going to allow to run, you know what I'm saying? That's why it's the Paranoia Purse, see? They're gonna cheat, Shifty."

"You overlooked one thing, Weasel," I said, as the horses were led into the paddock, where the owners and their entourages awaited them.

"What's that?"

"Ducato's animal is a go," I said. "He's the best horse in here, and he'll win."

"I'm throwing him out," the Weasel snapped. "These foreign imports ain't like Jap cars. They always need a race over here first. And Ducato's a crook, too, like the rest of them."

"That's real paranoia, Weasel," I told him. "Why don't you bet both the horses you like? You're getting five to two on Mitchum and three to one on the other one."

"Yeah, that's one way to go," he conceded, "unless they slam the money in at the last minute on the one they're trying with and knock the price to pieces."

"I can't help you, Weasel," I said. "I like Prince Willy."

"Ah, you're full of shit," he barked, and abruptly walked away from me.

I had never seen a horse more ready to run than Prince Willy. He was a rangy, full-bodied four-year-old colt with a magnificent-looking head and he was on the muscle, just so full of himself, his coat gleaming, ears pricked, a running machine primed to explode out of the gate. I glanced up at the board; he was the favorite in the betting, at eight to five. I watched Ducato, inscrutably surly as always, give his rider, Tim McArdle, a leg up, and then I headed toward the betting windows to put a hundred dollars on him to win.

The crowd knocked the price on Prince Willy down to even money on the last blink of the lights, but it turned out to be easy loot. Prince Willy broke well out of the gate, tucked in second along the rail behind the cheap speed, then moved out at the half-mile pole, went to the lead, and won in hand by six easy lengths. The Weasel's horses ran second and third, both trying hard but clearly outclassed. So much for paranoia.

− 15 −

Losers

Gerard T. Hopkins was apparently a man of easy enthu-
siasms. No sooner had I mentioned the name of Giorgio
Donabella than he burst into bloom. He bounded up from
behind his desk, rushed away into the stacks, and returned
almost at once with a large black volume that he set down
in front of him and began quickly leafing through. "An
extraordinary artist," he exclaimed, his small pink features
aglow, as if I had plugged him in an turned him on like a
lamp. The impression was further accentuated by the thick
fringe of curly orange hair that framed his otherwise bald
head. I guessed that he was in his early thirties, but he could
just as easily have been twenty or sixty; he was an authentic
pixie, who would not have looked out of place sitting on a
toadstool in an Arthur Rackham illustration of something
by the Brothers Grimm. When I had called him at the County
Art Museum for an appointment that morning, he had been
kind, soft-spoken, and efficient. "The research library is in
the Bing Building," he had explained, "to the right as you
enter, on the ground floor. Oh, you'll probably get lost.
Just ask one of the security guards and they'll get you to
us." And he hadn't even bothered to ask who I was or what
artist I was interested in. It had been enough for him to
know that I needed information for an article I was thinking

of writing on an important artist; he was the perfect librarian.

"Does this catalog have a list of all his paintings?" I asked.

"Oh, yes," Hopkins replied. "Of course, it's a bit more complicated than that. You'll need most of the day to sort this all out. And then there are several monographs on him, all rather scholarly and dull. It's quite frustrating, really."

"In what way?"

"Well, you see, what is desperately needed is a full-scale biography," he explained. "There hasn't been one, if you except the one in German by Professor Heinrich van Ratten, which ought to be pronounced rotten. It's a dreadful mishmash, written sometime in the sixties and wildly inaccurate, in view of what we now know about the man. You aren't thinking of doing one, are you?"

"I'm afraid not. All I have a commitment for is a possible magazine article, you see."

"Oh, too bad." He looked pained, as if I had betrayed him. "Well, never mind," he said, rallying gallantly. "I suppose now I should simply leave you to go through all this."

"I don't have a lot of time," I said apologetically. "Could you sort of sum up what you know about him for me? I mean, before I look at the catalog?"

"Yes, I suppose so. What would you like to know?"

"Just a bit about his life, for instance."

"Well, yes. It was a bit mysterious, actually." He paused a moment to gather his thoughts, then plunged in. "All we know about his family is that they were originally Neapolitan, but we don't know much else about his childhood or early years. We don't know what made him leave Italy, but we find him in Amsterdam in 1636, working as a carpenter and painting in his spare hours. He was a friend of Rembrandt's, and apparently they shared a studio for a while, even used some of the same models. Unlike the work of some other painters of the time, however, such as Lievens, who was also a friend of Rembrandt's, Donabella's work was always very distinctive. I mean, it couldn't be mistaken for anyone else's. Because he worked and had a family to support, a wife and two children, he really painted very little. He was also a heavy drinker, probably an alcoholic. Eventually, he quit his job, or was fired, and devoted the rest of his brief life to painting. He had very little success and died penniless in his late thirties, leaving a wife and son behind. She remarried, to a rich grocer, and lived a long, relatively happy life. Donabella was apparently crushed by the death of his daughter and he went rapidly downhill after that. Most of his paintings, at least the ones that have survived and we know about, were executed during the last ten years of his life, between 1640 and 1650." Hopkins checked the catalog. "There are twenty-seven oils and several dozen sketches or studies for paintings. We have one, the *Lazarus,* which I presume you've seen, in the Halsey Gallery."

"Oh, yes, that's the one that got me interested in him," I said. "It's a magnificent picture."

"Almost certainly modeled on the artist's father, but we don't have proof," Hopkins said. "All we know about Donabella comes from what his friends and colleagues said or wrote about him at the time. His wife never mentioned him at all. It's very frustrating, because I'm sure there must be material available in the Netherlands, perhaps also in Naples, in various public and private libraries and collections, but no one has yet done the necessary research. Professor van Ratten's book was really a sort of novel *à la* Irving Stone, but not that good, utterly useless as a factual account of the man's life and work. A couple of years ago I tried to interest Mr. Halsey in financing such a study or project, but I wasn't successful. You know, that still puzzles me."

"Why?"

"He seemed actually opposed to any attempt to research

into the artist's background and work. Strange, since he owns nearly half the Donabellas in the whole world."

"How many, exactly?"

Hopkins scratched his ear and consulted the catalog again. "Twelve in all, including the *Lazarus*," he answered. "The other eleven are in his house in Malibu. Have you been up to see them?"

"Not yet, but I'm planning to go."

"Oh, you must. They're extraordinary. Probably the greatest single collection of any major artist in private hands." He suddenly giggled and rubbed his palms together. "I know this is wicked of me to say, but we expect to get them all, eventually."

"Why wicked? The old boy's in his late seventies, isn't he? He can't live forever."

"That's what I meant, but it's not kind to say, is it?"

"He *is* going to will them all to the museum?"

"So we understand."

"Do you know Julian Meade?"

"Not really, but I know who he is, of course," he said. "He left the museum the year I came here. We've been introduced once, but that's all."

"I guess he was very instrumental in helping old man Halsey acquire his pictures."

"So I've been told. You know, it's really amazing that an artist of this stature has only become world-famous in the past decade or so," Hopkins observed, leaning back in his chair and tapping his fingers nervously together. "Everyone in the art world, of course, knew about Donabella and treasured his work, but so little of it was on view and it was scattered about here and there, in various collections and a handful of museums. When Mr. Halsey began acquiring them, however, and put together his own collection, it provided the focus that was needed. We could now see

the man's work as a whole and understand the importance
of it. Actually, in style, I think he's closer to Vermeer than
to Rembrandt, but there's no mistaking his originality. The
ten religious canvases are the most famous, especially our
Lazarus, Abraham's Sacrifice, which is in London, and the
Judas in Amsterdam, but personally I prefer the portraits
and the genre pictures. You know, what is remarkable about
Donabella is that he stood alone. Even Rembrandt had his
imitators and collaborators, but not Donabella. Every picture is unique and bears his unmistakable characteristics."

"What would you say those are?"

"Well, apart from the sheer virtuosity of the talent, his
use of light. He had a stronger feeling for the nuances of
light than almost all of his contemporaries. Then there's the
attention to detail and all that. Most of all, it's the life, the
energy in the work. You feel that you *know* the people he
paints and that you would recognize them instantly if you
ever saw them again. He was unique. He founded no school
and he had no imitators." Hopkins fluttered his delicate
hands in the air; he had been rendered temporarily speechless
by his own eloquence.

"He's a miracle, you see," he finally added. "I would
die, if I could paint like that."

"It killed him, in a way."

"I suppose you're right. I hadn't thought of it in that
respect. I suppose his talent did kill him. He was ignored
and unappreciated, much like Rembrandt, who also died
very poor."

"Rembrandt lived longer and painted more," I said. "Tell
me, do you know a man named Chambers, Fred Chambers?"

"No, I'm afraid not. Never heard of him."

"He was a painter. His name used to be Camerini, Federico
Camerini. He changed it. Or rather Americanized it."

"No, I don't know him. Why?"

"Just curious. He does some restoring for Julian Meade, and I think he's worked on some of the Donabellas, including the one here."

"Really? Well, that's quite possible. I remember being told that some of the pictures needed work. They'd been neglected for so long. Your friend is a restorer now?"

"Yes, he's apparently very good. Tell me, do you think it would be easy to forge a Donabella?"

"Easy? Almost impossible these days. We have such incredibly efficient scientific techniques now for detecting forgeries of all kinds—X rays, infrared beams, all sorts of things. I'm really not up on that subject at all. Why? Are you interested? I know that we have quite a lot of stuff on that. And I could point the way. You don't think there's a forgery connected with any of the Donabellas?"

"Just speculating," I assured him. "By the way, you said something about the artist's daughter? That she died and Donabella grieved for her?"

"Oh, yes, that was an almost legendary story about him. He was apparently so devoted to her, he adored her. She died in 1645 or 46."

"How old was she?"

"Twelve or thirteen. She probably had tuberculosis, but it could have been leukemia. Hard to tell, medicine being as primitive as it was in those days." He paused and rubbed a long index finger thoughtfully along the bridge of his nose." I think there's a letter of Rembrandt's to a friend describing Donabella's grief at the little girl's death. I could probably look it up for you."

"I don't think that will be necessary, thanks," I said. "What did she look like? Did he ever paint her?"

"Oh, yes, it's one of his most famous pictures," Hopkins declared, lighting up again. "It's also his smallest and absolutely exquisite. It was painted a year or two before she died. You'll find a very inadequate reproduction of it in the catalog." He tapped the black volume with one finger. "Would you like to see it?"

"I've seen it."

"Ah, then you've been to the Villa Bonpensante in Lugano," he said. "Isn't it a marvel? I think it's the finest painting in the whole museum, even though it isn't anywhere near as flashy as some of the pictures in that collection, especially the El Grecos and some of the Goyas. I was talking to Renzi about it last year, and he agrees with me."

"Renzi? Who's he?"

"Ah, of course, you wouldn't know." Hopkins said. "Guido Renzi is the curator of the Bonpensante, which I think is one of the finest private museums in the world, originally owned by the Bonpensante family in Lugano. Certainly it has a most important Flemish and Spanish collection. People come from all over to visit it. Renzi was here a few months ago and I had a delightful chat with him. He's a Ticinese, you know, a Swiss of Italian descent, which makes him a little less Swiss and a bit more human, if you know what I mean. Switzerland is *not* my favorite country." He giggled and again rubbed his palms together, obviously delighted with himself.

"Does Renzi know old man Halsey?" I asked.

"Oh, yes, I'm sure he does. I know that he went up to see Mr. Halsey and also to look at the Donabellas. Renzi wrote one of the monographs, by the way."

"I'm surprised Halsey didn't try to pry his Donabella away from him."

"Ah, but he did. Years ago, I understand, he offered a great deal of money for it. Renzi wanted to sell it to him, because the money would have enabled him to buy other pictures for the museum, but the Bonpensante family and the trustees blocked the deal."

"What was Renzi doing here, by the way?"

"He came to study security techniques used by our American museums," Hopkins explained. "Apparently, we have the best in the world, which I find hard to believe. Renzi told me they'd had a break-in last year."

"Really? What did they take?"

"That's the odd part of the story. Nothing. They came in through an attic window and overpowered the guard, drugged him and tied him up. No one knows how long they were in there, but nothing was missing, nothing had been touched. It was obviously a prank of some sort, perhaps involving university students. But it could have had serious consequences. That's the tragedy about museums these days, we have to turn them into fortresses." The telephone on his desk rang and Hopkins reached for it. "Excuse me a minute."

"Listen, you've been terrific," I said. "I'll just look through the catalog, if you don't mind."

"Be my guest."

"Does it have a list of all the places exhibiting the paintings?"

"Yes, of course."

"Well, thank you so much," I said, picking up the volume. "You've been a great help." I had to make some notes and to jot down names and addresses, but Hopkins, in his chatty manner, had already told me most of what I needed to know. Everything, however, depended now on Freddie surfacing. Otherwise, I would have to go to the police with my painting and a very strange, purely hypothetical story I had trouble believing myself.

That night I called Max to make sure I had no messages and that no one had been around asking for me, then I moved out of the small motel where I'd been staying and moved into another one a few blocks closer to Allyson's place. And very early the next morning, the day of Windy's first race for her, we drove out together to Santa Anita to see him. It was cold and clear outside, with pale sunlight casting a golden glow over the empty grandstand, the track, the horses and riders, the rugged background of mountains, but we had no time to appreciate this familiar but glorious scene. Allyson had barely half an hour before she had to drive back to her office and we hurried along the rows of stables to Boris's string.

Prairie Winds was sulking at the back of his stall, but no sooner had he heard Allyson's soft, caressing voice than he turned, thrust his head over the stall gate and began bobbing up and down in what I interpreted as equine glee. She walked right up to him and began talking to him and patting him, as if he were a big friendly dog. "Why, Windy, honey," she said, "just look at you, you pretty thing. You're all shiny and clean and all. Now, what have you and Boris been up to? What do you think of all this craziness out here? What do you think of all these folks at the track, huh?" The horse thrust his head high in the air and snorted loudly; I could have sworn he was laughing. Smiling, Allyson turned toward me. "Honey, get him a couple of carrots, will you? He can't have coffee on a race day—the caffeine." I started off on my errand. "Oh, and get him a lump of sugar too," she called after me. "He'll just sulk otherwise."

I came back with the goodies and watched the horse chew them noisily out of Allyson's hand. She went right on talking to him all the while, apparently serenely confident that he understood every word. I thought of Jay Fox at home, already up and poring over his pyramids of statistics, and it made me want to laugh.

"How's he going to run today?" I asked her. "Has he told you anything?"

"Oh, he knows he's going to run," she said. "He's feeling so good, Lou. Look at him. He's just a different animal than he was, don't you think? Boris has done a terrific job with him, and in such a short time."

"It isn't Boris," I said, "it's you. This damn horse is in love with you."

"I'm the first person who's talked to him in a while, that's all," she said. "Animals need to have attention paid to them, just like people. I didn't do anything special."

Boris returned from the track with a horse he'd been galloping and joined us. His furry face exuded delight. "You look at him and what you see?" he said to us. "He is feeling so good now, I don't be surprised if he win today."

"You're not serious?" I said. "You know this horse hasn't got any speed anymore. And he never could sprint."

"No, but he want to run now," the trainer said. "I have to run him or he kick down the barn. This is good work for him."

"There's no danger somebody will take him, is there?" Allyson asked, suddenly staring at Boris in alarm.

"No, no," Boris assured her. "He is in there for twenty thousand dollars. Nobody that crazy here, for this old gelding who don't win in two years."

"I don't want to lose him, Boris."

"You don't worry," he said. "I worry, okay? This race be like good gallop for him, that's all. One, two weeks from now, we find right race and boom!"

"Let's hope it rains," I said. "You know he moves up twenty lengths in the mud. I suppose Allyson told you."

"Oh, sure, I know," Boris said. "I go back and look up whole record. If it rains good, I put him in allowance race, you see. We keep him feeling good, you going to win money, Allyson."

"I don't care about that," she said. "I just don't want anything bad to happen to him, that's all."

"What can happen?" Boris asked. "He is old but he tough sonbitch. If he don't like you, nothing to be done. He is old and mean, but he one smart horse, I tell you."

"You'd have to be a dummy not to like Allyson," I said, simply as a statement of fact.

Allyson had one final exchange of confidences with Windy, then we said goodbye to Boris and started back toward the parking lot. As we turned the corner of the barn, Mel Ducato suddenly confronted us. "What do you think you're doing?" he asked, his face dark with anger.

"I don't know," I said, "what do *you* think we're doing?"

He ignored me. "How can you run that horse in a sprint? Don't you know anything?"

Allyson walked past him and he put a hand on her arm to stop her. "Don't you touch me," she said, "or I'll knock the shit out of you."

"You dumb broad," Ducato said. "You and that dummy trainer of yours!"

"Why don't you mind your own business?" I said. "You couldn't do anything with the horse when you had him. What do you care what we do with him?"

"I don't," he said. "But I can't stand stupidity."

"That should make it real tough for you to live with yourself," Allyson said. "It's your ego, little man. You can't admit you failed at anything, can you? Why don't you just pay attention to your own expensive horses, and we'll take care of ours."

"You can claim him back today for twenty thousand," I said, "if you want to."

"You gotta be kidding," he answered. "I don't know how some people get licenses out here. It's criminal."

I started to say something fairly rude, but Allyson stopped me. "Forget it, sweetheart," she said, taking my hand and pulling me after her. "Don't waste your time on him."

"I'm glad you cut in when you did," I told her, as we left the glowering trainer behind. "I might have had to hit him and my hands are the only capital I've got."

"He just can't stand to be wrong about anything," she explained. "There are lots of people like that. He knows that we've probably found what's wrong and it's bugging the shit out of him. I was afraid he might claim Windy back."

"And risk failing again with the horse? And if he succeeded, how would he explain it to his previous owner?" I pointed out. "Either way he's a loser, honey. No, he won't take him back. But he's rooting very hard for you to fail."

"He's a little man," she said.

"A spiritual pygmy," I agreed, "like so many of the winners we know."

I took Allyson to her car and kissed her goodbye. "See you later," I said.

"I'm not sure I can get out here later," she said. "We have a very full schedule."

"You don't want to see him lose, anyway, do you?"

"No. But how will you get back to town?"

"Jay will give me a ride, don't worry about it. There's always someone."

"You're sure?"

"Absolutely."

After she left, I went back to the track cafeteria, had breakfast and read the paper; then, with over two hours still to kill before post time, I walked into the empty grounds to study the *Form*. Although I had no intention of risking a dime on Prairie Winds, who was entered in the fifth and listed at odds of twenty to one, I rather liked my chances the rest of the day. With the sun now high overhead and warming the air to a comfortable seventy degrees or so, I found an empty bench behind the grandstand and stretched out for a quick snooze.

I must have fallen into a deep sleep, because, when I woke up, people were swarming into the premises all around me. I quickly sat up and glanced at my watch; about an hour had passed and now the track announcer's voice boomed out over my head, welcoming everyone to Santa Anita for another exciting racing day. "And now, if you have your programs handy," he intoned, "here are the overweights and changes for today."

I reached into my pocket for my program, which I had bought earlier at the cafeteria, and it was then that I noticed the folded sheet of paper at my feet. It must have been lying on my chest or stomach and slid to the ground when I sat up. I opened it to find a hastily scrawled note in pencil. "Shifty," it read, "I've been looking for you. I figure you've moved out. Don't try to find me here, as I stay out of sight and you wouldn't recognize me anyway. But I have to talk to you. You can meet me tonight, after ten p.m., in the public parking lot at the foot of Rose, on the beach in Venice. Please go there, park at the south end, and wait in your car. I'll find you, okay? Just make sure you aren't followed. Freddie."

Despite myself, I stood up and looked around for him. He was, of course, nowhere to be seen. I decided to take his advice and jammed the folded note into my pocket. Then I went to look for Jay.

"What the hell is that dumb Cossack doing?" were his first words to me, as I sat down beside him. "Didn't you tell him about the horse?"

"The horse is feeling good, Jay," I explained. "He needs the race, he's kicking the barn down. Think of it as a workout, that's all."

"If I was a religious man, I'd go to church and pray for a storm," he said. "You're sure this guy knows what he's doing?"

"I hope so, Jay."

"I hope he doesn't tip his hand."

"The race will be over about the time Windy gets into gear," I said. "There's a bunch of speedballs in here."

"Windy?"

"That's what Allyson calls him."

"I see. She still dreaming?"

"Yeah, she is."

"Well, don't tell me about it. I don't want to know."

"Why not? Afraid?"

"Don't be silly," he said. "I just don't want my concentration disrupted by foolishness, that's all."

"All she does, Jay, is dream winners. Is that bad?"

"I don't want to hear about it, but anytime you want to cross-book her action with me, let me know."

"Anyway, I don't need her or anyone today," I stated. "I like four horses on this card and I'm going to bring at least three of them in."

"Good," he said. "Just don't tell me about that either."

"I wouldn't think of doing that," I told him. "I may need a ride home later, okay? Allyson might be stuck at the office."

"Sure," he said. "Just catch me before the feature and let me know."

Would that I had kept quiet about my four good horses. One broke down on the clubhouse turn and the other three lost in photo finishes. At the end of the day, I was four hundred dollars poorer and feeling extremely foolish. I should have remembered that the track is a great humbler and that arrogance in the face of the Dummy God rarely goes unpunished.

Allyson did not make it back for Windy's race. I went down to the paddock to see him and he looked wild, so full of himself that the groom could hardly hold him. Boris gave his rider, an undistinguished journeyman jock named Art Lancelot, no instructions, and it was evident to me that the jockey entertained no hope of picking up even a small piece of the purse. He only rode two or three winners a meet anyway and he had obviously read *The Racing Form*. So had the crowd. Prairie Winds went off at thirty to one. He broke midpack, fell back to last, then made up a little ground in the stretch and finished eighth in the eleven-horse field, beaten about twelve lengths. "Hey, he can run a little," Lancelot told Boris after the race. "You ought to try him going long."

"Yeah?" Boris answered, feigning surprise. "You think so?"

"Yeah," the jockey said. "He didn't know where the other horses went the first part of the race."

"No kidding?" Boris said. "I'll be sonbitch. I try that for sure."

The track is a microcosm of the world. It is full of fools spouting the obvious and clever men outwitting themselves.

___ 16 ___

Forging On

I didn't immediately recognize the face at the window of my car that night, but I had to assume it was Freddie. It was clean-shaven, small, white and round, but the pale blue eyes were the same. I opened the passenger door for him, and he slipped into the seat beside me. "Let's go, Shifty," he said. "Let's get out of here."

"Where to?" I asked, as I backed out of my slot and headed for the street. A stiff breeze was blowing in off the ocean and spraying sand against what was left of my paint job. "This is great for my car."

"Go anywhere," he said. "Just keep driving."

"Who are you afraid of? The tall, pale blond man?"

"So you've met Klaus, have you?"

"Not really met him, Freddie," I said, "but he was at the Magic Castle the night Boom Boom and Pembroke were there. And he came by my place looking for me after the killings. What the hell have you gotten me into, Freddie? And who is Klaus? Klaus who?"

"I don't know his last name," Freddie said. He glanced behind us as I drove slowly out of the lot up Rose. "Turn right," he instructed me, as I reached the corner. "Drive out toward the Marina. Just keep driving. I don't want to stop anywhere."

"I haven't got much gas."

"You can get some after you drop me off. This won't take too long."

"Are you sure? I have a lot of questions to ask."

"Don't ask too many," he said. "You shouldn't know too much. There's some real money in this for both of us."

"I'm always interested in money, Freddie," I said, "but I'm not sure I like your way of making it. Why is this guy Klaus trying to kill all of us?"

"Not all of us," Freddie said. "His job is to get the BW back."

"It's not a BW, Freddie. It's just a little girl."

"You saw it, then?"

"You didn't think I wasn't going to open it, after what happened?"

"I guess I wasn't being realistic."

"An understatement, Freddie." I turned left on Washington Boulevard and headed up toward Lincoln. "Come on, Freddie, I want the whole story."

"I can't tell it to you. You don't want to know."

"Okay, I'll tell you what," I said. "I'll ask the questions I want answers to, and you answer them."

"If I can."

"If you can't, Freddie, I'm going to the cops."

"Jesus, don't do that." He shifted around in his seat to stare at me, his face bluish-white in the reflected glow of the passing street lights. "I'm counting on you, Shifty. You know what we're sitting on here, man? A couple of hundred thousand bucks, easy. A hundred thousand apiece, Shifty."

"I have to know more, a lot more than I know now," I told him. "Otherwise you can include me out, as the man once said, and I *will* go to the police."

"You'd ruin everything," he said, "and they won't be able to prove a thing. All you'd do is blow our chances at the money. Get smart, Shifty. I did."

I didn't answer. But instead of turning right on Lincoln toward the Marina again, I crossed the avenue, drove another block and a half and swung into an open parking space at the curb. "There's nobody following us, Freddie," I declared, "and I can't concentrate if I'm driving around. As you said, this may not take too long."

I doused the lights and we sat in silence inside the car for a couple of minutes, while we waited to make absolutely certain no one was after us. "Okay?" I finally asked. "You ready?"

"Yeah," he said, slumping into his seat, "I guess so."

"First of all, Freddie, you look like shit. Where have you been? Why didn't you try to get a message to me earlier?" I realized suddenly that I was more than a little angry at him; he had presumed too much on my friendship and put both Allyson and me in danger, the full extent of which I still didn't know. "How long did you think I could wait for you?"

"I was pretty sick," he explained. "After I left the hospital, I had like a relapse. I was in a cheap motel down near the airport for a couple of days. I didn't have a phone in the room, and I couldn't get out of bed."

"Ed Hamner said you had a concussion."

"Yeah, I guess I did. But I couldn't stay in that damn hospital and wait for Klaus to show up."

"You could have warned Boom Boom, the poor kid. You didn't think about anybody else, did you?"

He looked stricken; I had obviously plucked at a raw nerve. "Jesus, you're right," he said. "But I had no idea. ... She didn't know anything, see? I just gave her this key to keep, in case I couldn't risk using it myself. I had to assume I was being followed. I didn't know it was Klaus. I figured it would be just some private investigator working for Julian."

"Who does Klaus work for?"

"Halsey."

"And you know him."

"I met him in Italy. But he's a Swiss, from around Zurich. He's a hired gun."

"So I gather. And he wants Halsey's picture back."

"It's not Halsey's, okay?"

"I guess I knew that."

"Listen, Shifty, how much do you know?"

"Quite a bit, Freddie. I've been doing some research."

"So ask me your questions. I'll answer them, if I can."

"You've got to answer them, Freddie."

"If I do, will you promise not to go to the police?"

"No, I won't promise. I'll make up my mind after I hear your answers. That's all I'll promise, Freddie."

He started to protest again, but thought better of it and sighed. "Okay," he murmured, again slumping down into his seat, as if he wanted to blend into the upholstery. "Go ahead and ask."

"How long have you been forging Donabellas, Freddie?"

He took a deep breath and let it all out at once, like air escaping from a punctured bladder. "About five years," he confessed. "I started thinking about it seven or eight years ago, when I was starving to death. Then, during all the time I was grinding out all that crap for the wholesalers, all those fucking clowns and horrible little kids and phony Parisian street scenes, I started experimenting. I rented the loft downtown and holed up in there. I worked five, six hours a night. After about a year and a half, I could do it. I tried one out, a sort of copy of the one in the museum, and I took it to Julian."

"And what happened?"

"He couldn't believe it. First he thought I'd stolen the goddamn thing, then he realized it was a fake."

"How did he realize it? You told him?"

"No, it wasn't hard. You see, I didn't have the right

materials," he explained. "I'd been experimenting with normal paints, the kind you can buy in any store. In Donabella's
time, the artists mixed their own colors, using various veg-
etable and mineral elements and grinding them up in their
own mortars. Then there was the question of the oils, which
are sensitive to moisture in the air, measurable by today's
instruments. They are fragile and, as they dry out, those
tiny little cracks begin to appear that indicate the age of the
painting. You see, the harder the color mass appears, the
older the picture looks. I had only begun to understand all
that and what I had to do when I started painting my Donabellas. Julian was an expert. I fooled him at first, but then
he could tell. I didn't care about that. All I wanted him to
know was that I could paint a Donabella. I was sort of
getting even, proving something. To myself, I guess, as
much as to him."

"So what did he do, when he realized you could paint
like that?"

"He kept the picture around for a week or so. I left it
with him at his request," Freddie continued. "And then he
came to see me. He just knocked on my door one night."

"Where was this?"

"I was living in Venice at the time. Not far from where
you met me tonight, a couple of blocks east of Lincoln.
There's a big slum section in there called Ghost Town. You
got to remember, Shifty, I was really hurting for money."

"You were blowing it all at the track."

"I had some big winning days," he protested.

"Freddie, have you ever kept a record of your day-to-day
losses?"

"When I win, Shifty, I win big."

I started to enlighten him, but then I realized I was wasting
my time. I've never met a track junkie anywhere who could
ever admit, even to himself, the extent of his addiction. As
for expecting a confirmed loser like Freddie to confess that

his persistent money troubles could possibly stem from his betting losses, I might as well have anticipated Ronald Reagan avowing a loss of faith in the American system of enriching the rich. Besides, I didn't want to sidetrack our discussion into irrelevancies. "Okay, so you were broke," I said. "So what did Julian want you to do?"

"He said he had a couple of clients, very rich clients, who were Donabella freaks," Freddie explained. "He said that these people were willing to pay very well, up to ten percent of the market value of a given painting, for an exact rendering of same. He meant exact in every sense. In other words, a painting that would not only look like the original, but would be almost indistinguishable from the original. Was I willing to try it? Well, I told him I couldn't do it. I told him I didn't have the right materials and that, even if I did, it would take me some time to learn and to master all the techniques of a true forgery."

"That didn't stop him?"

"Oh, no," Freddie confirmed," not at all. He said he was prepared to finance all of my researches for up to a year. Whatever I needed would be provided, whatever I spent would eventually be deducted from the sale of the paintings."

"What if there were no sales?"

"That possibility was never considered," Freddie said, with a dry little chuckle. "Julian knew I would have to go abroad for what I needed, and he told me to get a passport. Two days later, he handed me twenty-five thousand dollars in cash. I blew five thousand at Hollywood Park that week. You wouldn't believe how many photos I lost."

"Oh, yes, I would."

"I bought travelers' checks with the rest of it and I took off for London, where Julian had a connection for me."

"A dealer?"

"No, no. He was a professional restorer. I realize now

that he must have worked for Julian, maybe for Halsey himself. He specialized in Vermeers. He died suddenly last year."

"Klaus?"

"No, a heart attack. He was pretty old. Anyway, he was a big help. He had volumes on all the techniques used in Flanders at the time. Based on those and on what I knew already, I was soon able to get to work and experiment. I went to Rome, because I could get everything I needed there and Julian had a studio for me on the Via Margutta, right in the center, where I could work in peace. In fact, he came over to see how I was getting along. By that time, a couple of months later, I was ready to get to work."

"How did you do it?"

"Well, I started by discarding all the synthetic paints," Freddie explained. "I researched all the natural colors, like ultramarine and powdered lapis lazuli. All the blues Donabella used came from this kind of stuff. Most of the pigments I needed I was able to pick up in a drugstore in London. The rest I found in Rome. One of my great discoveries was a kind of white known in Italian as *bianco di biacca*. Not only was it sensitive to cracking and aging, but you can't X-ray it. I began to paint in Rome, using these real old canvases from which I'd scraped everything but the base, with all the cracks. After I had painted over them, you see, I baked the canvases in a special furnace I built, at a temperature of about a hundred and twenty degrees centigrade. After a very slow drying out period, these pictures picked up all the fine age lines of a Donabella or a Vermeer. You couldn't really tell the difference, not with the naked eye. But I wasn't finished, see? The age lines were clean, while in a real Donabella they'd be filled with dust. So, after baking the canvas, I experimented with a light, almost invisible coating of varnish. As soon as that dried, I covered it with a very finely grated dried China ink, which looked exactly like the dust that piles up on old paintings and that settled beautifully in the lines themselves. Then I'd wash the picture very carefully with soapy water, let it dry, and give it one more coat of varnish. I guess I make it sound easy."

"No, you don't, not to me."

"I worked pretty hard and I had to experiment a lot. I had some failures, more than just a few. In fact, it was six months before I was even ready to try a real Donabella and by that time I was broke again. I called Julian and he flew over. He brought me some lire this time, about ten thousand dollars' worth. Six weeks later I had my first Donabella to show him."

"Which one was it?"

"It was an original, Shifty. It was loosely based on the *Judas,* in Amsterdam, but it was mine. Julian arranged to have it shipped out to L.A. I had to wait to hear from him. I was broke again and I couldn't go anywhere."

"Let me guess," I said. "You went to the track in Rome, right?"

Freddie laughed. "How did you know? You ever been racing in Italy?"

"No."

"Well, it's crazy," he said. "There's just no way to pick a winner there. There's no *Form* and no past-performance charts and no workouts. The racing is mostly on turf and they run clockwise, the opposite of ours. The main course at the Capannelle is a mile and three-quarters around, Shifty, and the stretch is six furlongs long. They do all the real running in the last part of the race, on the straightaway. And the cheating that goes on, you wouldn't believe it! You just can't win there."

"But you went anyway."

"What else was I gonna do, Shifty? It was the only place they were running, right?

"Okay, so you were broke again. Then what happened?"

"Julian came back and told me we had a deal. He'd pay me fifty thousand dollars a picture, on delivery. I accepted. It seemed like a lot of money to me at the time."

"When was this, exactly?"

"Three years ago last summer. During the Del Mar meet. You didn't miss me?"

"No. You always used to disappear from time to time, Freddie, whenever you tapped out. You always showed up again, eventually."

"I kept a low profile, Shifty. I mean, I had to hide the money at first."

"You've been flaunting it pretty well this go-around."

"I got tired of not enjoying it. I decided the hell with it, I'm gonna spread out a little. And then, with girls like Boom Boom . . . I mean, I was getting drained at both ends, if you know what I mean."

"You went on working in Rome?" I asked.

"The first two pictures, yeah. I had a good setup there. The last two I did in Lugano. Julian had a good connection there, too, through the Villa Bonpensante."

"Guido Renzi?"

He looked surprised. "You've been doing a lot of research."

"Yeah. Tell me, Freddie, how were you able, or how were they able, to get these pictures over here?"

"That's easy. There are all kinds of ways. There's a very big international racket in smuggled art going on," he explained. "You roll the canvas up and stick it inside a metal or a cardboard tube containing papers of some sort—posters, calendars, whatever. One of the big canvases, the *Lazarus*, was inserted into a shipment of carpets. The BW I took out of Lugano myself, in an umbrella. Of course, it's not usually me, Shifty. I mean, except for that one time, I don't do it myself. Julian has a whole organization working for him."

"Julian or Bernard Halsey?"

"I don't know. Does it matter? They work together, don't they?"

"I imagine that Julian works for Halsey, wouldn't you say?"

Freddie nodded. "Yeah, sure. It's Julian I deal with."

"They never asked you to execute an original?"

"That's right."

"Why Donabella, Freddie? How'd you happen to pick him?"

"I always loved his stuff. I loved the way he used color, I loved the detail, the precision, the intensity of the work," he said, "as if in every single painting he was trying to sum up everything he knew, everything he felt about art. He's a terrific painter. It was the same thing I was trying to do in my own work, which nobody liked."

"Why not?"

"I don't know," he admitted. "It wasn't flashy, it didn't try to make gigantic statements, see? I was trying for something else, Shifty. I didn't consciously plan what I was doing, not at first. I had this collection of bottles and jars and other small objects at home and I just started painting them. I painted all the time, Shifty, but it was always the same—still lifes of all these little pieces of bric-a-brac I owned. I didn't want to paint anything else, see? I was interested in the way these objects worked in with the background. I wanted to carve a space for them, something very clean and neat. I was trying to make something out of the air. It's what a lot of modern artists, like some of the Abstract Expressionists in New York, were doing in a much splashier, much more spectacular way, see? Am I making any sense?"

"Not really, but what do I know about art?"

"You're a magician, Shifty, you deal in illusions, but you work inside a very small frame. It's you and your hands and a few small objects. Is that right?"

"Yes, it is."

"Okay, but there are other magicians who deal in the big illusions—animals that disappear, women sawed in half, right?"

"Yeah. So?"

"So you can think of me as a close-up artist, if you like. I was trying to do what I wanted to do in my own limited, very unspectacular way." He took a deep breath and plunged on. "Tell me, Shifty—who makes the big bucks in magic?"

"The big-splash artists."

"Just like in art," Freddie pointed out. "I was a better artist than most of my more famous contemporaries and I was starving to death. I couldn't sell my work and I had to make a living as a hack, grinding out motel art for a few bucks a pop. And I had all the talent in the world. I really didn't start out to be a forger, Shifty. I just wanted to prove at last that I could paint as well as anyone. And I did."

"Where's your own work now, Freddie?"

"I destroyed it. I had it all carted away and burned."

"That's too bad. I'd have liked to see it."

"No, you wouldn't," he said, irritated. "You wouldn't have given it a second glance. Maybe it wasn't any good, I don't know. Anyway, Federico Camerini is dead. Long live Freddie Chambers."

"Just a couple of more questions, Freddie, okay?"

"Sure."

"At what point did you learn it was Halsey who was really behind this scam?"

"After about a year. I read one day in a magazine where he had this fantastic collection of Donabellas. Until then I had figured that Julian was dealing with several clients, not just one."

"And that's when you figured you were being underpaid for your work."

"Right."

"And now?"

"I'm negotiating, Shifty," he said. "I need to know the BW's safe. Is it?"

"For a while."

"I'll have an answer for you very soon. I've been in touch with Julian."

"So have I. He knows I've got the picture stashed away. I told him it would be turned over to the police, if anything happened to Allyson or to me."

"Allyson? What's she got to do with this?"

"She's involved, Freddie. She's involved because I'm involved."

"Just sit tight, please. I know they'll come up with the money, but they want to be absolutely sure I can deliver the painting."

"Did they ever think you wouldn't?"

"There's something special about this one," Freddie admitted, with a wicked little grin. "It's old man Halsey's personal favorite. He wants it so bad he can smell it. When a collector like Halsey wants something, he won't stop until he gets it. This is the guy who tried to corner the emerald market a few years ago, remember? He and those Arabs. He's a promoter of cartels. And what he wants, he usually gets."

"That's what I'm afraid of, Freddie."

"If it's out of reach, he'll deal, don't you see? He'll pay whatever he has to."

"What's he paid you so far, Freddie?"

"Twenty-five thousand, half. I was supposed to get the rest on delivery, but I'm holding out. I want two hundred thousand. You can have half, Shifty. I need you. But you've got to sit tight till I can finalize the deal. Please..."

I closed my eyes and leaned my head back against the seat. I was suddenly very tired and still more than a bit confused. I needed some time to think things through and I have to confess that the prospect of a hundred thousand dollars, a lot more than the average Pick Six win or than I could ever hope to earn in any two years of close-up magic, weighed heavily on me. "You've got two weeks, Freddie," I finally heard myself say.

"Great. It should be wrapped up before then."

"But I have to discuss it with Allyson," I warned him. "She's also involved."

"You've got to persuade her, Shifty."

"I'll try. Now listen, I have to know how to get hold of you. Where are you staying?"

"I move around," he said. "Right now I'm in a motel in Santa Monica, but I won't be there tomorrow." He reached into his pockets and came up with a business card for an answering service in West Hollywood. "I bought this service for a month. You can call anytime and leave a message for me."

I took the card from him and turned on the ignition. "Where to?"

"You can drop me at Rose and the beach," he said. "My car's in the lot."

"I didn't see it."

"I had to sell the convertible," he explained. "I got an old VW instead. But when we put this one over, Shifty, we'll both be in the chips. There's always fresh, right?"

"You ought to stay away from the horses, Freddie," I said, as I pulled away from the curb. "You can't beat 'em and they got you into this mess. Even if you pull this off, you'll just give it all back at the track."

"I haven't been lucky, Shifty. You wouldn't believe how many photos I lost, how many times I run one-three in Exactas."

"I believe you."

Freddie launched into a harrowing account of his recent

misfortunes at the pari-mutuel windows, but I had stopped listening to him. I had heard these horror stories so many times before, and not only from Freddie, but from all the losers I knew. It was old news to me. I concentrated, instead, on trying to figure out what it was about Freddie's account of his career as a forger that bothered me. Something in his tale had been omitted, but I didn't yet know what it was. By the time I dropped him off in Venice, however, I had remembered to query him on one more point. "The BW," I asked, as Freddie opened the car door and started to get out, "what did you mean by it?"

"Mean by it?"

"Yeah. The picture is that of a little girl. BW stands for Beautiful Woman, I gather. What does it mean? You aren't a pedophile, are you?"

Freddie laughed. "If you spoke Italian, you'd know exactly what it means."

He got out of the car and I leaned over the seat after him. "Okay, Freddie, so what does it mean?"

He didn't answer, but walked swiftly away from me into the darkness. He looked very frail as he leaned into the wind now blowing hard off the ocean.

"Freddie, take care of yourself!" I called after him. "You look like an old plater full of bute!"

–17–

More

The house itself, I discovered, was not visible from the highway. I followed the instructions I had been given over the phone that morning and drove about thirty miles up the coast beyond the Trancas traffic light, then turned right through an open iron gate and into a paved driveway flanked by two rows of tall, dark-green cypresses. The road meandered up through the hills for about a mile and a half, then led through another gate in a high stone wall and past a small, manned watchtower from which a uniformed guard followed my progress through binoculars. I proceeded for another several hundred yards through groves of lemon and orange trees and I still couldn't see the place. Suddenly, however, I turned a sharp corner and found myself in a pebbled courtyard between the wings of an enormous English manor house. I had been told that Bernard Halsey had bought it ten years ago in Surrey, had it transported brick by brick to his California property and meticulously reconstructed, the sort of architectural whim in which the very rich like to indulge themselves. But I hadn't known what a manor house was. I had envisioned something warm and Tudory, cozily ancient and hung about with trellised vines, not this cold and forbidding keep.

With sinking heart, I parked, got out and walked up to

the front door, a massive construction of wood and iron. The late-afternoon sun glinted off the windows and the wind blew icily off the stone walls, kicking up miniature dust storms at my feet. Not a human voice or a comforting civilized sound could be heard. The enormous house basked in its ominous silence, staring at me through its huge, blind windows. I had a terrible feeling that I had somehow wandered into the remote countryside of Transylvania, with the sun about to set and me without a garlic clove or a crucifix. I had to force myself to ring the bell.

After what seemed an eternity, I heard bolts being laboriously drawn and the door creaked open. A pallid and expressionless manservant ushered me into a dim corridor. He led me down a series of hallways into an empty, luxuriously furnished drawing room and abandoned me. I edged nervously about the room and studied the paintings on the walls, mostly pastoral landscapes of the Flemish school. I was engrossed in a small canvas by one Hendrick van Avercamp when I heard a door open behind me. I whirled around and found myself confronted by a mousy-looking little brunette of about forty dressed in a gray flannel business suit and sensible English pumps.

"I'm sorry," she said. "I didn't mean to startle you."

"It's okay. I really don't believe in vampires."

"I beg your pardon?"

"Just joking."

She did not smile. "I'm Miss Larrimore, Mr. Halsey's secretary. Mr. Halsey will be tied up for a while. Would you like to see the collection?"

"I certainly would. Especially the Donabellas."

She thrust a four-page pamphlet describing the contents of the house at me, then walked me briskly into the hallway. "This way, please."

We trotted through the enormous rooms. The house, I learned, was called Cadman Place. It was built between

1520 and 1525 by Sir Phillip Dutton, a courtier of Henry VIII. "It was one of the earliest English manor houses to be erected solely as a dwelling," I read, "and with no provision for defense." Sir Phillip had imported Italian craftsmen to work on it and designed it in the form of a quadrangle. "Mr. Halsey has added a wing of private offices and bedrooms, but otherwise the house remains basically what it was when it was built."

"It's not exactly homey, is it?" I said, as we entered the so-called Great Hall.

"The Hall is fifty feet long, twenty-six feet wide, and thirty feet high," Miss Larrimore said, in her finest tour-guide manner.

"You could stable a horse in that fireplace."

"That would not be appropriate," Miss Larrimore answered. She was obviously not programmed to become a bundle of fun.

The whole East Wing consisted of two rooms, the Long Gallery and the library, each a hundred and sixty feet long and twenty-four feet wide. "You'd need a Sherpa and an oxygen mask to get to the top shelves," I observed. Silence from Miss Larrimore. "Where are the Donabellas?"

"This way, please."

We strolled past priceless furniture—Venetian, German, Italian, Chinese, English, and French. One room was adorned by a Greek marble head of the third century B.C., set down among other statuary and enclosed by sixteenth-century tapestries. We toured through rooms of Italian, Flemish, Dutch, and English paintings, among which were a Rubens and a Vermeer, until at last Miss Larrimore opened one more door and led me into a relatively small end room containing the Donabellas.

There were eleven of them, all but three of them religious canvases. I went from one to the other, checking each of them against the list I had brought with me. I also studied each of them carefully, although I really had only an amateur's feel for what I was looking at. It was an extraordinary experience, however, to be suddenly exposed so overwhelmingly to the masterpieces of a single great artist. I could have looked at them for hours, but for some reason my absorption in Donabella's work seemed to make Miss Larrimore uneasy. She hovered by the door, her eyes unwaveringly fixed on me. "I think we'd better go now," she said, after about ten minutes. "We don't want to keep Mr. Halsey waiting."

"Oh, no, indeed," I agreed. "We mustn't do that."

We returned to the drawing room and Miss Larrimore left me. "It won't be long," she said, easing herself efficiently out. "Would you care for some tea?"

"No, thanks."

She shut the door behind her and I sat down to wait. I could see the pale sun setting beyond the hills and the ocean below and I leaned my head back against the sofa. What in God's name was I doing here? I asked myself. I had the uncomfortable feeling that I was out of my league and that I had chosen now to play in a game that I could only lose. Was that what Allyson had meant when she had argued with me over what I proposed to do? Was it the ethics of my position that she had objected to or had she been moved by concern for my safety as well? And why couldn't she understand what I had tried so hard to make clear to her?

"I owe it to Freddie," I had told her. "He trusted me to act for him and that's what I'm doing."

"Why don't I believe you, Lou?"

"I don't know. Why don't you?"

She had risen from her chair to pour herself a second glass of wine, but also, I now feel, to give herself a little more time to think. When she turned back to face me, I could see the resolve in her eyes. There was hurt in them, too, but mainly a determination not to give way, not to yield to sentiment. "We haven't heard from Freddie," she said. "It's been ten days now and we haven't heard from him."

"I know," I told her. "That's why I can't wait any longer."

"That's why we should go to the police."

"What do we have to tell them? Nothing."

"We can tell them exactly what we know and let them act as they see fit," she said. "It's not up to us to do anything, Lou."

"I really don't see it that way."

"Two people are dead," she said. "Their deaths may have had something to do with Freddie and his painting. And now Freddie is missing. We *have* to go to the police now, don't you see?"

"That's not going to help Freddie. They're not going to find him." I took a deep breath and again tried to explain my position to her. "If I'm right about what's going on, then we have what these people want—the BW," I said. "At some point they're going to have to deal with us."

"You, not me. I don't want any part of this anymore."

"Okay, me. I'm not asking you to be a part of this, except for taking care of the picture. You don't have to be involved and I'd rather you weren't, frankly." I was suddenly too nervous to go on sitting there, so I stood up and began to pace around the room as we talked. Allyson watched me from her position in the kitchen doorway. "You see, I don't think they've gotten to Freddie," I said, "or by this time they'd have come looking for me again. They know I have the painting. Freddie's probably been in touch with them."

"Then why haven't we heard from him?"

"Well, he may be sick. He may be holed up somewhere. He looked like hell the night I saw him. Maybe he's dead, even, but if he is, I'd bet it's from his injuries and not anything that's happened to him since."

"It's all guessing, Lou. And if you're wrong, we could

be in real trouble. And I don't like what you're doing. I don't like what Freddie is doing, that's what I mean."

"And that I'm helping him."

"Yes. It's wrong."

"What's wrong about it?"

"You really don't know?"

"Tell me. I'd like to know, Allyson."

"Okay." She set her glass down on the dining table and sat down. "I'm sorry, but I guess this is going to be difficult."

"Go ahead."

"We're not sure of much, but we are sure of one thing," she said. "We know that this picture we have is a forgery and/or that it was stolen. Either way a crime has been committed and is being perpetuated. The fact that a friend of yours asks you to help him doesn't outweigh that simple fact, don't you see? What Freddie is doing and has done is wrong and you're wrong to help him. I see that as an absolute. I just don't see any way around it."

"The nuns sure did a good job on you."

"Yes, I guess they did. I've felt this way ever since we first became involved in this mess and it's been growing inside me every day ever since. And then there's the other aspect."

"Which is?"

"The money, Lou. You can smell it, I know you can. You haven't stopped thinking about it since Freddie told you what was at stake, have you?"

"It's an added consideration," I admitted. "I'm almost forty, Allyson. I don't make a lot of money. Luckily, my needs are modest. But I wouldn't turn down a chance to make an easy hundred thousand dollars."

"Not even if it's a crime and you know it's a crime?"

"We haven't committed any crimes, Allyson. We don't know anything."

"We know enough," she said. "We know too much. What we are doing is holding stolen goods and keeping quiet about information that could lead to the solving of two possible murders. We're as guilty as everyone else involved."

"Do you really think that?"

"I do."

"You have lofty principles, Allyson," I said. "I'm not sure I can live up to them."

"I know. I know I sound like some kind of terrible goody-goody, but that's the way I was raised," she said. "I can't help it. I just can't do what I don't think is right."

"I guess I know that about you," I said. "Or you wouldn't have gone through the trial and all that."

She looked up at me and I saw that she was having a hard time controlling her emotions. It surprised me, but it shouldn't have. "You'd have settled, wouldn't you?" she asked. "You'd have accepted the plea bargain."

I nodded. "Yes. Like your husband, I'd have paid the man the two dollars."

She got up and moved toward the bathroom and I tried to block her way, to take her in my arms. "Don't," she said, "please don't. I'll be all right, Lou. I just need a couple of minutes." And she brushed past me and disappeared into her bathroom. I poured myself a glass of wine, drank most of it in one gulp, and waited nervously for her to come out.

When she did, I could tell that she had herself in control, although it had clearly cost her some tears. I wanted to comfort her, but I knew she wouldn't let me and then she said, "I'm sorry, Lou. I don't want to set myself up as some kind of holy saint or something. I'm not. And I guess I understand, or I'm trying to. But I can't go along with you on this."

"What *are* you going to do?"

"I want you to take the painting," she said. "I'll bring it home tomorrow. I want you to take the painting and I don't want to know any more about any of this. You can do what you like, but please don't tell me about it."

"Okay, I'll go to the police, if you want me to."

"No, you won't. You'll do what you really want to do. I know you, Lou. I guess I know you better than you think. I guess I know you better than you know me."

"I've always known you were a straight arrow, Allyson."

She ran a hand over her eyes and turned away from me. "Please go now," she said. "I'm very tired."

"You don't want me to stay?"

"No, not tonight. I'll see you tomorrow."

I walked to the door and opened it, then turned back. I wanted to tell her that I loved her and that she shouldn't worry about me. But she had disappeared into her bedroom and closed the door behind her.

"Mr. Anderson?"

I jumped to my feet and turned around. I hadn't heard him come in and now he stood facing me in the center of the room. "Yes. Mr. Halsey?"

"Please sit down." He did not offer to shake hands, but walked quietly over to a chair across from me and sank into it, his pale gray eyes regarding me with the calm assurance of a man holding four aces in a table-stakes poker game. Behind him, Miss Larrimore hovered, steno pad in hand, obviously unsure of herself. He turned his head briefly toward her. "We won't need you, Miss Larrimore," he said. "This shouldn't take long."

She scurried for an exit and I concentrated on him. Bernard Halsey was a big man, I realized, taller than he seemed from the pictures I had seen of him, which these days usually displayed him at charity functions or gallery openings, where he tended to stoop over the bevies of attractive young women who seemed inevitably to flock to him. He had been married and divorced four times, I recalled, with, strangely enough, only one child from all these unions. But he didn't look like a ladies' man. He was dressed in a dark blue business suit of old-fashioned cut and his thick, gray hair was combed straight back. He had large, strong-fingered hands and a sharp, shrewd, melancholy face with a long nose, thin lips, and a small, pointed chin. His voice was dry and raspy and he didn't seem like a man to whom laughter came easily. The accumulation of the vast Halsey fortune had obviously left him little time for casual entertainment. "Well now," he said, as the door clicked shut behind Miss Larrimore's back, "what is this all about?"

"I think you know, Mr. Halsey," I said, "otherwise you wouldn't have consented to see me in private like this. I imagine you have more creative ways to spend your time."

"You imagine correctly. I presume you've come to see me about the painting you say you are holding for your friend."

"The BW, yes."

"The what?"

"That's what Freddie called it," I explained. "It took me a while to figure out what it meant. It's the artist's name."

"Indeed?"

"Yes. Freddie told me I'd know if I could speak Italian," I continued. "So I bought a dictionary and solved the puzzle. The word for woman in Italian is *donna,* with two n's. *Bello* or *bella* is the word for beautiful. Donabella is spelled with only one n, but it's close enough. The BW, or Beautiful Woman, is a Donabella."

"Very interesting. Would you get to the point, please."

"Sure. I'm not absolutely certain how Freddie acquired this particular painting, but I have a pretty good idea."

"There's no mystery about that," Halsey said. "He executed it on commission for me. You're probably aware that your friend Chambers is an expert restorer and recreator of other artists' work. He's especially fine with Donabella.

I've used him before in both capacities and paid him very well for his services."

"I have another word for what Freddie does for you."

"What's that?"

"Forgery."

The pale gray eyes continued to regard me as calmly as before, without the least evidence of surprise or concern. I had just raised into his pat hand, but he had no doubts at all about the outcome of the play. "That's an unpleasant word, Anderson," Halsey said. "And false, as well. This man Chambers has executed several paintings for me, exact copies of works that I admire and want to have in my collection, but which are, unfortunately, unavailable to me. They are not for sale. I have tried to buy them, but was unable to acquire them, Mr. Julian Meade, my dealer, brought me a sample of Chambers' work a few years ago. He assured me that, given the proper ingredients and training, this man would be able to make nearly perfect, very authentic-looking reproductions of these pictures for me. He has been very well paid to do that, but evidently, again according to Mr. Meade, he has come to believe that he has been underpaid for his work and that he's been exploited. He is asking an outrageous sum for the picture you're keeping for him, Naturally, I am not prepared to be held up. The fee agreed on was fifty thousand dollars, of which he has been paid half. I will pay the second half on delivery of an acceptable painting. I imagine the one you're holding for him is as fine as the others he has executed. I'm willing to pay the balance on the deal once the picture is turned over to me, or to Mr. Meade, either by you or Chambers or anyone who brings it to us."

"Fifty thousand dollars is a lot of money for a copy."

"Perhaps. But, as I indicated, Chambers' work is first-rate. The normal fee, I imagine, would be about a third or even a fourth of what I'm willing to pay, but I don't care about that. I'm willing to pay well for top-quality work. In business as well as in art, I've found it counterproductive to be cheap. It doesn't pay off, with people especially."

"What am I worth to you?" I asked.

For the first time the eyes showed a flicker of surprise. "It depends on what you have to sell and what your price is," he said. "If you're here to deliver my picture, I'll pay you the twenty-five-thousand-dollar balance I agreed to pay. How you choose to divide it with Chambers is your business. If you're here to negotiate a higher price, you're wasting your time and mine. Why don't you get to the point, Anderson?"

"I'd like to see these copies of yours. Why aren't they with the other Donabellas?"

"Because they are copies, that's why."

"So where are they?"

"I had them executed for my personal pleasure, Mr. Anderson," he said. "They are not for public viewing." He glanced irritatedly at his watch. "Now will you please get to the point. My time is limited."

I reached into my pocket and pulled out a list I had made before driving out there of the dates, numbers, and names of all the telephone calls I had made all over Europe during the previous ten days. "By my count, you have six of these so-called copies," I said, "including the one you had made of the *Lazarus* in the County Art Museum."

"I gather that Chambers has been consistently indiscreet," Halsey said. "He will not be working for me again."

"Probably not," I agreed. "I haven't heard from him for over ten days now. I hope nothing has happened to him." I paused to look straight into those impassive, pale gray eyes. "I hope you've called off your man Klaus."

Halsey sighed, shook his head, and leaned forward, as if about to push himself to his feet. "There really isn't much point prolonging this unpleasant meeting."

"I think you'd better hear me out," I said, "because I don't think you'd want a police search to be made of these premises."

Halsey laughed. It was a dry, hollow sound, a puff of wind out of a deep cavern, but utterly without mirth. "I understand you're a magician," he said, "but you should have taken up comedy." He did, however, remain seated.

I glanced down at my list. "I telephoned all nine of the museums and private collections that own Donabellas," I declared. "Five of them in four different countries—England, Switzerland, Belgium, and the Netherlands—all admitted having had break-ins during the past three years. What is extraordinary is that in each case nothing was taken. A couple of minor vandalisms were reported, but nothing serious. Now why would anybody go to the trouble and risk of breaking into a museum or private house and not bother to take anything? Don't you find this unusual?"

Halsey did not answer; he sat stonily in his chair, the cold eyes unblinkingly fixed on me. I plunged on. "Maybe I should back up a bit," I said. "You may want to know what led me to make all these calls. The first hint I had came from Freddie himself, when he kept referring to his picture as 'the BW.' Why would a man refer to a forgery the way he might to an original? Then there was the time I met him by chance in the Halsey Gallery at the museum, just before Christmas. We were looking at the *Lazarus* and Freddie was there, too. He was upset and moved. He also told me I was wrong, when I observed to Allyson, apropos of the picture, that nobody painted like that anymore. He looked to the canvas and spoke to it. 'I love you,' he said. 'You're the best of the lot.' And then he rushed out of there, still very upset. Why do you suppose he was upset, Mr. Halsey?"

"I have no idea."

"Because he was looking at his own picture," I said. "He

had stopped by to admire his own work. As a serious artist, he had never received any recognition and never been able to make a living, except by turning out cheap junk art for wholesale houses supplying decorations for commercial establishments. And now he had an authentic masterpiece hanging on the wall of the L.A. County Museum that he couldn't sign his own name to or tell anybody about. Why wouldn't he be upset?"

"Are you actually telling me that my *Lazarus* is a forgery?"

"Not *your Lazarus,* Mr. Halsey," I answered. "The one you donated to the museum, yes."

"And how do you suppose that came about?" Halsey asked. "By osmosis?"

"No, it was easy. It was probably the easiest of your operations," I said. "The picture needed restoration. It was carried out under the direct supervision of Julian Meade, then still a curator at the museum. The *Lazarus* was probably the first of Freddie's real forgeries on your behalf. It was easy to make the swap, after which you and Meade conceived the larger scheme—that of commissioning the other forgeries and arranging to have them substituted for the real Donabellas. That's why no actual thefts were ever reported. The forgeries were simply substituted for the originals, which were then smuggled out across various borders and into the U.S. You didn't commission just copies, you commissioned forgeries that had to be executed so skillfully that they would be able to fool the experts and could be detected only by the most meticulous scientific investigation. But why would anybody suspect that the pictures hanging in their accustomed places were no longer the originals? They looked exactly the same. The ingredients used to create them were mostly the same. When I went to get the BW at Freddie's loft in downtown L.A., I found a little notebook in which Freddie had scrawled notes to himself when he was working on the *Lazarus*, phrases like 'watch flesh tone right hand' and 'folds blue robe too bright, tone down,' stuff like that. A man executing a simple copy wouldn't take that much trouble, he wouldn't be quite that meticulous, would he?"

"I really don't know," Halsey said calmly. "Anything else?"

"Yeah. Freddie got to feeling not only unappreciated, but underpaid," I continued. "Considering what the originals were worth, that is. He might have been okay, except that he lost so much money at the track. He also squandered it on women. It's a losing parlay, as my friend Jay Fox might put it. It takes Freddie several months to study, prepare, and then paint a perfect Donabella, but Freddie is the sort of hard knocker who can go through fifty grand in a matter of weeks. And so he decided to cross you up. He went along on the break-in in Lugano, as he had on all the others, but this time he had two pictures to substitute. One is now hanging on the wall of the Villa Bonpensante in Lugano, one was smuggled out to you here in Malibu and one, the original, Freddie kept, figuring that he could up the ante on you and make you pay him a more realistic fee. Have I got this right so far?"

"Hypothetically, it's a fascinating account," Halsey said. "But who would believe it?"

"Well, Klaus, your Swiss hired gun, got a little too enthusiastic in his work," I pointed out. "I mean, it was okay for him to try to find Freddie and deal with him, but two murders in one night struck you as excessive. The police could take a strong interest in a terminal event like that, I imagine, even if the story struck them as farfetched. I suppose we won't be hearing or seeing any more of Klaus for a while, will we?"

"I have no idea who he is," Halsey said and sighed. "Ah, well . . . is that it, Anderson?"

"No," I said, "there remains the question of motive. I

mean, I know why Freddie and Julian Meade and everyone else acted as they did. It was for money. But you? The one thing you definitely don't need is money. So why did you go to all this trouble?"

Halsey rose to his feet. "I think this has gone far enough," he said. "I'll have someone show you out."

"The only thing I could come up with was greed," I said, ignoring his bluff. "At first, that sounded preposterous to me. But then the behavior patterns of the very rich have always struck me as preposterous. I mean, here you are, with all the money and all the possessions anyone could want, enough loot to feed a starving African country or bail a Latin American nation out of debt, and all you do is pile up more for yourself. Your charitable contributions and your museum donations, even the genuine ones, are all tax-deductible. You are seventy-fucking-eight years old and it's still not enough. What is it with you people? I looked up your bio and read up on you. Your whole career is a big story of greed. Whatever you set your mind to, you went out and got. You bought it or merged it or swallowed it or bullied it into your clutches. Your whole history is spiced with dazzling attempts to corner the action, create little cartels of one kind or another. When you couldn't do that, when you found the competition to be as cunning and un-scrupulous as yourself, you made deals, you rigged prices, and God knows how many people you've paid off in the process."

Halsey ignored me. As I rambled on, he strolled delib-erately across the room to an antique French escritoire set against the wall, opened a drawer and withdrew a fat, sealed brown envelope. He casually dropped it on the table in front of me, as I paused for breath. "Take it," he said. "There's twenty-five thousand dollars in there. Take it and bring me the painting."

"What if I'm not for sale?"

"Everyone and everything is for sale. That's the golden rule of business. It's only a question of finding the correct price."

"What do you do with your pictures, Halsey? Do you just sit there by yourself in your hidden little room some-where in this big castle of yours and get your jollies off looking at your Donabellas, knowing that you, and only you, have eighteen of them, two-thirds of all the Donabellas in the world?" I asked. "Does it matter that much to you? Is the answer to your riddle the single word 'more'? Is it to be always more, more, more? Isn't it ever going to be enough?"

He paused at the door and turned to look at me. "Your story is a comic-strip invention, absurd from beginning to end," he said. "Furthermore, there is no way that you can substantiate any of it. No one would believe you and if you persist in it, I'll do whatever has to be done to put a stop to it."

"I know that. I knew it before I came here," I said. "Only the poor go to jail, only the hard knockers lose."

"If you don't deliver my painting to Mr. Meade within three days, you will return this money to him." He started to open the door.

"Wait a minute," I said, also standing up. "You said everyone and everything had a price. You haven't met mine."

"No?"

"No, you're not even close. You think you're holding all the cards, but you're not. Cards, by the way, is my specialty. I can do anything with a deck of cards. I have something you really want. Let's call that the hidden ace. Do you want to negotiate with me or do I go to the police and cause a lot of inconvenience for all of us with a story the press is sure to snap up?"

Halsey thought the matter over and then nodded almost imperceptibly. "These negotiations are better carried out abroad," he said, with a wintry little smile. "I can arrange payments most easily through my representatives in Lugano. I have an office there and they'll handle the matter for me. Telephone Miss Larrimore here tomorrow morning. She will make all the arrangements."

"I'm looking forward to meeting your man in Lugano," I told him. "Would his name be Renzi, Guido Renzi?"

Halsey did not answer. He walked out of the room, leaving the envelope stuffed with money lying on the table in front of me. I left without even opening it.

_ 18 _

Mud

It began to rain the morning after my visit to Halsey's transplanted manor house, and it was raining six days later, when I got back from Lugano. I called Allyson at the office from the airport and her voice sounded friendly and relieved, but distant, as if we now inhabited different planets. "Are you all right, Lou?" she asked.

"I'm fine," I said. "I'm about to fall down from lack of sleep, but otherwise I'm fine. Everything went very well. I have Freddie's money."

"I don't want you to tell me about it," she said. "Please."

"Okay, I just thought you'd want to know."

"Freddie's showing a little improvement," she said. "He can't talk yet, but he recognizes people and he can nod yes or no and—"

"What? Where is he? What's happened?"

"You mean you hadn't heard? They found him the day after you left. You didn't know? I sent you a telegram."

"I didn't get it."

"He was in a motel in North Hollywood and had a relapse," she said. "It must have been nearly a full day before anybody found him. That was about twelve days ago, not long after you saw him. He was in a coma. They took him to the nearest hospital, somewhere in the Valley. By the time we heard about it, he'd been transferred to the VA facility in Westwood, right next to where I live. They'd identified him and found he was a veteran, so he's entitled to medical care there."

"But what happened to him? Did he have a stroke?"

"No, but the effect is the same. Listen, Dr. Hamner is right here. He can tell you."

Before I could ask her when I could see her, she handed the phone to Ed Hamner, who sounded briskly cheerful, even as he poured out the bad news. He would have announced the end of the world as the last two minutes of a boring football game. "He's putting up a good fight, but he's not going to make it all the way back," he bubbled. "He'll eventually be able to get around some, but he's not going to go dancing and his speech will be permanently affected. I don't think he'll be able to paint again. He's right-handed and the hemorrhage was on the left side of the brain."

"So he had a stroke, is that it?"

"What he had, Shifty, was a subdural hematoma. He never should have walked out of Cedars the way he did."

"You may think I understand this secret language you people speak, but I don't have a clue as to what's wrong with him. You want to enlighten me?"

"What he had was a slow leak in his head," Ed explained. "The beating he got when he was mugged apparently weakened a blood vessel, which ruptured sometime after he left the hospital. He may have taken a fall or bumped his head again. He'd have been all right if he'd stayed in bed, as he was supposed to do. If it develops slowly and is not treated, the blood leaks into the brain and puts pressure on it. The first symptom is a bad headache. Eventually, you lapse into a coma. The ultimate effect can be like a stroke. If they hadn't found Chambers in time, he'd have died. As it is, he's paralyzed on the right side of his body and his speech is affected. He'll improve with treatment and therapy, but it's too early to tell how much."

"Can he have visitors?"

"I don't see why not."

"Can I talk to Allyson again?"

"She's with a patient now. Why don't you call her back later?"

"Tell her I'm going to see Freddie and I'll call her tonight at home."

"What do you think of Windy's chances?"

"Who? Oh, you mean he's running?"

Ed laughed. "You bet. He's in the seventh tomorrow. It's an allowance at a mile and a sixteenth, but there's only six horses in the race."

"An allowance? What's the track like?"

"It's a swamp out there. Where have you been?"

"Out of town."

"Allyson said the horse is doing fine. She dreamed he'd win by ten."

I took a taxi straight from the airport to the VA hospital and found Freddie at the end of a long ward full of patients in various stages of permanent debilitation. He was sitting up in bed, with his paralyzed right arm and twisted fingers resting helplessly on the mattress at his side. His face was wasted and pale above a gray stubble of a beard, but the blue eyes were alive and alert to my presence. No sooner had he seen me walking toward him than his lips began to twitch and he tried desperately to talk. I sat down beside him and put a calming hand on his shoulder, "Freddie, it's okay," I said. "I've got good news."

I pulled a screen around the bed and sat down close to him, so no one not actually intent on spying on us could overhear what I had to say. Freddie's eyes looked like small blue lakes seen from a tremendous height, as I leaned in to give him an account of my meeting with Halsey and my subsequent negotiations on our behalf in Switzerland. "They knew I was coming, of course," I told him, "and it was fairly smooth going. Renzi himself came to see me at the hotel they'd booked me into, a little place off the main piazza there, in Lugano. I guess you stayed there, too. Say, Freddie, he's a pretty smooth customer. Very erudite, very cultured, very suave. And a crook to the tips of his manicured nails."

Freddie grunted and his mouth twisted to one side. It wasn't pretty to see, but I realized I had made him laugh; his shoulders were shaking and his eyes reflected merriment.

I continued with my account. "They had upped the ante to fifty thousand more by the time I got there, but I gave Renzi what W. C. Fields used to call a noncommital answer," I said. "I told him to go fuck himself. I decided, however, to be reasonable, Freddie. I wasn't sure we could get two hundred thousand and I didn't want to push too hard. I figured they might sick Klaus onto us again. So I demanded another hundred and five thousand and that's what I got." I could see the questioning look in Freddie's eyes and I grinned at him. "It's okay, Freddie, the hundred thou is for you. The five is for me. I just want my expenses covered, okay?"

Freddie nodded, his eyes never wavering from mine. A thin trickle of saliva was running down his chin from the immobile right corner of his mouth and I dabbed it away with a wad of Kleenex. "That was the easy part," I said. "The tough part was working out the logistics of the deal. It wound up with me telling them they'd have to trust me. First the money, then the picture. It took two days to convince them, but there was no way I was going to turn over the BW before I had the money. Finally, Renzi got an okay, presumably from old man Halsey, and then we spent the next two days working out the details. Your hundred grand is in a numbered Swiss bank account in Lugano, Freddie.

It's in both our names. You can draw on it anytime you want to, or I can do it for you."

Freddie began to cry. The sight of his tears shook me, but I had determined to keep the mood light. "Goddamn it, Freddie, cut the sentimental crap, will you?" I snapped at him, in mock anger. "We're running out of Kleenex."

I cleaned him up again and threw the wads of paper into a wastebasket. "Now listen," I said, "you're okay here, huh?"

He nodded and gurgled, the closest he could come to speech, but I was happy to see that he was trying. "So here's what I'm going to do," I continued, "and don't argue with me. I'm going to arrange to transfer this money for you into an American bank here, where you'll get the best interest possible on a long-term savings certificate. This'll give you ten or twelve thousand a year to fool around with, okay? You won't be able to touch this money for at least three months, but you're out of action for a while anyway. By the time you're up on your feet again and ready to go, you'll be holding. But I'm going to keep a hand on it, Freddie. I know you. You'll blow the hundred grand in two months, if I let you. You're going to have about a thousand a month to play with and that's it. I'm going to make a smart horseplayer out of you, Freddie. Your junkie days are over. But don't worry—if anything happens to me, the money is all yours. That's the way it'll be set up."

I stood up to go, but he was making a tremendous effort now to communicate; the blue eyes were mad with the intensity of his desire. "If you're worried about the BW," I said, "it's in a self-service storage locker in Culver City. Tomorrow morning I'm turning the key to it over to Julian Meade." Freddie sank back against his pillows, all passion spent. He looked suddenly mortally frail, as vulnerable and brittle as spun glass. His bony chest heaved up and down from the physical strain of our meeting.

I made one last effort to cheer him up. "It's not a bad arrangement, Freddie," I said. "You've got free medical care and you've got Social Security and you've got no expenses anymore and you've got action money. What more could you want? And I'll tell you something else: Allyson's horse, Prairie Winds, is running tomorrow at Santa Anita. He's going to be the longest shot in the field and he's a mud lark. I'm going to bet a thousand dollars on him for you out of my five grand, okay? I'll let you know how we do."

And before he could try to say anything else, I turned and walked quickly away from him. I was three days behind in my sleep and all I could think about was getting home. I made the taxi stop at a liquor store on the way, however, so I could buy *The Racing Form*. I wasn't *that* tired. . . .

It stopped raining sometime during the night, but nothing had really begun to dry out by the time I drove into Santa Anita, less than an hour before opening post time the next day. The racing strip was a dark-brown mass of oozing mud that glistened under a pale yellow sun. It was a cold, clear day, with a hint in the air of more rain to come, perhaps by nightfall. I went up into the stands and found Jay already on the scene, cheerfully at work finalizing his plans for the day. "Where you been, Shifty?" he asked. "I got a nice double and, if it wins, I'm risking a thou on the dreamer's horse."

"I don't know about your double, but I'm with you on Prairie Winds."

Jay smiled broadly. "You know what's so nice about this play?" he said. "It doesn't matter whether the Russian puts mud stickers on him or not. He won his first race in the goo slickshod and the other two with the caulks on. Also, he's got Lancelot up on him, which will keep the odds honest. We're sitting on a big win, Shifty. This is the play of the meet."

"The only horse I'm worried about is Prince Willy," I said. "He won his first race in this country easily and he's bred to like the off going. He's got a lot of class, even if his owners don't."

"He's never run in this stuff," Jay assured me. "It's a real mess out there."

"What are they calling it?"

"It's muddy now. By the seventh, it'll be thick goo, just what my broker ordered."

Pinhead and Action Jackson came swooping toward us. "The flies to honey," I observed.

Jay winked at me. "We have a nice double," he announced, as they arrived. "And that will be our play for the day."

I spent most of the rest of the afternoon running two thousand dollars, Freddie's action and mine, through the machines a few bucks at a time, always in a different location. The morning line had Prairie Winds listed at twenty to one and it would not do to alert even one mutuel clerk to the fact that anyone thought enough of this animal's chances to be willing to risk real money on him. I worked my way up and down the windows on the ground floor, where I wasn't likely to bump into anyone I knew, and never bet more than twenty dollars a pop at any one place. By the end of the sixth race, I'd unloaded all but six hundred of my capital, the balance of which I planned to bet in one lump sum just before post time. I knew that Jay would be following roughly the same tactic, but even so the first blink of the odds dropped Prairie Winds to eight to one. Jay Fox wasn't the only sharpie on the grounds who kept records.

I headed for the saddling stalls and found Allyson sitting alone on a wet bench by the paddock. She was wearing a black raincoat, against which her face looked pale and drawn with fear. I sat down next to her. "What's the matter?" I asked. "You all right?"

"I'm fine, Shifty. I'm just scared."

I took her hand. "Don't worry," I said. "He's going to win."

"If anything happens to him, I'll just kill myself, that's all."

"Nothing's going to happen to him. Allyson, why didn't you answer the phone last night?"

"I—I couldn't talk to you."

"You don't want to see me again, is that it?"

"I don't know, Lou. Not for a while."

"Listen, it's all over. I got Freddie his money. I only took enough to cover my own expenses and make one bet, that's all. Is that wrong?"

"I just can't talk about it now."

"I know you think what I did was wrong," I continued, "but I didn't make the rules of this game. It's rigged to be won by the Bernard Halseys of this world. I'm a betting man, Allyson, and I don't bet into a sure losing proposition. I'm also a magician, but I can't turn the pigs into people. And anyway, isn't it nice? All over the world lovers of art are going to be looking at Freddie's beautiful paintings. His name won't be on them, but they'll give just as much pleasure as the real Donabellas would have. So at least he has a form of recognition and some money in his pocket. Is this so terrible? Museums everywhere are full of beautiful fakes. The fact that they're fake doesn't make them any the less beautiful, does it?"

"It's wrong, Shifty. You know it as well as I do. What you did is wrong."

"Oh, God save me from the virtuous people of this world," I said. "You're not talking virtue, Allyson. You're talking money. Don't you see that?"

"Shifty, I have to go now," she said, standing up. "I have to go to Windy."

"Will you never see me again?"

"I don't know. I can't think about it now." She started to walk away from me.

"Is it true you dreamed he'd win by ten lengths?" I called after her.

She didn't answer and I let her go. It wasn't until later, when I was standing at the paddock rail and watching Prairie Winds and his group of rooters that I realized our love affair was over. For only the second time since we'd met she had called me Shifty. It's not that I'm ashamed of that nickname, but it was indicative in this case of how Allyson now felt about me. It hurt quite a lot.

I stayed away from her and her doctors after that. On my way back to the grandstand, however, I found myself riding up the escalator directly behind Julian Meade and his snobbish girlfriend. I hadn't seen him since ten o'clock that morning, when I had stopped by the Masters to turn over the key to my storage bin. "Well, fancy meeting you here," I said. "It's a small and cruel world."

Linda Halsey glanced back at me in horror and Meade simply ignored me. "It's too bad about your horse today," I said, as we stepped off the escalator and they headed for the Turf Club. "Old Windy is going to blow mud right up his ass."

I waited by the Large Transaction windows until a minute before post time and then stepped into line behind the Weasel. "Hello, Shifty," he said. "You're gonna bet Prince Willy again, ain't ya? You was right about him the last time. He's a lock here, you know what I'm sayin'?"

"If you say so, Weasel."

"Can't lose. But you know what's a laugh? That dumb Polack trainer of your girlfriend's puttin' that cheap pig in here against class and with that bum Lancelot up. What a laugh!"

"He's going to win, Weasel."

"Willy? You're damn right he's gonna win. I'm bettin' four bills on him. Even if he is odds-on. No way he can lose."

As I was waiting to make my final bet, however, Dr. Will Thompson came swooping up to me. He looked like a nervous filly being loaded for the first time into a starting gate. The sweat was pouring down his face and the program in his fingers was shaking. "Hi, Will," I said. "You washed out on your way to the post."

"*I* washed out? You should see Prince Willy. He's soaking wet."

"Is that so?"

"It's an Exacta race," he exclaimed. "I boxed him with Allyson's horse. What do you do when they get that wet?"

"You fuck 'em," the Weasel said. "No foreplay." He snickered. "Just bet Prince Willy, doc. Wet or dry, he's a lock here."

"Oh, God," Thompson moaned. "I should have bet him straight."

Windy went off at fourteen to one. When the gate opened, he immediately dropped back to last, about fifteen lengths behind Prince Willy, who popped out of his stall and opened up six around the clubhouse turn, with the other horses strung out single file behind him. It looked like a harness race. By the time they hit the backside, Prince Willy had opened up ten, but he was rank and working too hard in the soft going. Half a mile from home, Windy took off on the outside, galloping along in the muck like Eliza dancing across the ice floes. He swept past the other trailers, then loomed up alongside Meade's horse as they turned into the stretch. From there to the wire it was simply no contest. The mudlark skipped through the goo, opening up ground with every stride. He won by twelve lengths. The exhausted Prince Willy staggered through the stretch, trying to hold on to second, but he fell apart at the sixteenth pole and lumbered in fourth. "That," said Jay, "is the easiest fourteen grand I have ever made."

I stood up and watched Allyson and her doctors group around Prairie Winds in the winner's circle. Ed and Charlie were jumping up and down, hugging her, each other, Boris, and Art Lancelot, who was beaming like a gargoyle. The jockey was, after all, sitting on his first winner of the meet, I realized. I kept my eyes focused on Allyson. She turned around once and glanced briefly up into the stands. I thought she might be looking for me, but maybe not. She was standing right next to Prairie Winds, her hand resting lightly on his neck, and I had a feeling she was talking to him.

"Can you believe that?" the Weasel snarled at me two minutes later, as I headed for a payoff window. "That fuckin' Commie bastard! What did he shoot into the pig? His picture oughta be on every fuckin' post office wall in the country!" He must have read the truth in my eyes, because he suddenly stopped raving and his jaw dropped. "You had it? You bet on him?"

"Well, Weasel, actually . . . yes," I admitted. "I did have a small wager on him."

The Weasel's mouth snapped shut and the hostile yellow eyes glittered dangerously. "Fuck you!" he said. "Fuck all of you!" And he scooted away in impotent fury.

At the track, not only is it important to win; it is also important that your friends and enemies hear about it. After all, as the Fox once so eloquently put it. "Everybody's got a horse story out there, but the only one worth listening to is the one in which you've cashed a ticket. . . ."

Prairie Winds never ran again. Allyson told Boris that the horse had earned his right to a gentle old age and, anyway, she couldn't have stood it if anything happened to him or she lost him to anyone else. So she sent him to a ranch in

Riverside County, where he now carries small children around on his back and grazes placidly in a fenced-in meadow under the warm year-round sun of Southern California. Once every couple of weeks, Allyson drives out to see him. She brings him his coffee and they stroll around the corral talking to each other. I asked her about it not long ago and she said that he doesn't miss the track. And neither does she. "I haven't gone back there since that day," she said. "It was a part of my life once and now it's over."

"You don't dream winners anymore?"

She shook her head. "That all stopped, too, Shifty. I think you stole my soul."

We're friends now, but it took me a long time to get over Allyson. A week after I returned from Lugano, I went to Las Vegas for six weeks to work at the Golden Nugget, while my friend Vince Michaels, the resident magician there, took a vacation. I didn't get the TV-series job either; the producers gave the part to an actor and hired another close-up artist to double the stunts and illusions. At my request, Happy Hal Mancuso booked me out on some cruises and it was early July before I got back to town.

I went to see Freddie at the VA and found him getting around with a walker and talking. He was also painting again, very slowly and laboriously, but only his own stuff now. The pictures, mainly of tiny horses and jockeys, were exquisite, but he didn't care about selling them. He never talked about the Donabellas; he, too, had made his peace with ambition. Of course, he was still losing at the track. The grand a month he was allotted to play with was usually gone by the end of the first week, but this left him plenty of time to paint. "You're better off," I told him. "You never had any luck with the horses."

My third day back, I went out to Hollywood Park and bumped into Ed Hamner. He brought me up to date on Allyson. She was getting a divorce from Julian and seeing some guy she'd met at a dinner party somewhere. He was a middle-aged, free-lance magazine writer, who had recently moved out to California from New York. "He's a nice guy," Ed said. "He likes the horses, too, but nobody can get Allyson out to the track anymore. I guess her time with you finished all that."

"Is she going to marry this guy?"

"Who knows?" Ed answered. "Who cares? Let's talk about something important. Who do you like in the fourth?"